Silver Glimpse

Belle Wren

Published by Belle Wren, 2024.

This is a work of fiction. Similarities to real people, places, or events are entirely coincidental.

SILVER GLIMPSE

First edition. October 31, 2024.

Copyright © 2024 Belle Wren.

ISBN: 979-8224586738

Written by Belle Wren.

Chapter 1: The Inheritance

The air was heavy with the scent of salt and decay, mingling with the faint aroma of damp wood and distant pine. As I stepped out of the car, the sea breeze tousled my hair, pulling at the edges of my carefully curated city life. My stiletto heels sank into the gravel driveway of the Glimmering Tide Inn, the once-vibrant sign creaking like an old sailor in the wind. It hung askew, as if even the name was reluctant to claim ownership of this fading establishment. I took a deep breath, inhaling the past, nostalgia clawing at my throat like a persistent memory.

Nana had always dreamed of turning this place into a sanctuary for weary travelers, a haven that boasted more than just ocean views. But what remained was a skeletal structure, peeling paint revealing shades of faded charm beneath the years of neglect. The ocean waves crashed rhythmically against the rocky shore, echoing the unease stirring in my stomach. I felt like an imposter here, an urbanite in a world where everyone else seemed to know their role—except me.

"Are you lost, or just here to gawk?" a voice drawled from the shadows.

I turned, half-expecting a local to rise from the mist like a character in a folktale. Instead, it was Jack, the handyman—a name that sounded far too mundane for a man who looked like he had stepped straight out of a rugged romance novel. His tousled hair, dark as storm clouds, framed a face chiseled by both sun and labor. He leaned against the dilapidated railing, arms crossed, a smirk playing at the corner of his mouth as if he'd found amusement in my predicament.

"I'm here to inherit," I replied, summoning the kind of confidence I typically wielded in boardroom meetings, but it came out a little shaky, like a poorly balanced wine glass on a wobbly table.

"Ah, the heir," he said, his tone dripping with sarcasm, the way only a true local could manage. "Welcome back to the glamorous life of a hotel owner. You'll want to watch your step. The last time I checked, the staircase was still in the process of falling down."

I shot him a look, half annoyed, half intrigued. "I thought this was your job," I said, raising an eyebrow, a gesture that had often struck fear into the hearts of lesser men in the city. "You're the handyman, right? Shouldn't you be fixing things instead of standing there criticizing?"

His eyes narrowed, an unspoken challenge hanging in the salty air. "I can only fix what's worth fixing. This place," he gestured broadly, "is a different story. It's like a shipwreck waiting for a tide to sweep it away."

I glared at him, the defiance boiling just beneath the surface. "Then maybe I should find someone who cares enough to help me sell it before it sinks. I'm not planning to stay long, you know."

"Oh, I figured as much. You city types never do," he replied, pushing off the railing to step closer, the warm breeze ruffling his shirt in a way that made me acutely aware of my own prim attire. "You'll sell it, and then what? Back to your high-rise apartments and crowded subway rides?"

"Exactly," I said, arms crossed tightly against my chest, warding off the cold that had nothing to do with the weather. "I have a life in New York. I can't be tied to this place."

Jack's expression softened, revealing a hint of curiosity mixed with pity. "You think that's all there is? A life in New York? This town has its charms, if you're willing to look. But it's not for everyone. Most people who leave never come back."

I took a step back, feeling the walls of my carefully constructed identity begin to tremble. "I didn't leave because I didn't love it. I left because I wanted something more—something better," I shot back, the hurt in my voice betraying my facade.

"Right," he said, nodding slowly, as if contemplating the depths of my claim. "Better is subjective. What's better for you might be a trap for someone else."

Just then, a loud crash echoed from the interior of the hotel, startling us both. We exchanged looks, and I felt a strange impulse to investigate, as if the noise were a siren call drawing me back into the inn's depths, into the chaos I so desperately wanted to avoid. "Maybe that's the ceiling collapsing. Or it could just be the ghosts of the past trying to get your attention," he suggested, half-joking, half-serious.

I inhaled sharply, the weight of my heritage looming large. "If I have to deal with ghosts, I'd prefer them to be the friendly kind."

With a reluctant grin, Jack waved me forward. "Then let's get on with it. I promise I won't let you drown in nostalgia... or dust. Probably."

The interior of the Glimmering Tide Inn was a time capsule, each room echoing stories long forgotten. The floral wallpaper peeled in places, revealing stark white drywall, and the floorboards creaked underfoot like old bones. I could almost hear Nana's laughter as I moved through the lobby, her spirit lingering in the corners, urging me to breathe life back into this fading dream.

"See?" Jack said, following closely behind. "It's got potential, if you're willing to invest a little sweat equity."

"Right now, I'm just trying not to trip over the past," I muttered, but my heart raced at the thought. As he pointed out the features—the grand fireplace, the sweeping staircase—each moment sparked a flicker of warmth that had been absent since my arrival.

Yet with every charming detail, an undeniable truth settled heavily in my chest: I was here to sell, not to stay. But as Jack's eyes glimmered with an earnest hope that perhaps I could be the one to revive this place, I couldn't shake the feeling that my plans were about to unravel even further.

The sun hung low in the sky, casting a golden hue over the Glimmering Tide Inn as I stepped further into the heart of the hotel. Dust motes danced lazily in the fading light, swirling around me like ethereal spirits caught in a moment of timelessness. I was both an intruder and a guest in this sacred space, the remnants of my grandmother's laughter echoing softly in the corners. Each creak of the floorboards beneath my feet seemed to whisper secrets, tales of laughter and love, disappointment and hope.

Jack's footsteps echoed behind me, and I felt his presence like a warm breeze, equally infuriating and intriguing. "You know, for someone who claims to be just here to sell, you're getting awfully sentimental," he remarked, a teasing lilt in his voice.

"Sentimental?" I scoffed, rolling my eyes. "I'm merely assessing the situation. I don't do sentiment; I do facts and figures." But the truth was, beneath the cool veneer, I could feel something stirring, a thread of connection weaving its way through my heart.

"Sure you do. Let's see how long that lasts when you discover the state of the rooms." He gestured toward a hallway, his tone a mix of challenge and mischief. "Or do you want to play a game of 'guess what the last guest left behind' first?"

A reluctant smile tugged at my lips. "Lead the way, oh seasoned handyman. I'm sure your inventory of broken furniture and questionable stains is legendary."

As we ventured deeper into the inn, Jack opened the door to the first guest room, and a wave of stale air rolled out like a shroud. Inside, the space was an unfortunate testament to neglect. The floral bedspread lay in tatters, and the once-gleaming dresser was now a graveyard of dust bunnies. I wrinkled my nose at the sight, imagining the endless cleaning and renovations that awaited me.

"Well," Jack said, leaning against the doorframe with a nonchalance that could only be earned through years of experience. "What do you think? Good investment or potential disaster?"

"More like a potential disaster," I admitted, stepping further into the room, the floor creaking ominously beneath me. "But I suppose it could be charming with a little TLC. A complete overhaul, mind you."

"Charm is just a fresh coat of paint away," he replied, his voice dripping with irony. "And maybe a complete gutting of the plumbing, electrical, and structural integrity."

I shot him a playful glare. "Don't you have something more constructive to say? Like, 'you can turn this place into a beautiful paradise'?"

"I could, but I prefer honesty. It's much more entertaining." He grinned, a flash of mischief lighting his eyes. "Besides, you'll figure out soon enough that renovation is really just a test of patience and creativity. More of an art than a science, if you will."

"Patience isn't exactly my strong suit," I sighed, peering out of the window at the tumultuous waves crashing against the shore. The ocean's wild beauty pulled at me, threatening to unravel my carefully curated life once again. "I might need to consult with a real estate agent instead of getting into this mess."

"A real estate agent won't care about the history of this place," Jack countered, stepping beside me. "They'll see numbers and not the stories that haunt these walls. If you're going to sell it, you need to understand what you're letting go of first."

His words settled into the silence, stirring emotions I had buried beneath deadlines and conference calls. There was a truth in what he said, a truth I was loath to confront. I glanced at him, our shoulders brushing slightly, an electric connection that caught me off guard. "And what's your story, Jack? Why are you here, slumming it with the ghosts of broken dreams?"

His expression shifted, a flicker of something deeper crossing his face before he masked it with his usual bravado. "Just a guy trying to earn a living in a place that's been left to rot. Not everyone gets to play the big shot in the city, you know."

I studied him, intrigued. "And yet, you seem to care more about this place than I do. Why is that?"

"Someone has to," he replied, his tone suddenly serious. "Nana had a vision for this hotel. I think that's what keeps it alive, even in its current state. But it's a battle, and sometimes you can't tell if you're winning or losing."

I felt a pang in my chest, as if the weight of his words had struck a chord. "You're really passionate about this, aren't you?"

He shrugged, but the flicker in his eyes revealed more. "Let's just say, every building has a soul, and sometimes that soul just needs a little encouragement to shine through."

In that moment, as the ocean roared outside, something shifted. I could see the possibilities—beyond the peeling wallpaper and broken furniture lay a future brimming with potential. Maybe I wasn't just here to sell the Glimmering Tide Inn; perhaps I was here to uncover the layers of stories waiting to be told.

With a newfound sense of purpose, I turned back to Jack. "Okay, let's do this. If we're going to make something of this place, we might as well get our hands dirty."

His eyebrows shot up in surprise. "You really mean that? You want to dive into the chaos instead of just tossing it all to a broker?"

"Why not?" I smiled, a spark igniting within me. "After all, who doesn't love a good challenge?"

"Or a disaster waiting to happen," he teased, a grin spreading across his face. "Welcome aboard, Captain. Let's set sail into the storm."

The camaraderie we forged in that moment felt effortless, a connection that swirled in the air between us like the ocean breeze. I could sense the weight of what lay ahead—the renovations, the decisions, and perhaps a little uncharted territory in my own heart.

As we began our impromptu tour of the remaining rooms, I felt a renewed sense of determination, ignited by the idea that maybe, just maybe, I could breathe life back into this place. The vision of a thriving inn nestled along the coast danced tantalizingly in my mind, twinkling like the stars above the crashing waves.

Jack's witty banter and the shared glances that lingered too long made me forget, even for a moment, the tight grip New York had on my future. I found myself hoping this wasn't just a detour on my journey but rather a new chapter waiting to be written, one filled with laughter, renovations, and perhaps a little unexpected magic.

The sun dipped lower, casting long shadows across the weathered floors of the Glimmering Tide Inn as Jack and I ventured further into the heart of the hotel. The promise of change loomed heavy in the air, mingling with the salty breeze filtering through the cracked windows. Each room we explored was a reminder of what could be—if only I were willing to embrace the chaos. A soft thrill of possibility coursed through me as I glanced at Jack, who was surveying the space with an artist's eye, envisioning the potential hidden beneath layers of dust and neglect.

"Let's make this place sing," I said, feeling the excitement bubble to the surface. "We could strip down these walls, paint them fresh, and bring in some coastal charm. Think breezy whites and seafoam greens."

Jack raised an eyebrow, a skeptical smile forming on his lips. "And you thought you were just here to sell? Look at you—already dreaming of décor."

"Don't mock my vision," I replied, feigning offense. "Every great transformation starts with a dream."

He chuckled, and the sound warmed me more than the sunlight streaming through the room. "Okay, Dreamer. But you know it's going to take more than a can of paint and a few throw pillows, right?"

"Throw pillows are key," I said with mock seriousness, and we both laughed, the sound echoing in the otherwise quiet hall. But as the laughter faded, a different kind of weight settled over us, the unspoken acknowledgment that this journey would require more than just vision—it would demand commitment.

"Alright," he said, turning serious again. "If we're doing this, we'll need to dig deep—both into the hotel's history and our own skills. Have you ever renovated anything before?"

"Does rearranging furniture count?" I shot back, recalling the hours spent perfectly aligning my city apartment's minimalistic design. "I may not have the manual labor experience, but I'm a marketing expert. I can sell the vision."

"Selling the vision is the easy part," he replied, running a hand through his hair, the gesture both exasperated and endearing. "Turning that vision into reality? That's where the real work comes in. Are you prepared to roll up your sleeves and get dirty?"

"Let's just say I'm not afraid of a little dust," I said, determination hardening my resolve. "Or the inevitable splinters from this lovely old wood."

"Splinters can be a badge of honor," he replied with a grin, crossing his arms. "Just don't say I didn't warn you when you're knee-deep in sawdust and frustration."

The energy between us crackled, a blend of camaraderie and challenge that ignited my enthusiasm. I felt a strange kinship with Jack, one that went beyond our mutual interest in reviving the inn. As we moved through the remaining rooms, I started to see beyond the faded wallpaper and cracked tiles; I envisioned a space where laughter and warmth could flourish once more.

"Let's start with the lobby," Jack suggested, his tone shifting as he gestured toward the grand space that had clearly been the inn's heart once upon a time. "It needs the most love—and the most work."

The lobby was a cavernous room, with a fireplace that loomed large, its once-proud mantle now a graveyard for dust. In its heyday, I imagined it bustling with guests, the air filled with laughter and the scent of fresh-baked cookies. Now, it was a husk of what it could be, but even in its neglected state, I felt a flicker of hope.

"Imagine the potential," I said, stepping closer to the fireplace. "A cozy seating area, hot cocoa by the fire, a warm welcome for everyone who walks through the door."

"Or an accidental fire hazard," Jack replied dryly, but his eyes sparkled with a hint of mischief. "I'll help you make it cozy, but I'm not responsible for any marshmallow-related disasters."

"Marshmallow-related disasters?" I echoed, chuckling at his peculiar phrasing. "You must have an interesting history with hot chocolate."

"Let's just say my culinary skills don't extend beyond a microwave," he admitted, leaning against the wall. "But I can build a fire, and that counts for something, right?"

"Absolutely. Fire is essential for life," I declared with a mock solemnity. "And if we can manage to keep the marshmallows out of the flames, we'll be golden."

We shared a smile, our banter weaving a thread of connection between us, and for a fleeting moment, I forgot about my original plan to sell the inn. The idea of transforming this place into a vibrant retreat began to consume my thoughts, and the notion felt more enticing than any corporate ladder I had climbed in New York.

As the afternoon slipped into evening, the shadows lengthened, casting a romantic glow over the space. I found myself lost in a daydream, envisioning guests returning to the inn, filling it with laughter and life once more.

But as the sun dipped below the horizon, reality crept back in, heavy as a storm cloud. "I still have to figure out how to get this place sold," I said softly, the words slipping out before I could stop them.

Jack's expression shifted, the lightness giving way to something more serious. "And if you don't want to sell?" he asked, his voice barely above a whisper. "What then? Are you ready to stay?"

I opened my mouth to respond but found the words caught in my throat, a truth I wasn't ready to face bubbling to the surface. The idea of staying—of rooting myself in this crumbling paradise—scared me more than I cared to admit. "I—I don't know," I stammered, my pulse quickening as his gaze bore into me. "This place is a lot to take on, and it's... complicated."

He stepped closer, and the air between us crackled with tension, the reality of my indecision hanging heavily. "Complicated can be good," he said softly, a challenge lingering in his tone. "Sometimes it's the things that scare us the most that end up being the best."

Before I could respond, the sudden crash of thunder rolled through the sky, shaking the walls of the inn. A bolt of lightning illuminated the room, and the power flickered ominously before plunging us into darkness. My heart raced, a jolt of adrenaline flooding my senses as I fumbled for my phone, its screen casting a faint glow.

"Great timing," Jack said, laughter threading through his voice even in the shadows. "Looks like the storm is coming to join the party."

"Perfect," I replied, anxiety creeping in. "Just what we needed."

The wind howled outside, rattling the windows as I moved cautiously toward the lobby doors, my phone light flickering over the dusty furniture. "We should check the back to make sure everything's secure," I said, though my voice trembled slightly.

"Right behind you," Jack replied, but there was an edge in his tone that made me pause.

As I reached for the door to the back hallway, a loud bang echoed from the kitchen, followed by an eerie silence that settled like a thick fog. "Did you hear that?" I asked, my heart racing.

Jack nodded, his expression now serious. "Stay close to me."

We stepped cautiously into the hallway, the dim light from my phone casting eerie shadows on the walls. Every creak of the old inn sounded amplified in the silence, the darkness wrapping around us like a shroud. As we approached the kitchen door, I felt an inexplicable chill creep down my spine, an instinct that warned me something was amiss.

"On three, we open the door," Jack whispered, his breath warm against my ear. "One, two..."

But before we could reach three, the door swung open with a thunderous crash, revealing a figure shrouded in shadow, silhouetted against the flickering light of the emergency exit sign. My heart dropped as a sharp gasp escaped my lips.

The storm outside raged on, thunder cracking like a whip, but my focus was solely on the mysterious figure before us. "Who are you?" I called, my voice steadier than I felt.

As the figure stepped into the light, my heart raced with a mixture of fear and recognition.

Chapter 2: The Town That Time Forgot

My heels sink into the gravel parking lot, a far cry from the polished marble lobbies I'm used to. The town is smaller than I remembered, a place where time seemed to have stopped, preserving itself in quaint nostalgia and heavy layers of expectation. Local shops, colorful wooden buildings, and streets lined with vibrant geraniums and cheerful daisies exude an undeniable charm. They whisper tales of sun-drenched afternoons and laughter that floats through the air like the sweet scent of funnel cakes from the nearby fair. Yet, I refuse to let it win me over. I am not here to indulge in quaintness or sentimentality. I am here with a mission that feels as heavy as the bags under my eyes.

Every shopkeeper knows my name, their faces lit with recognition that sharpens into a kind of pity when they realize why I've returned. Mrs. Thompson, with her wild silver curls and a penchant for wearing floral dresses that seem to bloom just as much as her garden, ushers me inside her tea shop with a warm smile that falters as she offers me a cup of chamomile, my grandmother's favorite. "Your Nana always said tea cures everything," she beams, though her eyes betray a hint of sadness. I know that look all too well. It's the same one my mother wore after the funeral, as if she were trying to stitch together the frayed edges of our family history with nothing more than hope and a cup of something hot.

"Thanks, Mrs. Thompson, but I'm okay," I reply, my voice lacking the buoyancy I desperately want to project. I glance around the shop—tea tins lining the shelves, each labeled with whimsical names like "Earl Grey Delight" and "Lemon Zinger," as if promising comfort with every sip. But I can't linger here, not when the air is thick with unspoken memories that gnaw at me like a ravenous dog. Instead, I choose to retreat, exiting into the warm embrace of the afternoon sun that feels far too bright for my mood.

Outside, the familiar sound of laughter drifts from the nearby park, where children play beneath the dappled shade of towering oaks. Their carefree spirits remind me of summers spent in this very town, weaving daisy chains and chasing fireflies. Those days are now ghostly echoes, each memory tinged with a bittersweet hue. I shake my head, trying to clear the fog of nostalgia that threatens to cloud my purpose. The weight of expectations presses on me, but none more than Jack's, whose silent scowl follows me everywhere.

Jack, with his broad shoulders and perpetually furrowed brow, has become the embodiment of my childhood rivalries, a living reminder that some things never change. Our encounters were often filled with spirited debates and unspoken attractions, an electric tension that would sizzle in the air between us. But now, it feels as if a chasm has opened, filled with unacknowledged grievances and the burden of our respective choices. He stands outside the old hardware store, arms crossed and face set in that familiar grimace, as if I've just walked into the wrong neighborhood and he's about to call the cops.

"What are you doing back here?" Jack's voice cuts through the afternoon, sharp and accusatory, as if I were a thief caught in the act of stealing something precious.

I take a deep breath, the familiar smell of cedar and fresh paint reminding me of the last summer I spent here, when everything was simpler, and our arguments had a different flavor. "Nice to see you too, Jack," I reply, trying to inject some humor into the tension, but it falls flat. "I'm here for the estate. You know that."

His expression hardens, a fortress against whatever emotions bubble just beneath the surface. "You mean you're here to destroy the last thing my grandmother loved." His words cut through the air like a knife, revealing a vulnerability I hadn't expected. The accusation hangs between us, and I can feel the heat of anger flaring within me.

"I'm not here to destroy anything," I retort, my voice rising slightly, fueled by a mix of frustration and hurt. "I'm just trying to figure out what to do with it." The truth is, I've inherited my grandmother's quaint little inn, a charming establishment that has seen better days and now stands as a testament to the life she built.

Jack shifts uncomfortably, and I can see the tension in his jaw, the way his hands clench into fists at his sides. "You're just going to sell it, aren't you? Turn it into some corporate monstrosity."

"Do you think I want to?" I counter, my tone sharper than intended. "Do you think I want to feel like a stranger in my own family's legacy? I don't want to be the villain here, Jack."

For a brief moment, the air between us crackles with something unnameable, a flicker of understanding amid our shared past. I can see the hurt reflected in his eyes, a mixture of betrayal and sorrow. I want to reach out, to bridge the gap that has grown between us like a wide river, but I'm not sure how to swim across it without sinking.

"I don't know what you want," he replies, the edge of his voice softening slightly. "But whatever it is, just know the town isn't what you remember. People are counting on you to do right by her. Do right by the inn."

With that, he turns and walks away, his retreating figure leaving a trail of unresolved feelings in his wake. I stand there for a moment, watching him go, my heart racing with a mix of anger and something else—something that feels like longing. The town that had once seemed like a nostalgic refuge now feels like a battlefield, every corner filled with reminders of what once was and what might never be again.

As the late afternoon sun dips low, casting a warm, golden glow over the town, I decide to make my way to the inn. The path is familiar yet foreign, each step leading me deeper into a landscape that was once my sanctuary but now feels like an unraveling thread. The scent of fresh pine wafts through the air, mingling with the floral notes from the nearby gardens, coaxing forth memories I had buried beneath layers of ambition and distance. I used to love wandering these streets, my laughter mingling with the sound of rustling leaves. Now, it feels like I'm traipsing through a graveyard of my own youth, where every ghostly whisper serves as a reminder of my responsibilities.

The inn stands at the end of the block, a sturdy structure that has weathered many storms, both literal and metaphorical. Its white paint is chipped in places, revealing the raw wood beneath, but it retains a certain charm that pulls at my heart. The wraparound porch, adorned with wicker chairs and flower boxes overflowing with vibrant blooms, beckons to me like an old friend. I step onto the porch, the familiar creak of the floorboards beneath me both comforting and unnerving, and push open the door.

The musty smell of old furniture and fresh paint hits me as I enter, a testament to both neglect and the attempts at revival my grandmother made in her later years. Dust motes dance in the slanting light, a ballet of forgotten memories. I run my fingers along the polished banister, feeling the grooves and scratches that tell stories of countless visitors and family gatherings. My grandmother's voice echoes in my mind, urging me to cherish the moments, to savor the little things. But those little things feel impossibly heavy now, like weights dragging me down into uncertainty.

"Hello?" My voice cuts through the silence, but it is met only with the whisper of the wind outside. The inn is eerily still, its warmth swallowed by the shadows that lurk in every corner. I walk into the parlor, where the grand fireplace, usually the heart of the home, stands dark and unlit. The faded floral wallpaper and mismatched furniture are relics of a bygone era, yet they hold a comfort I hadn't anticipated.

A soft thud catches my attention, and I turn to see a figure emerge from the kitchen. It's Rose, the inn's cook, who has been more of a second mother to me than anyone else in this town. Her cheeks are round and rosy, the kind that invites secrets and laughter.

"Well, if it isn't my favorite troublemaker!" she exclaims, her voice a melodic blend of warmth and mischief.

"Hi, Rose," I reply, a smile breaking through my tension. "I see you haven't changed a bit."

"Why would I? I'm too old for that nonsense." She chuckles, wiping her hands on her apron. "What's with the long face? Come here and give me a hug!"

I step into her embrace, and the world feels a little less heavy for a moment. Rose's hugs are legendary, enveloping you in a cocoon of comfort that feels like home. "I'm just trying to figure out how to keep this place from falling apart without Nana," I confess, my voice barely above a whisper.

She pulls back, her dark eyes sparkling with wisdom. "Your grandmother built this place with love. You've got it in you too. Just remember, it's not about the bricks and mortar. It's about the heart."

I nod, though the uncertainty lingers. "Have you heard from the town council yet about the renovations?" I ask, shifting to practicalities. "I want to make sure they don't have any objections before I start tearing things up."

"Oh, they've been buzzing like bees. I heard Jack's been quite vocal about it," she says, a knowing smile playing on her lips. "He's protective of this place, you know. Has been ever since he was a boy."

"Protective or possessive?" I mutter, and Rose raises an eyebrow, clearly unimpressed with my sarcasm.

"Tomato, tomahto," she replies, waving a hand dismissively. "You'll figure it out. Just remember, if you need help, I'm here. And don't be too hard on him. He lost his grandmother too, you know."

I swallow hard, the thought hitting me like a punch to the gut. Jack's scowl may have stung, but beneath it lay his own grief, tangled up in the legacy we both now share. "I'll keep that in mind," I murmur, though my mind races with a multitude of possibilities, each one more complicated than the last.

Just then, the door swings open, and a gust of wind bursts into the room, bringing with it the crispness of the coming evening. I turn, half-expecting another unwelcome visit from Jack, but instead, it's a delivery person, laden with boxes and packages. He's a lanky young man with a messy tuft of hair and a distracted demeanor, completely at odds with the picturesque setting.

"Delivery for the inn," he announces, his voice barely above a mumble.

"Perfect timing! What have we got?" I move toward him, curiosity piqued. The boxes are marked with various suppliers' labels—bedding, toiletries, decor—essentials for breathing life back into the inn.

"Looks like everything you ordered, plus a few extra pillows. Can't have your guests sleeping uncomfortably, right?" He flashes a grin, momentarily illuminating the dim room.

"Pillows are always essential," I quip, leaning against the counter, suddenly feeling lighter. "Especially for drowning sorrows."

He chuckles, his laugh echoing warmly in the space. "That's one way to look at it. You know, I've always loved this place. My family used to stay here every summer when I was a kid. It's like a second home."

"Then I'll do my best to keep it standing," I say, grateful for his unexpected enthusiasm. "You know, people around here are a bit... skeptical of change."

The delivery guy shrugs, his carefree attitude palpable. "Change can be good. Just like how too many pillows can cause neck cramps. You've got to find the right balance."

I smile, savoring his words. In this moment, the weight of the town's expectations seems to lift, if only for a breath. I might not have all the answers yet, but I'm starting to realize that perhaps it's not just about the legacy I'm inheriting, but also about the community that surrounds it. I can feel the pulse of the town beneath my feet, thrumming with potential, and for the first time since I arrived, I feel a flicker of hope sparking within me.

Before I can overthink my next move, I glance at the delivery guy. "You're just the person I need. What's your name?"

"Ethan," he replies, straightening up and offering me a bright smile that feels like the dawn breaking after a long night.

"Ethan, welcome to the team," I say, unable to suppress my excitement. "How would you like to help me turn this place back into something spectacular?"

His eyes widen, and the playful grin returns. "As long as there are pillows involved, count me in."

With the weight of expectations still lingering, I know that the journey ahead won't be easy. But standing there, surrounded by memories and new possibilities, I can finally see a path forward.

The sun dipped lower in the sky, casting a warm glow that softened the edges of the quaint town, yet my heart felt heavy as I stood on the porch of the inn. With each passing moment, the memories of laughter and summer nights echoed in the corners of my mind, creating a cacophony that pulled at the strings of nostalgia. I glanced around, half-expecting to see my grandmother flitting through the garden, her silver hair glinting in the light, watering her beloved daisies.

But there was only silence and the scent of pine mingling with the promise of fresh beginnings. I turned to Ethan, who was busy unpacking boxes. His youthful energy was infectious, a breath of fresh air in an environment steeped in the past. "You know," I started, leaning against the doorframe, "if you keep that up, I might have to start calling you my official unpacking assistant."

Ethan chuckled, his face lighting up with genuine delight. "Assistant? I was hoping for a more prestigious title. How about Head of Inn Operations?"

"Head of Inn Operations? I like it! You can put that on your resume." I smirked, feeling the ice around my heart begin to thaw, even if only slightly.

As we worked side by side, the rhythm of unpacking began to feel almost therapeutic. Each item I unwrapped sparked conversations about my grandmother's favorite recipes, local legends, and the peculiarities of the town. Ethan shared stories of his own family visits, revealing a boyhood spent exploring the woods behind the inn and fishing in the nearby lake. I could hear the nostalgia in his voice, a sound that mingled with my own memories, forging an unspoken bond between us.

"Do you ever think about what it would be like to live somewhere else?" he asked as he set down a box of decorative plates. "I mean, this place has its charm, but sometimes it feels like we're all stuck in a time capsule."

I considered his question, gazing out at the peaceful street. "Stuck isn't the right word. It's more like... anchored. People here have roots, and they don't just pull them up because a new trend pops up somewhere else."

Ethan nodded, his expression thoughtful. "True. But roots can also keep you from growing. Sometimes I wonder if the town has too many of them."

"Is that your subtle way of saying you want to escape?" I shot back playfully, raising an eyebrow.

"Maybe," he admitted, his grin widening. "But what if I found a way to escape without leaving? Help you breathe new life into this place instead?"

"Now that sounds like a challenge," I replied, a spark of enthusiasm igniting within me. "I think I could get behind that."

Just then, the tranquility of our moment shattered as the door swung open with a dramatic creak, and in walked Jack, his presence filling the room like a dark cloud. "What are you two doing in here?" he demanded, his gaze sweeping over the unpacked boxes as if assessing a crime scene.

"Just making this place look a little less... lived-in," I replied, my voice lighter than I felt. "You know, giving it a little love."

Jack narrowed his eyes, his jaw tightening. "Love? This inn doesn't need love; it needs a miracle."

"Miracles come in all forms, Jack," I shot back, my patience thinning. "Some of us are just trying to do our best here."

"Your best, huh?" he scoffed, running a hand through his hair, a gesture that somehow managed to be both frustrated and defeated. "What you think is best might not be what's best for this town. This inn is a part of our history. You can't just slap a coat of paint on it and call it a day."

I crossed my arms, my heart racing. "And what would you have me do? Leave it to rot while I chase my dreams somewhere else? I'm trying to honor my grandmother, Jack, not destroy her legacy."

"Honoring her doesn't mean turning it into a tourist trap," he retorted, his voice low and tense. "People here care about this place. They have their memories tied up in every creak of the floor and every brick in the wall."

The tension between us was palpable, an electric charge that could ignite a fire. "And you think my grandmother would want me to let it die?" I shot back, my voice rising.

"I think she'd want you to understand the weight of what you're carrying," he replied, softer now, as if he were trying to reach the part of me that had grown cold and distant.

"Is that your way of saying I shouldn't be here?"

Jack's shoulders slumped slightly, and for a fleeting moment, the fight left his eyes. "I don't want to see you get hurt, that's all. This isn't just a business venture; it's part of who we are."

"Maybe it's time we redefine who we are, then," I said, the words escaping before I could hold them back. "This town can't stay stuck forever. We need to grow, evolve—"

"Or watch everything we love disappear," he interrupted, his tone thick with emotion.

The air grew heavy with our unspoken histories, the myriad paths we had taken that had led us here, standing on opposite sides of a chasm. I felt the weight of his words settle over me, mixing with my own uncertainties about the future.

"Let's find a way to do this together," I finally suggested, my heart racing as I took a step forward, extending an olive branch through the tension. "Maybe if we work together, we can honor her memory and make this place shine again."

Jack studied me for a long moment, his expression unreadable. Then he sighed, a reluctant concession. "Fine. But I'm not letting you turn this place into some cookie-cutter version of itself."

"Deal." I felt a flicker of hope, a tentative bridge forming between us.

Ethan, watching from the side, interjected with a grin. "I like this teamwork thing. It has a nice ring to it."

As we began discussing ideas, the atmosphere lightened, but just as I thought we might be turning a corner, a loud crash erupted from the back of the inn, a sound so sudden it made us all jump.

"What was that?" Jack's voice was sharp, and in an instant, the camaraderie we'd just built dissolved into concern.

"I don't know!" I exclaimed, my heart racing again as dread washed over me. "Let's check it out."

We hurried toward the sound, the three of us racing through the corridor, uncertainty clinging to us like fog. I could feel Jack's presence behind me, his protective instinct igniting as we moved, and Ethan's eagerness spurring us forward. As we reached the back door, the dim light revealed shattered glass and scattered boxes.

"What happened?" I gasped, my eyes scanning the wreckage.

Then, among the chaos, I saw it: a letter, fluttering on the ground, its edge stained with something dark and ominous. The name on the envelope sent a chill down my spine. It was addressed to me, the handwriting unmistakable.

"Open it," Jack urged, his voice tight with tension.

My heart pounded as I bent down to pick it up, dread settling heavily in my stomach. What lay inside could very well change everything I thought I knew about this place, and about myself. I hesitated, the air thick with expectation, before slowly tearing it open.

And as the words revealed themselves under the fading light, I realized I was not just standing on the edge of my grandmother's legacy. I was about to unearth secrets that could redefine everything.

Chapter 3: Storm Warnings

The wind howled like a wounded animal, a relentless force that rattled the windows of the old hotel, sending a chill down my spine. I pressed my palms against the cold glass, watching the storm morph the world outside into a blur of dark greens and grays. The once-vibrant garden was now a wild tangle of whipping branches, and I could almost hear the trees crying out in protest as they were battered by the elements. I took a deep breath, inhaling the scent of rain-soaked earth mixed with the musty aroma of the hotel's faded interiors—a combination that both grounded and unsettled me.

Jack stood nearby, a hulking figure in the dim light of the lobby, his arms crossed over his chest, a permanent scowl etched onto his handsome face. There was something undeniably magnetic about him, even as he radiated a gruffness that kept most people at arm's length. I had tried to catch glimpses of his softer side, those flickers of warmth hidden beneath his stoic demeanor, but he remained an enigma wrapped in a brooding silence. He was here to help, but I could tell he'd rather be anywhere else.

"Do you think it's safe to stay open?" I asked, my voice breaking the heavy stillness, forcing it to crack like the lightning outside.

He turned his gaze to me, his eyes dark and stormy, and for a moment, I felt a strange connection, a tether forged in the chaos of the storm. "We can't close now," he replied, his voice low and rough, like gravel sliding against itself. "Not when there are guests who need us."

The way he spoke felt both protective and accusatory, as if my very presence threatened the stability he so desperately tried to maintain. But there was a flicker of something else in his eyes—concern, perhaps. It ignited a spark of defiance in me, pushing me to lean into the challenge of the night ahead. "And what about you?" I challenged, trying to match his intensity. "What makes you so willing to stick around? This place is barely holding on."

His expression hardened, and he turned back to the rain-soaked window, a shroud of secrets falling over him once again. "This hotel isn't just a building, you know. It's history. A lot of people have memories tied to this place." The way he said "memories" felt heavy, weighted by a burden I couldn't yet fathom.

I wanted to press him for details, to peel back the layers that he so carefully guarded, but I stopped myself. The last thing I needed was to delve into the past—mine or his. I was merely a traveler passing through, and this hotel was just a brief layover on my journey back to my real life. The storm outside, however, seemed determined to keep me rooted here, as if the universe conspired against my plans.

"Fine," I relented, leaning against the counter with a sigh, the wood cool against my skin. "If we're staying open, we should at least be prepared. Let's grab some flashlights, check on the guests, and make sure everything is secure."

Jack studied me for a moment, and I could almost hear the gears turning in his head as he weighed my resolve. Then, to my surprise, a reluctant smirk tugged at the corners of his lips. "Look at you, taking charge like you own the place."

The compliment caught me off guard, igniting a flicker of warmth that spread through my chest. "Well, someone has to," I replied, injecting a playful note into my voice. "And it might as well be the only one who doesn't look like they've been marinating in a sour mood all day."

He chuckled—a deep, throaty sound that resonated within the walls of the hotel, making the air feel lighter. It was a welcome shift, and I found myself wanting to chase that sound, to uncover the humor lurking beneath his gruff exterior.

We moved together through the dimly lit corridors, the flickering bulbs overhead casting strange shadows that danced around us like mischievous spirits. Each step was accompanied by the steady drum of rain against the roof, a constant reminder of the storm's wrath. I could feel the tension between us, thickening the air like humidity before a summer storm. It made the mundane act of searching for flashlights feel electric, as if every lingering glance could spark something deeper.

As we rounded the corner, I spotted a group of guests huddled together in the small lounge area, their faces pale with concern. I stepped forward, forcing a bright smile to break through the worry I felt gnawing at my insides. "Hey there! We're just checking in. Is everyone doing okay?"

Their responses were muffled, a mix of nervous chatter and tentative reassurances, but I could see the anxiety reflected in their eyes. I glanced back at Jack, who had taken a step back, his arms crossed again, watching me with a guarded expression.

I turned back to the guests, determined to pull them from their apprehension. "Why don't we gather some games or movies? We can have a storm party right here!" My enthusiasm surprised even me, but I was desperate to create a moment of normalcy amidst the chaos.

Jack snorted softly, an amused light returning to his eyes. "Storm party? You're really something, aren't you?"

"Someone has to be the voice of fun around here," I shot back, unable to hide my grin. "Besides, I refuse to let a little rain ruin our night."

With the laughter that erupted among the guests, I felt a shift within myself, an awakening of the spirit I thought I'd lost somewhere along the way. The storm raged outside, but within these walls, I was determined to create a haven, even if just for a few hours. I glanced at Jack, who seemed caught off guard by the sudden levity. Maybe there was more to him than just a brooding exterior. Maybe, just maybe, this storm might force us both to confront more than the elements outside.

And as the wind howled louder, threatening to shake the very foundation of our sanctuary, I felt an unshakable resolve settle within me: this night would be about survival—not just from the storm, but from the shadows lurking in the corners of our lives.

The storm continued to lash at the hotel, and inside, the atmosphere hummed with a curious blend of tension and camaraderie. As I gathered the guests, I felt the electricity in the air shift, the storm outside mirrored in the way we huddled together, seeking warmth and connection amidst the chaos. Jack moved through the crowd with a reluctant grace, his body language still reserved, but his presence—strong and silent—offered an odd sense of security. I was beginning to appreciate how he silently filled the space around him, making the chaos seem a bit more manageable, though I wouldn't dare let him know that.

I rummaged through the front desk drawers, digging up a hodgepodge of board games and dusty card decks, hoping they'd spark some joy amidst the unease. "How about a game of Scrabble?" I suggested with a bright smile, lifting the box in triumph. "We can compete for the title of Storm King or Queen." The words flew from my mouth, buoyed by the giggles from a couple of kids huddled at their parents' sides.

Jack watched me with a bemused expression, arms crossed, leaning against the wall as if he were too cool to join in but too intrigued to walk away. "I thought you said you were going to be the voice of fun," he teased, raising an eyebrow. "Scrabble? Really? I've seen rain-soaked people make better choices."

"Well, you could always join the fun instead of standing there like a grumpy lighthouse keeper," I shot back, feigning a dramatic sigh. "But I get it; it's hard to shine bright when you're dimming the light of your own personality."

He chuckled, shaking his head in amusement. It was a sound that stirred something warm inside me. I was reminded that beneath his tough exterior lay a man capable of laughter, of finding joy in the absurdity of life—even if he was too stubborn to admit it.

A family with two children squealed in delight, pulling Jack toward the makeshift game table. "Come on! You can be our referee!" The little girl tugged at his hand, her face alight with the kind of fearless enthusiasm that only children possess. To my surprise, Jack complied, albeit with an eye-roll that suggested he was doing this entirely against his will.

As the game commenced, I began to feel a sense of normalcy returning, albeit briefly. The storm outside created a symphony of drumming rain and howling wind, but inside, the laughter rose, filling the hotel with life. Jack took on the role of an unwilling but strangely effective referee, keeping track of scores while throwing in quips that sent the children into fits of giggles. I observed him more closely, his face softening in the light of camaraderie, revealing a dimension I had not expected to see.

"Your turn!" I called, nudging the game board toward him, a playful challenge in my voice. "Let's see if the storm has stolen your Scrabble skills too."

He shrugged, still pretending to be unbothered. "I don't need a storm to mess up my word game. I'm quite skilled at doing that on my own."

"Your humility is inspiring, really," I shot back, a smirk playing on my lips. "But seriously, give it a go. You might just surprise us all."

Jack leaned over the board, his brows furrowing in concentration as he picked out his letters. "I'm not here to win. Just to keep the peace." The words held an edge of seriousness, and for a moment, I wondered what kind of battles he was truly fighting in his own mind.

The game continued, punctuated by bursts of laughter and the occasional groan of disappointment from misplayed words. I couldn't help but relish the sound of it all—the guests relaxing, even if just for a moment, lost in the storm's roar outside. The hours rolled on like the storm itself, each moment stretching the night into something almost magical.

Just as the atmosphere shifted, a loud crack of thunder reverberated through the hotel, and the lights flickered. The room plunged into semi-darkness before the emergency lights blinked to life, casting a dim, eerie glow over our gathering. A nervous hush fell over the group as the reality of the storm reasserted itself, the wind howling louder than before.

"Great," I muttered, rolling my eyes. "The storm is now auditioning for a horror film."

"Perfect timing for a spooky story," one of the children piped up, her eyes wide with excitement.

I turned to Jack, who was now enveloped in the glow of the emergency lights, his expression unreadable. "You seem like someone who would have a good ghost story up your sleeve," I challenged, a playful smile creeping across my face.

"Me?" His gaze sharpened, incredulous yet intrigued. "I don't do ghost stories. I leave that to the professionals."

"Professional grumpiness, you mean?" I shot back, and the room erupted in laughter. Jack smirked, shaking his head in mock disapproval.

"Okay, how about a tale from the hotel's past?" he finally relented, his voice low and gruff, the tension in the air shifting as curiosity took hold. "This place has its share of ghosts—real and otherwise."

I leaned closer, captivated, as he launched into a story about the hotel's founder, a reclusive old woman who was said to roam the halls at night, searching for something lost. "They say she was looking for a piece of her heart," he said, his voice dropping to a conspiratorial whisper, "something that had been taken from her long ago."

The children listened, rapt, eyes wide with wonder and fear. The storm outside seemed to pause, the world narrowing down to Jack's voice and the shadowy figures the storm conjured in our minds. He wove a tale of love and loss, of a hotel that held the secrets of its guests long after they had left.

As he spoke, I felt the weight of my own past pressing against me, the memories that lingered like unwelcome ghosts. But in that moment, as Jack's voice filled the air, I found a sliver of solace. I caught his gaze, and for the first time, the storm raging outside felt distant, like a backdrop to a story unfolding inside these walls.

The laughter and tension of the evening washed over me like the rain against the roof, and I realized how much I craved this connection, this unexpected bond that had formed amidst the chaos. The storm had brought us together, weaving our fates like threads in a tapestry, each one essential to the whole.

And as the thunder rumbled overhead, I couldn't shake the feeling that maybe, just maybe, this place held more than just history. It was a sanctuary, a turning point, and perhaps a home to something new.

The game of Scrabble had morphed into a full-blown spectacle, the remnants of the storm's intensity fading into the background noise as the guests rallied together in gleeful competition. Jack had somehow shifted from the aloof specter of authority to the reluctant hero of the evening, his dry humor and unexpected charm transforming the mood. He had even managed to draw the older guests into the fun, coaxing smiles from those who had initially appeared daunted by the storm outside. The hotel had taken on a new life, vibrating with laughter and the shuffle of game pieces.

I was perched on a stool, observing Jack as he interacted with the guests. He was no longer just the gruff handyman I had first encountered; he had become a bridge, connecting everyone in the room, his charisma pulling us together in a way I hadn't anticipated.

My heart did a little flip at the sight. Who knew the man could light up like that? Just when I thought I had him all figured out, he tossed another surprise into the mix.

"Okay, how about this?" he announced, resting his hands on the edge of the table. "The next word must include a color. And if you can't come up with one, you have to tell us your worst hotel experience."

I leaned forward, intrigued. "Oh, that's clever. Now we're going to hear some juicy gossip." I winked at the guests, spurring them on. "Who doesn't love a good horror story?"

The room erupted into a flurry of excited chatter, everyone eager to share tales of their misadventures in the hospitality world. One elderly woman recounted a mishap where she accidentally flooded her hotel room while trying to create the perfect bubble bath. Another guest told a comical story of being locked out of their room in nothing but a towel. Laughter echoed against the walls, ringing out like music in the storm's shadow.

"Alright, my turn," Jack said, a smirk creeping onto his lips as he leaned back against the counter. "There was this one time I was called to fix a leaking sink in the middle of the night. The owner had a guest who decided it would be a great idea to make spaghetti at two a.m. Just a little garlic and olive oil, nothing crazy, right? Well, it turned out she didn't know how to boil water. The kitchen looked like a tornado hit it, and the worst part? I had to clean it up."

Everyone burst into laughter, and I couldn't help but join in, the image of Jack, usually so composed, navigating the chaos of a midnight pasta party forming a delightful picture in my mind. The storm outside raged on, but in that moment, we were cocooned in a warmth that belied the tempest.

The playful atmosphere persisted until a sudden gust of wind slammed against the building, rattling the windows and stealing our breath for a moment. The laughter faded to whispers, the mood shifting like the clouds outside. Jack's expression turned serious as he surveyed the guests, gauging their reactions.

"Alright, let's all take a breath," he said, voice firm yet reassuring. "The storm is bad, but we're safe in here."

I glanced around the room, my heart tightening as I sensed the worry creeping back in. The weight of the storm pressed against us, and the shadows danced eerily along the walls. I felt a knot forming in my stomach, a mix of anxiety and an urge to protect this fragile sense of community we had built.

I cleared my throat, raising my voice to break the tension. "How about we all grab our flashlights and tell ghost stories instead? It'll be fun!"

"Good idea!" someone called out, and soon everyone was scrambling for the dim emergency lights and their phones, the glow creating a sense of intimacy in the darkness.

Jack stepped beside me, his shoulder brushing against mine, a jolt of electricity shooting through me. "You really think that's a good idea?" he murmured, a hint of skepticism in his voice.

I turned to him, daring a smile. "What's the worst that could happen? We scare away the ghosts, and then we have to deal with just you."

His laughter rolled out like thunder, low and resonant. "You're brave, I'll give you that."

As the stories unfolded, I noticed how Jack's gaze lingered on me more than the others, a fleeting intensity that sent shivers down my spine. The guests spun tales of hauntings and lost souls, and I found myself leaning into the rhythm of their words, captivated not just by the stories but by the way Jack's laughter intertwined with mine, creating a melody that was both comforting and exhilarating.

After a particularly hair-raising tale about a spectral maid who still swept the hallways, I felt emboldened. "I'll share one," I declared, my heart racing as I took a breath. "This hotel has its own stories, right? What if we had a resident ghost?"

Jack shot me a look, his brow raised. "Are you volunteering to play the ghost?"

"Only if you promise to help me haunt the guests," I shot back, laughter bubbling up. "We could be the dynamic duo—ghosts with a sense of humor!"

The room erupted into laughter again, and for a brief moment, the storm outside felt like an afterthought. I launched into a lighthearted tale about a ghost named Mildred who only appeared during storms, her favorite pastime being to hide the guests' shoes. I mimicked Mildred's ghostly antics, flailing my arms and pretending to glide across the floor. The guests roared, and even Jack let out a genuine laugh, his eyes sparkling with mischief.

But just as the atmosphere reached its peak, a deafening crack of thunder echoed through the hotel, followed by a sudden, ominous silence. The lights flickered and then went out completely, plunging us into darkness. Gasps erupted around the room, and I felt a chill race up my spine.

"Everyone okay?" Jack's voice sliced through the panic, steady and commanding. "Stay close to one another."

Panic rippled through the crowd, and I instinctively reached for Jack's arm, the warmth of his skin grounding me in the chaos. "This is a little too dramatic for a ghost story, don't you think?"

"I don't think this is part of the act," he replied, his voice a low rumble that set my nerves on edge.

Before I could respond, the hotel shook violently, as if the storm had decided to join our ghost story. The windows rattled, and a low rumbling echoed from deep within the structure, a sound that felt foreboding and alive. My heart raced, and I turned to Jack, whose eyes were wide with a mixture of concern and determination.

"Stay here," he ordered, and before I could protest, he slipped away, moving through the darkness toward the front desk, his silhouette swallowed by the gloom.

"Jack!" I called, but my voice felt feeble against the roar of the storm. The guests huddled closer, fear evident on their faces, and I felt the knot in my stomach tighten further.

The lights flickered back to life momentarily, revealing Jack halfway to the door. But then, in an instant, everything went black again. The storm was now screaming, drowning out the laughter and camaraderie we had built, leaving only fear in its wake.

I stumbled forward, heart pounding, desperate to follow him into the chaos. "We can't just stay here!" I shouted, but my words were swallowed by the tempest outside.

Then, the hotel groaned ominously, and with a deafening crash, something shattered. The floor beneath us trembled, and the atmosphere thickened with impending dread, pulling me back as if the very building were warning me to stop.

Suddenly, a bright flash illuminated the room, revealing a figure just outside the door—a silhouette framed against the raging storm. My breath caught in my throat, and I froze, caught between the safety of our group and the unknown that lurked beyond.

"Jack!" I yelled, but my voice faltered as the figure moved closer, the storm's wrath amplifying the tension that crackled in the air. The shadows closed in, and I could only stand there, heart racing, as the darkness seemed to swallow everything around me, leaving only the haunting question of who—or what—was about to step through that door.

Chapter 4: A Promise Made

The morning light spilled into the hotel lobby, casting sharp angles on the remnants of what had once been a vibrant gathering place for the town's summer tourists. The floral wallpaper, once cheerful and bright, now faded into muted patterns, whispering of a time when laughter echoed off these walls. Dust motes danced lazily in the sunbeams, floating over overturned chairs and scattered debris, remnants of a hastily abandoned breakfast service. The sight of it all felt like a gut punch.

I rubbed my temples, trying to stave off the growing headache that accompanied each confrontation with the weight of responsibility that now sat on my shoulders. Nana had left me this sprawling mess, a hotel that was a patchwork of her whims, and beneath it all, the scent of mold mingled with stale coffee. I took a deep breath, inhaling the bittersweet aroma of memories. Somewhere in this wreckage, I could still smell the lilacs she planted each spring and the sound of her laughter as she flitted about, making every corner feel alive. But the laughter felt like a ghost now, leaving me stranded with the specter of my choices.

"Why don't you just admit it? You're running away again," Jack said, his arms crossed over his broad chest, the sunlight accentuating the sharp lines of his jaw. He was as much a part of this hotel as the creaky floorboards, always here, always stubbornly tied to this place. His dark hair fell into his eyes, the warm brown depths of them piercing through the morning haze with an intensity that made my insides twist. He had that infuriating knack for knowing exactly which buttons to press, and I wasn't in the mood to indulge him today.

"I'm not running away," I shot back, my voice sharper than I intended, echoing against the bare walls. "I'm trying to salvage what's left of my life. This isn't my home, Jack. It never was."

His brow furrowed, frustration etched into every line of his handsome face. "It could be. You just have to stop looking at it as a burden. You act like it's a punishment. It's your heritage, Alice. Your history."

"And what do you know about my history?" I spat, the heat of the argument igniting my temper. "You've been here for what, years? You know every nook and cranny, but you don't know me. You don't know what it feels like to walk away from a family legacy that you never wanted in the first place." My words hung between us, a charged silence that crackled like a summer storm brewing overhead.

Jack opened his mouth to respond, but I held up a hand, cutting him off. "I didn't ask for this. I didn't ask to inherit this decrepit building or the memories that come with it. This isn't a storybook where everything gets wrapped up in a neat little bow. It's a burden, and I don't want it."

The challenge in his gaze softened momentarily, revealing the man who had grown up in this town, who had seen the beauty of its simplicity and its flaws. "You think I haven't felt the same way? This place has its problems, but it's not just a hotel; it's a community. It's family. And you're running away from that."

"Don't you get it?" I replied, my voice lowering, a tremor of uncertainty slipping in. "My family isn't here anymore. They left me with this, with nothing but reminders of what I've lost." My voice broke, and I hated how vulnerable I sounded. I was teetering on the edge of a cliff, and the last thing I needed was for him to shove me off.

"Maybe it's time you stop thinking of it as a loss," he countered, stepping closer, the tension thickening the air between us. "Think of it as a chance. A chance to make it your own, to breathe new life into it." His voice dropped, intimate, compelling. "You can't keep hiding behind anger forever, Alice."

I shifted my weight, the worn floor creaking underfoot. Jack was always good at digging into the parts of me I preferred to keep buried, the feelings I'd wrapped in layers of bitterness. "And what would you know about hiding?" I challenged, desperation creeping into my tone. "You've never left. You're tethered here, and maybe that's easy for you. But for me? I've spent my whole life trying to find a place where I fit. And every time I think I might, something pulls me back, reminding me I don't belong."

The air was thick with unsaid words, and his eyes searched mine, challenging me to find the courage buried deep beneath my fears. I could feel the intensity of our connection, electric and unnerving. In that moment, everything shifted—my resolve wavered, and for the first time, I wondered if running away was truly the answer.

"Maybe you're right," I finally whispered, the admission tasting foreign on my tongue. "But it feels so much easier to walk away." My heart raced, pounding against my chest as if trying to break free from the shackles of indecision.

"I know it does," he said, softer now, an understanding lacing his words. "But sometimes, the hardest things are the most worth fighting for."

As the sun rose higher, illuminating the dust motes swirling around us, I felt the weight of his gaze, anchoring me in the moment. A flicker of resolve sparked within, igniting a determination I hadn't known I still possessed. I couldn't walk away—not yet. Not while there was still so much to uncover, so much to reclaim from the ashes of my past.

The atmosphere in the hotel shifted like the changing tides outside, an ebb and flow of tension and unspoken words. I could still feel the heat of our argument lingering in the air, clinging to my skin like the humidity of a summer afternoon. With a resigned sigh, I turned my back on Jack and moved toward the bar, the heart of the establishment where laughter once spilled like champagne. Now, the polished wood was dull, a thin layer of dust accumulating in the corners, waiting patiently for someone to restore it to its former glory.

I reached for a damp cloth, my fingers brushing over the cool surface of the counter. A ghost of a memory flitted through my mind—Nana, apron tied around her waist, would be standing right here, concocting the most extraordinary cocktails, her laughter bubbling over like the fizz in her favorite drink. I could almost hear her teasing me about my serious nature, a knowing smile playing on her lips. "Life's too short to be so grave, Alice," she'd say, always a little dramatic, her voice lilting with affection.

A soft thud interrupted my reverie, and I turned to see Jack leaning against the doorframe, arms crossed, looking as if he'd been caught in a storm. "What's the plan? Are you really going to just wipe your hands clean of all this?" His eyes bore into me, a tempest of frustration and concern swirling behind them.

"Why does it matter to you?" I shot back, trying to inject my voice with a bite, but it faltered under the weight of my uncertainty. "You've made it clear that this place is your lifeline. I'm not part of your grand vision for whatever this hotel could become."

His brows knitted together in that infuriating way that meant he was about to deliver one of his philosophical lectures. "Because, Alice, whether you like it or not, you are part of it. This hotel isn't just a building; it's a piece of your family's legacy. You can't just dismiss that."

I rolled my eyes, letting out a frustrated huff. "Legacy? Is that what you call a dilapidated structure with peeling paint and broken dreams? That's a romanticized way to describe a sinking ship." The sarcasm dripped from my tongue, but beneath it lay a kernel of doubt. Deep down, I wondered if I was indeed dismissing something important, something that could change everything.

Jack pushed off the doorframe and stepped closer, his gaze unyielding. "So, what's the alternative? You think you can just pack up and run? You'll always be tied to this place, whether you want to be or not."

I glanced around the room, noting the remnants of what once was. The chandelier, though dust-laden, still held the charm of its youth, waiting to shine again if only someone would bother to care. "I want to leave, Jack. I want to go back to a life where I don't have to constantly defend my choices or feel guilty for wanting to find my own path."

"Finding your path doesn't mean turning your back on the past," he insisted, his voice softer now, almost coaxing. "You can reclaim it. You can make it your own."

"You don't get it," I said, my voice rising as emotions swirled in my chest. "I spent years trying to carve out a place for myself. I went to college, I got a job, and every time I thought I could breathe, I felt this pull back to a life I didn't choose."

"Maybe it's time you chose differently." He paused, his gaze unwavering. "There's so much potential here. You just have to want to see it."

The silence that followed was thick with possibility, and I could feel my resolve starting to crack. A small part of me itched to stay, to see if I could breathe new life into this old hotel, to transform it from the remnants of a bygone era into something fresh and vibrant. But could I really do that?

"What if I fail?" The words slipped out before I could stop them, revealing the trepidation I harbored beneath my bravado. "What if I invest my time and energy, and it all comes crashing down? It's easier to walk away than to risk disappointment."

Jack took a step forward, his expression earnest. "But what if you succeed? What if this place becomes something incredible because you chose to fight for it? I've seen the spark in you, Alice. You're stronger than you think."

His encouragement was like a lifeline, but it also made me uncomfortable. The idea of success felt too far away, too abstract. "You're talking about dreams, Jack, and dreams are a luxury I can't afford."

He took a deep breath, running a hand through his hair in that endearingly frustrated way. "I get it. I do. But sometimes, the things that scare us the most are the things worth fighting for. You've got a chance to do something real here, not just for you but for this town, for your family."

The thought was intoxicating and terrifying all at once. I glanced out the window toward the small park that bordered the hotel, where children played under the watchful gaze of their parents. Could I really be a part of something bigger?

Just then, a loud crash echoed from the kitchen, breaking the fragile moment. Jack and I exchanged glances, the tension momentarily eclipsed by curiosity and concern. Without thinking, we rushed through the doorway, propelled by instinct.

The scene that met us was a chaotic blend of overturned pots, a cloud of flour in the air, and the unmistakable sight of Tom, the hotel's part-time cook, trying to right a massive mixer that had toppled over. Flour coated his hair and clothes, and he looked like he'd just stepped out of a slapstick comedy.

"Tom! What in the world?" I exclaimed, trying to suppress my laughter.

He looked up, flour-covered and sheepish, hands raised in surrender. "I was just trying to whip up a batch of muffins! It seems I have more skill with a frying pan than this contraption."

Jack chuckled, shaking his head. "And you thought it was a good idea to wrestle with a mixer? You're going to scare the tourists away before they even arrive."

"Hey, I thought it might impress Alice!" Tom shot back, his tone defensive yet playful. "Muffins are a staple around here. What's a hotel without good muffins?"

A smile tugged at the corners of my lips, and I felt the tension from earlier dissolve into the air. Maybe this was what I needed—a reminder of the community that surrounded me, the people who were just as much a part of this hotel as the walls themselves.

"Alright, let's see what we can salvage," I said, rolling up my sleeves, determination igniting within me. Maybe I wasn't ready to walk away just yet. Perhaps it was time to start piecing together not just the hotel, but my own fragmented dreams, one muffin at a time.

As the flour settled and the chaos of the kitchen slowly transformed back into something resembling order, I couldn't shake the realization that I had just stepped into a scene I never knew I needed. Tom, still dusting himself off, beamed with the kind of enthusiasm only found in someone who had just successfully salvaged a disaster. "Alright, where's that mixing bowl? We're going to need a lot of flour to make up for my earlier faux pas," he quipped, grinning like a child on Christmas morning.

I grabbed a bowl from the shelf and tossed it toward him, unable to suppress a laugh. "Just don't knock over anything else, alright? I've had enough of hotel disasters for one morning." The banter hung in the air like a warm hug, and I could feel the tightness in my chest ease just a bit.

Jack leaned against the doorframe, arms crossed, a bemused smile playing at the corners of his lips. "I'm pretty sure Tom's kitchen skills have never been better demonstrated. Should we be concerned about the state of our breakfast?"

"Only if we run out of muffins," I replied, my voice teasing. "In that case, I'd say we should all be worried."

Tom snorted and began gathering ingredients with renewed vigor, tossing flour and sugar into the mixing bowl like a mad scientist. "I promise you, this time I won't let anything explode. Well, unless you count my attempts at baking."

As I joined in to help, the rhythm of our movement created a kind of unspoken camaraderie. The scent of sugar and vanilla wafted through the air, an intoxicating reminder of simpler times, as I caught Jack watching me, a contemplative expression on his face. I wondered what thoughts were brewing behind those deep brown eyes. Maybe he saw the shift in me, the flicker of hope igniting where frustration had reigned just moments before.

"You know," he said, breaking the comfortable silence, "there's something undeniably charming about a hotel that serves muffins for breakfast."

"Is that what you'd call it? Charming?" I shot back, raising an eyebrow. "I'd say it's more of a 'why did I decide to come back here?' kind of charm."

He chuckled, and the sound reverberated through the room, warming the space. "It's not just about the muffins, Alice. It's about the people. This place has heart. You just need to look beyond the dust and broken fixtures."

"I appreciate the sentiment, but I still have to figure out how to make it financially viable," I countered, slipping into practicality. "And I still don't know how to run a hotel. Not to mention, I've been out of this game for years."

"Maybe you don't have to do it alone," Jack suggested, his tone earnest. "You've got me, and I know this place better than anyone."

"Great, so I get to run a hotel with my unpaid intern," I replied, crossing my arms dramatically. "I hope you're not expecting a salary anytime soon."

"Hey, I've got years of experience in hard labor," he replied, grinning. "Consider it a volunteer opportunity."

The banter continued, flowing easily between us, like a melody that had been dormant for too long. But as we began mixing the batter, a sudden weight pressed down on me, a reminder that beneath the laughter, uncertainty still loomed. There were bills to pay, repairs to consider, and a town whose memory of my family had woven itself into the fabric of their lives. I could feel the knot in my stomach tightening as I pushed those thoughts aside, focusing instead on the moment at hand.

Just as Tom popped the muffins into the oven, a sharp knock echoed through the kitchen. The sound was insistent, the kind that demanded immediate attention. We all turned toward the door, and I felt a flicker of dread. Visitors had been few and far between lately, and the last thing I wanted was another reminder of the mess I was tangled in.

"Who could that be?" I asked, casting a sideways glance at Jack. He shrugged, concern flickering across his face.

"I'll check," he said, moving toward the door with a purposeful stride.

As he opened it, a rush of cool air swept in, mingling with the warmth of the kitchen. A tall figure stood silhouetted in the doorway, backlit by the sunlight. I squinted against the brightness, trying to make out the features of the newcomer.

When Jack stepped aside, the figure moved into the room, revealing a woman with sharp features, dark hair pulled back in a tight bun, her eyes glinting with a mix of curiosity and judgment. She was dressed impeccably, the kind of tailored outfit that screamed "I mean business," and my heart sank.

"Good morning," she said, her tone cool and clipped, scanning the room with a critical eye. "I'm Margaret Lane, the new representative from the town council. I've been hearing quite a lot about the state of this establishment."

"Oh great," I muttered under my breath, exchanging a worried glance with Jack. "What did I do this time?"

Margaret didn't seem to notice my discontent as she continued, "I understand there's been quite a bit of upheaval since your grandmother passed. It's unfortunate, really." Her gaze landed on the counter strewn with baking supplies, and a slight grimace crossed her face. "But the council is concerned about how this will affect the community."

"Is that so?" I replied, fighting the urge to bristle. "And how do you suppose my grandmother's passing affects the entire town? Are muffins now a public concern?"

Her lips pressed into a thin line, and I could see the challenge sparking in her eyes. "Your family's hotel has always been a cornerstone of this community, Alice. If it falls into disrepair, it would impact everyone. We can't have that."

The tension in the room thickened, Jack standing protectively beside me, a silent support against the unexpected onslaught. "We're working on it, Margaret," he said, his voice steady. "But we could use some time and maybe a little support from the council."

"Oh, I'm sure you'll need more than just time," she replied, her gaze flicking between us. "The town is considering options. Options that might not include this hotel in its future."

The weight of her words landed like a stone in my stomach, the gravity of the situation crashing down around us. "What options?" I managed to ask, my voice steady despite the tumult within.

Her lips curved into a slight smile, but it didn't reach her eyes. "Let's just say, if you can't show us that you're committed to reviving this place soon, we may have to explore alternative solutions."

The implication hung heavy in the air, each word echoing in the silence that followed. I could feel the ground shift beneath me, and suddenly, the muffins we had been so cheerfully preparing felt like a distant memory, lost in the shadow of impending decisions.

As Margaret continued, my mind raced, grappling with the looming threat of losing everything my family had built. The room faded away, leaving just the weight of her words and the reality of what lay ahead. With every beat of my heart, the uncertainty coiled tighter, the stakes higher than I had ever imagined.

"Let's schedule a follow-up meeting," she concluded, her tone final. "You'll need to present your plan for the hotel and how you intend to uphold its legacy. I suggest you prepare thoroughly."

Just like that, with a confident nod, she turned and left, the door swinging closed behind her with a dull thud that echoed like a drumroll, marking the beginning of a new battle I hadn't anticipated.

I turned to Jack, my heart racing. "What do we do now?"

His expression mirrored my concern, determination mingling with uncertainty. "We fight, Alice. We fight like hell."

And as I stood there, staring at the door that had just closed on my hopes and fears, I realized that the fight was only beginning. The weight of my family's legacy pressed heavily on my shoulders, and I knew that walking away was no longer an option. The stakes were too high, the potential too great. I was in this now, and there was no turning back.

Chapter 5: Secrets Beneath the Surface

Sorting through Nana's belongings was like peeling back layers of a life I thought I understood, only to discover the hidden complexities beneath the surface. Each item held a story, from the yellowing postcards she had collected over the years, filled with the scrawled loops of her friends' handwriting, to the vintage brooches that sparkled like memories from another era. The scent of lavender still lingered in the air, a ghost of her presence that clung to the fabric of the quilt draped over the armchair, a piece she once told me was made from scraps of old dresses she cherished. I was almost certain I could hear her laughter echoing in the background, a comforting reminder of the summer days spent nestled in her embrace, listening to her recount tales from her youth.

It was in that armchair, beneath the quilt, that I stumbled upon something unexpected—a small wooden box, its lid slightly ajar, as if inviting me to pry deeper into its contents. My fingers brushed against the smooth, polished surface, the grain telling stories of its own. Inside, nestled among a collection of dried flowers and faded photographs, was an old leather journal, its cover worn and soft like a cherished favorite. The sight of it sent a shiver of anticipation down my spine. Nana had always kept journals, chronicling everything from daily musings to the weighty truths of her heart. I felt a thrill, mingled with trepidation, as I flipped open the cover, the crisp pages crackling in protest.

Her handwriting danced across the paper, a mix of neat loops and hurried scrawls that revealed glimpses of a life lived boldly. The entries were like whispered secrets spilling from the past, painting vivid pictures of laughter-filled evenings at the hotel she had owned, where the hum of conversation and the clinking of glasses had created a tapestry of life. She wrote of the guests—their joys and heartaches woven together like the threads of her beloved quilts.

Each line felt like a tether to a time I could only imagine, a world filled with flickering candlelight and the rich aroma of her famous apple pie wafting through the air.

Yet, as I delved deeper into the pages, I found something that struck a dissonant chord. Amidst the jovial accounts of bustling summers and cozy winters, there were mentions of a promise—a vow made long ago to someone whose name was only hinted at, lost within the delicate lines of her cursive. The details were vague, almost shadowy, hinting at a love that had once burned brightly but seemed to have flickered out, leaving behind an ember of unfulfilled longing. I read and reread the words, my heart quickening with each sentence, feeling an inexplicable connection to this long-forgotten promise. It gnawed at me, this sense that there was more to Nana's life than the warm nostalgia I had clung to.

Jack, the gruff handyman who had always been a fixture at the hotel, floated to mind as I pondered the journal's revelations. I could picture him now, his rugged features softened by the fading light, yet there was an impenetrable wall behind his dark eyes. There was a history there, a shared knowledge that seemed to dance just out of reach. Each time I had asked him about the past—about Nana, about the hotel—he had brushed it off with a casual wave of his hand, deflecting my curiosity with a gravelly chuckle or a muttered remark about the weather. But now, armed with the journal's secrets, I felt a surge of determination. I needed to confront him, to peel back those layers of his carefully constructed facade.

When I finally found him in the maintenance shed, tinkering with an ancient radiator, the tension crackled in the air like the static before a storm. "Jack," I said, my voice steady despite the butterflies swirling in my stomach. He looked up, brow furrowed, a tool pausing in mid-air. "I found something—Nana's journal."

His expression shifted, a shadow crossing his features. "That old thing? Best to leave it be," he replied, his tone gruff, but I noticed the flicker of fear that ignited in his eyes. It was a fleeting moment, but it told me everything I needed to know.

"No," I pressed, stepping closer, the journal clutched tightly in my hands. "There are things in there—things about a promise she made, something that meant the world to her. I think you know what it is." My heart raced, the stakes suddenly higher than I'd anticipated.

Jack's jaw tightened, the gruff exterior I had come to recognize shifting into something more vulnerable, almost fragile. "You shouldn't be digging into things that don't concern you," he warned, his voice low, gravelly.

But I saw through the facade, the fear lurking just beneath the surface. "And why not? It's about my family, about her. How can I not want to know?" The air between us was thick with unspoken truths, secrets swirling like dust motes caught in the sunlight filtering through the cracked window.

He set down the tool, his shoulders sagging as if the weight of the world pressed down upon him. "Some promises are better left unbroken, Sophie," he said, his voice rough like the wood of the shed, and in that moment, I could see the shadows of his own burdens reflected in his eyes. It was a poignant reminder that we all carry our histories, threads of grief and joy woven together in complex patterns.

"Then tell me," I urged, desperate for the truth. "What did Nana promise? Who was she to you?" I stepped closer, the distance between us shrinking, and for a heartbeat, it felt like we were two souls standing at the edge of something profound, teetering on the brink of revelation.

Jack hesitated, his gaze drifting away, as if the weight of my question had sent him spiraling into the past. "You're not ready for that," he murmured, his voice barely above a whisper, but the challenge in my heart burned hotter. What lay beneath the surface was not just about Nana's promise—it was about understanding the threads of our own lives that connected us, even when we felt worlds apart.

Jack's reluctance hung in the air like the humidity before a summer storm, electric and thick with unspoken truths. His eyes flickered back to the journal, the weight of it palpable between us, a tangible connection to a history he seemed desperate to keep buried. "You think you're ready for this, Sophie?" he asked, his tone low and rough, each word tinged with a protective urgency that only deepened my curiosity.

"Ready or not, it's part of my history too," I shot back, a fire igniting in my chest. "You might think you're protecting me, but you're just keeping me in the dark." The truth was, I was tired of shadows, tired of unanswered questions that loomed over me like the low-hanging clouds threatening to spill rain at any moment.

His shoulders stiffened, and for a brief moment, I thought he might close off entirely. But instead, he took a deep breath, as if steeling himself for the plunge. "Fine," he said finally, the resignation in his voice ringing louder than any accusation. "But you need to understand that some stories come with a cost."

"Everything worth knowing has a price," I replied, crossing my arms defiantly, my heart racing with anticipation and anxiety. "What's the worst that could happen? Just tell me what you know."

Jack shifted his weight, glancing toward the door as if considering an escape route. Instead, he leaned against the workbench, arms folded tightly across his chest. "Nana was special, Sophie. Not just to you, but to this place. She carried secrets like a traveler carries a heavy bag—wearily, yet with a sense of purpose." His eyes softened for a moment, and I caught a glimpse of something raw and painful behind the bravado.

"I get that," I urged, taking a tentative step closer. "But she wrote about a promise, Jack. What was it? Who was it to?" My voice cracked slightly, desperation threading through my words.

With a sigh that seemed to echo the weight of decades, Jack began to speak, each word drawing me deeper into a story I had never fully understood. "Years ago, before you were born, there was a man—Derek. He and your Nana were... close. More than close, really. They were in love. But life happened, as it always does. He was the kind of man who could charm the socks off anyone, but he had a wandering heart."

I felt my breath catch, the images of a young Nana laughing, her eyes sparkling with joy, swirling in my mind. "And the promise?" I pressed, feeling as if the ground beneath me had begun to shift.

"He promised to return, to make a life together." Jack's gaze turned distant, like he was searching for memories lost to time. "But life took him away, and Nana was left with nothing but that promise. I think it haunted her." The words hung between us like a spectral presence, heavy with implication.

"Haunted?" I echoed, my heart pounding. "Did he ever come back?"

Jack shook his head, a sadness washing over his features. "No. He got swept up in his own life—adventures, dreams, whatever they call them. And Nana, she kept that promise alive, waiting for him to return. I don't think she ever stopped loving him, even when she moved on."

I tried to process this revelation, the reality of Nana's unfulfilled love hitting me like a wave. It was easy to see her as the strong matriarch, but this story painted her in shades I had never considered. "What happened to him?" I asked, my voice barely above a whisper.

Jack met my gaze, a mixture of empathy and caution in his expression. "He became a traveler, chasing after dreams and escapades, leaving behind a trail of broken promises. But the truth is, Sophie, sometimes it's not the promises we make that define us; it's the ones we don't keep."

The air thickened with the weight of his words, and I could feel the walls of my childhood crumbling around me, revealing a more intricate foundation. "Do you know where he is now?" I ventured, almost afraid of the answer.

Jack shrugged, his indifference seeming to mask a deeper sorrow. "Last I heard, he was in New Orleans, living a life full of music and adventure. But that was years ago. Who knows where he is now? Maybe he's still wandering." The name of that vibrant city conjured images of jazz-filled nights and beignets dusted with powdered sugar, contrasting sharply with the stark reality of a lost love.

"And what about you?" I asked, the question slipping out before I could rein it in. "You've been here for as long as I can remember. Did you love her too?"

Jack's expression flickered, the defenses he had built so carefully beginning to crack. "Nana was like family to me," he replied, a hint of vulnerability softening his voice. "I was her right hand, helping her keep the hotel running. But love? That's a different story."

"Different how?" My curiosity was piqued, the threads of his emotions weaving into the fabric of my own burgeoning understanding of this tangled history.

He sighed, rubbing the back of his neck as if trying to shake off a weight. "I cared for her, in my own way. But she was always waiting for someone else. It's hard to compete with a ghost." His honesty struck a chord deep within me, reverberating with an empathy I hadn't expected to feel.

"I had no idea," I murmured, feeling a pang of guilt for prying into a life I had only seen through a narrow lens. "But she was happy, wasn't she? I mean, she had us."

Jack nodded slowly, his expression softening with nostalgia. "She was happy enough, but you could see the flicker of loss in her eyes. It was like she carried two lives inside her—the one she lived and the one she let slip away."

The atmosphere shifted, charged with a tension that felt both fragile and electrifying. I could sense the weight of our shared history, how our lives intertwined through threads of love, loss, and unfulfilled promises. "Do you think she ever stopped hoping he would return?"

Jack met my gaze, his eyes reflecting a storm of emotions. "Hope is a tricky thing, Sophie. It can either lift you or crush you beneath its weight."

His words hung in the air, a poignant reminder of the stories that shape us, often in ways we can't comprehend. I felt the remnants of Nana's promise echoing in my chest, and it stirred something within me—a determination to uncover the truth, not just for her, but for myself. The layers of our shared history were unfurling, revealing a tapestry of interconnected lives that had weathered the storms of time, and I was resolute in my quest to stitch together the fragments that remained.

The air between us was thick with unresolved emotions, each moment stretching out like an elastic band ready to snap. I could sense the tension simmering beneath the surface, igniting my curiosity and frustration in equal measure. Jack stood there, his rugged exterior betraying an internal battle, and I couldn't help but wonder what other secrets the old hotel held—secrets that could rewrite our family history.

"Why are you so intent on keeping me in the dark?" I asked, a little more forcefully than I intended. The vulnerability I had glimpsed in Jack's eyes was now a distant memory, replaced by the familiar mask of gruff indifference.

"I'm not keeping you in the dark," he replied, his voice steady but lacking the warmth I had hoped for. "I'm trying to protect you from the shadows that linger here." He gestured around the cramped shed, and I could almost see the specters dancing in the corners, haunting the very air we breathed.

"Protect me? Or protect yourself?" I countered, my voice laced with irritation. "It's easy to hide behind walls when you've built them high enough to keep everyone out."

His eyes narrowed, and for a moment, I thought he might bite back with something sharp. But instead, he sighed heavily, the weight of his years pressing down upon him. "Look, I get it. You want answers. But some things are better left undisturbed. Your Nana's story isn't just a love tale; it's a tragedy that could tear apart the very fabric of what you believe to be true."

"Then let me decide what's worth tearing apart," I insisted, refusing to back down. "I owe it to her to find out the truth. And you owe it to yourself to stop being her guardian and start being honest with me."

Jack looked away, running a hand through his tousled hair. "You think you're ready for that?" he asked, more to himself than to me. "You think the truth will set you free? Sometimes, the truth just chains you to the past."

I could see the struggle etched on his face, a man caught between loyalty to my Nana and his own buried feelings. "If you really loved her, why didn't you ever tell her? Why let her cling to the memory of someone who never came back?" The words slipped from my mouth before I could rein them in, but the question lingered in the air, charged with emotion.

Jack's jaw tightened, and for a moment, I feared I had crossed a line. But then, a flicker of something crossed his eyes—regret, perhaps? "Love doesn't always manifest in the way we expect, Sophie. Sometimes it's about sacrifice, knowing when to step back. I didn't want to be the reason she forgot about Derek."

"Derek," I repeated, tasting the name on my tongue. It was a name that had been whispered through the corridors of the hotel, lost in the echoes of laughter and memories. "And what if she never forgot him? What if her life was just an elaborate stage set, and she was the only actor left standing?"

Jack stepped closer, the distance between us shrinking to nothing. "You're digging into a grave that's been left undisturbed for too long. What do you expect to find? Closure? Answers? Sometimes, the best thing to do is to let the past stay buried, even if it means sacrificing your peace."

The heat of the moment ignited a fire within me. "Sacrifice peace? You mean sacrifice the truth? I refuse to believe that unearthing these secrets will bring anything worse than the shadows you're so afraid of."

He studied me, a mixture of admiration and concern flashing in his eyes. "You're stubborn," he finally said, a hint of a smile creeping onto his lips, though the weight of our conversation lingered. "Just like your Nana."

"Stubbornness runs in the family," I replied, a smirk breaking through my earlier frustration. "But I think we both know it's more than just stubbornness. I'm trying to understand the legacy she left behind. I want to know who she really was, beyond the quilts and apple pies."

Jack sighed deeply, the tension in his posture easing just slightly. "All right. But if we're going to do this, we need to tread carefully. You're right about one thing: secrets can be like a wildfire, consuming everything in their path. And once they're out, there's no putting them back in."

"Then let's douse that wildfire with truth," I declared, my resolve hardening like steel. "What do we need to do?"

"I'll take you to the old garden shed," Jack said, his expression shifting from apprehensive to contemplative. "It's where Nana used to keep her most personal things. If she wrote about her promise, there's a chance she may have stored something of Derek's there too—letters, photographs, anything."

My heart raced at the thought of uncovering more of Nana's past. "Lead the way," I urged, and without another word, he turned on his heel, his presence both daunting and comforting as we navigated through the sprawling grounds of the hotel.

The garden shed was a ramshackle structure at the far end of the property, hidden behind a thicket of wildflowers that had overgrown in a riot of color. As we approached, the familiar scent of damp earth and blooming petals enveloped us, creating an atmosphere thick with nostalgia. Jack pushed open the creaky door, and it swung inward with a groan, revealing a cluttered space filled with tools and remnants of the past.

"Here," he said, leading me deeper inside. "She kept a lot of old things in here." His voice softened as he pointed to an old trunk, its surface scuffed and worn from years of neglect. "This is where I think we'll find what you're looking for."

With trembling fingers, I knelt before the trunk, the air charged with anticipation. "What if it's nothing?" I whispered, uncertainty creeping in. "What if it's just more memories I'm not ready to face?"

"Then we deal with it together," Jack said, placing a reassuring hand on my shoulder. "Whatever you find, you won't have to face it alone."

Taking a deep breath, I lifted the lid of the trunk, the hinges protesting like ghosts disturbed from slumber. Inside, layers of yellowed fabric and brittle papers greeted me, the remnants of a life long past. As I sifted through the contents, a fragile envelope caught my eye, its edges frayed and yellowed, bearing my Nana's elegant handwriting.

My heart thudded in my chest as I pulled it free, and the moment I opened it, the scent of lavender flooded my senses, sending me spiraling back to the summers of my youth when she would sprinkle it on her linens. Inside was a letter addressed to Derek, words swirling like the memories of a life once cherished.

Suddenly, the creak of the door jolted me, and I turned to see a shadow silhouetted against the light. "Jack?" I called, confusion and dread mingling in my gut.

"Yeah?" he replied, but his tone was different—strained, almost urgent.

"I think I found something!" I exclaimed, holding the letter up like a treasure. But as I turned back to the trunk, a sense of unease settled over me, the atmosphere shifting abruptly.

"Where are you?" I asked again, but there was no response. Just silence.

And then I felt it—a presence in the room, cold and unyielding, wrapping around me like a shroud. I turned, and what I saw made my breath catch in my throat. Standing in the doorway was a figure I recognized all too well, a familiar face cloaked in shadows. The last person I ever expected to see.

Chapter 6: The Dance

The sun hung low in the sky, draping the small town in a golden hue that seemed to soften the edges of every bustling stall and laughter-filled gathering. The air buzzed with the excitement of the annual summer festival, a kaleidoscope of colors and sounds that blended together like a perfectly mixed cocktail. As I stood by the town square, feeling slightly out of place in my faded sundress, I could see the locals setting up booths adorned with homemade crafts and sweet treats that wafted enticing aromas through the warm breeze. I had always imagined myself as a charming stranger in a storybook, but today, I felt more like a misplaced puzzle piece, the edges rough and unfit for the vibrant picture before me.

"Come on, Emily! We need more hands at the pie-eating contest!" Ellen, one of the local matrons with a laugh that rolled like thunder, swept in with a determined look that brooked no argument. Her floral-patterned apron fluttered as she grabbed my wrist, pulling me away from my thoughts and deeper into the heart of the festivities. I tried to protest, a weak protest, really, because deep down, I knew it would be futile. These women had made it their mission to fold me into their community like a well-loved quilt.

I was swept along, weaving through the throng of townsfolk, each face familiar with the other as they called out greetings and shared teasing jabs, their bonds forged over years of shared experiences. I couldn't help but admire the way they moved together, a living tapestry of lives intertwined, vibrant and alive, while I was just a thread dangling on the fringe. I caught glimpses of Jack at the edge of the crowd, his tall frame leaning against a wooden post, hands stuffed in his pockets, an inscrutable expression crossing his handsome face. There was an undeniable shift in the air when our eyes met—a charged recognition that was both familiar and unsettling.

"Look who finally decided to show up," he said when I approached, his voice low and teasing, but there was something deeper behind his words. It was that subtle challenge wrapped in a playful smirk, a part of him that I was beginning to understand.

"Not everyone can be as dedicated to festivities as you, Jack," I shot back, grateful that my tone held a playful edge. It felt good to spar with him, to dance around the complicated feelings that simmered beneath the surface. His lips curled into a grin, and for a moment, the world around us faded—the laughter of children, the clink of glasses, the distant strum of a guitar melted away, leaving just the two of us suspended in a moment that felt almost intimate.

The shrill whistle of the contest started, and before I knew it, Ellen had dragged me into the chaos of the pie-eating frenzy. I watched as faces smeared with berry juices dove into the task with competitive fervor. I couldn't help but laugh, the sound bubbling up and spilling over. For all my initial reluctance, there was a warmth to being pulled into this chaos, a sense of belonging that sent a thrill through me, igniting a spark I thought had long extinguished.

Just as the laughter crescendoed, the music began—a lively folk tune that filled the air with energy, beckoning everyone to the makeshift dance floor. Before I could catch my breath, Ellen hoisted me up, her infectious enthusiasm compelling me into the crowd. I was surrounded by twirling skirts and stomping boots, the rhythm thumping in my chest as hands pulled me into the fray.

Then, through the swirling bodies and sparkling lights, I felt a familiar hand wrap around mine. Jack's presence anchored me amidst the joyous chaos. He spun me into the dance, and for a fleeting moment, the world became a blur of colors and sounds, a sensory delight that enveloped us. Our hands touched, and it was electric—a spark that traveled up my arm, igniting something deep within me that I hadn't dared to acknowledge.

"You dance like you were born to it," he murmured, a teasing glint in his eye, though I could see the seriousness behind his jest. My heart raced, caught in the whirlwind of the music and the connection crackling between us.

"And you dance like you're trying to avoid stepping on my toes," I shot back, a grin spreading across my face. He laughed, a deep, genuine sound that echoed in my ears, and I felt my earlier hesitations begin to melt away.

But as the song swelled, pulling us into its crescendo, reality came crashing back like a wave, threatening to drown me in uncertainty. The laughter of the festival faded, the faces blurred, and all that remained was Jack and me, locked in this moment where time seemed to stand still. I could see the challenge in his eyes, a flicker of understanding passing between us that hinted at something deeper, something I was terrified to explore.

The music began to slow, the vibrant notes tapering off, and just like that, the spell broke. The crowd reasserted itself, the laughter and chatter crashing in like a tidal wave, dragging me back to the reality I had tried so hard to escape. I stumbled back, trying to catch my breath, the weight of the world pressing down on me. I didn't belong here; I wasn't part of this life. I could feel the familiar urge to flee creeping up my spine, pulling me away from the warmth of the gathering and the intensity in Jack's gaze.

"I—" I started, my voice barely above a whisper, but Jack stepped closer, the energy between us palpable, charged with unspoken words and possibilities that left me dizzy. He opened his mouth to respond, but before he could say anything, I turned and fled the dance floor, my heart pounding like the distant drums.

I stumbled out of the dance like a startled rabbit, heart racing and breath hitching in my throat. The festival's lively energy buzzed around me, but it felt alien now, too vibrant against the gray cloud of my thoughts. I dashed toward the edge of the square, where the trees stood like watchful sentinels, their leaves whispering secrets in the wind. I needed a moment—a brief pause to collect myself before the weight of reality came crashing back in full force.

Leaning against the sturdy trunk of an ancient oak, I let the rough bark press against my back, grounding me in the present. The laughter and music faded into a distant hum, and I closed my eyes, allowing the cool breeze to wash over me. Yet, even in this moment of solitude, I felt the heat of Jack's gaze lingering like a shadow, an invisible tether binding me to that electrifying dance. The way our hands had connected—it had ignited something I wasn't prepared to confront.

"Hey, Emily!" a voice called out, pulling me from my thoughts. It was Lily, one of the town's youngest residents, with her wild curls bouncing as she approached, clutching a handful of colorful ribbons. "Are you okay? You look like you just saw a ghost!" Her innocence was like a balm to my frayed nerves.

"I'm fine, just... needed some air," I replied, forcing a smile that felt too tight. "What's with the ribbons?"

"They're for the maypole!" she chirped, practically bouncing in place. "You have to help! Come on!" She tugged at my sleeve, her enthusiasm contagious despite my lingering doubts.

The maypole stood in the center of the square, a tall, adorned pole surrounded by a patchwork of flowers. The townsfolk had gathered around it, eager to start weaving the ribbons in a colorful dance that represented unity and community spirit. I hesitated, glancing back toward the dance floor where Jack lingered, his silhouette etched against the sunset. He was deep in conversation with a group of guys, yet the distance between us felt like an unbridgeable chasm.

"Emily! You're here!" Ellen's voice boomed from the crowd, her presence as commanding as ever. "Come on! We need all hands on deck for this!" She waved me over, her apron swaying like a banner of authority.

With a sigh of resignation, I followed Lily to the maypole. The energy of the crowd enveloped me, and despite my initial reluctance, I felt a flicker of belonging sparking back to life. I knelt to help tie ribbons to the base, vibrant colors swirling together, reminding me of childhood summers spent weaving daisy chains and dreaming of fairy tales.

"Alright, everyone!" Ellen announced, clapping her hands to draw attention. "Let's show Emily how it's done!" The crowd erupted into laughter, and the light-heartedness of it all made me chuckle. The way they all rallied around, as if I were the guest of honor, sent warmth spreading through my chest.

As the music started again, a lively tune that begged for movement, I joined the throng of dancers weaving around the maypole, each twist and turn bringing ribbons together in a symphony of color. The air was thick with laughter, the sound bright and buoyant, pulling me into its rhythm.

"Careful, or you'll trip over your own feet!" Jack teased from the sidelines, his voice warm and playful, pulling me back into the space between us. He stepped forward, and before I could brace myself, he took my hand again, guiding me into the dance with a natural ease that belied my earlier panic.

"Or maybe I'll just trip over you," I shot back, the banter feeling effortless, a dance of words as we twirled beneath the gathering dusk. There was something exhilarating about the way he moved, every step charged with a playful challenge, each turn a silent agreement that we could share this moment without the baggage of our past.

But as the dance progressed, the joy began to twist into something more complicated, a tension that sparked between us like static electricity. His laughter echoed in my ears, but it only served to remind me of the distance I still felt within this vibrant community.

I was just an outsider trying to fit in, a shadow moving through the light.

As the last notes of the song faded, Jack leaned closer, his breath brushing against my ear as he said, "You know, you should stay. This place isn't so bad." His tone held an urgency that struck me, a plea wrapped in the fabric of playful challenge.

"I can't," I replied, my heart sinking at the weight of the truth. "I don't belong here, Jack. I don't know how to be what everyone expects." The words slipped out before I could rein them in, a confession that felt raw and exposed.

He pulled back slightly, searching my eyes with an intensity that made my pulse quicken. "What do you want, then? What would make you feel like you belong?" There was a softness in his tone, a curiosity that made it feel as if we were two explorers navigating uncharted territory.

Before I could answer, a commotion erupted near the edge of the square. A group of teenagers was gathered, voices raised in playful shouts, but it soon turned into something more heated. I could see a couple of them gesturing animatedly, and the laughter that had filled the festival was replaced by an uneasy tension.

"Let's check it out," Jack said, already leading the way, his hand brushing against mine. I followed, a mixture of excitement and apprehension bubbling in my stomach. The festival felt alive with possibilities, yet the looming confrontation ahead sent a shiver down my spine.

As we approached, I could make out the faces of the teens, their expressions morphing from playful to confrontational. It seemed like a harmless disagreement at first, but something told me it was about to escalate. Jack moved ahead, his posture protective, and I felt a strange mix of admiration and worry for him.

"What's going on?" Jack asked, his voice steady but commanding, cutting through the rising tension like a knife. I stayed a step behind, watching as the situation unfolded, aware that this small town was about to reveal more of its secrets, secrets that could either bind me closer to it or push me away entirely.

The thrumming energy of the festival intensified as I neared the gathering of teenagers, their laughter now tinged with a sharper edge. I could see Jack's posture shift, his body instinctively leaning forward as he assessed the situation. It was strange to see him step into this role—he was no longer just the flippant jokester who danced with me moments ago, but a protector poised to confront whatever drama was brewing. The air crackled with anticipation, and I felt the unease settle in my stomach like a heavy stone.

"Come on, let's just talk about this!" a tall boy with wild hair shouted, gesturing wildly as he squared off with another teen who stood defiantly, arms crossed, eyes blazing. The crowd began to gather, murmurs rippling through the onlookers, and the sense of community that had filled the festival moments earlier felt like it was fraying at the edges.

"What's happening?" I murmured to Jack, keeping my voice low as I stepped closer, hoping my presence would help defuse whatever tension lingered. He shot me a sidelong glance, his expression a mixture of concern and determination.

"Just a disagreement about who gets to play the lead in the town's upcoming play. It's been brewing for weeks," he replied, his voice steady despite the chaos unfolding before us. "But these things can escalate quickly. Just stay behind me."

I nodded, caught between wanting to step in and help and the instinct to hold back and watch as Jack navigated this fraught situation. The boy with wild hair was clearly trying to keep things civil, but the other boy, a stocky kid with a scowl etched onto his face, seemed intent on stirring the pot.

"You think you're better than everyone just because your dad's on the council?" the stocky boy sneered, taking a step closer, fists clenched at his sides. The challenge hung in the air like a thick fog, heavy with the unspoken tension of pride and ambition.

"Hey!" Jack stepped forward, placing himself between the two boys. "This isn't the place for this. We're supposed to be celebrating, not brawling in the streets." His voice rang out, firm but calm, drawing the attention of the gathering crowd.

The stocky boy opened his mouth to retort, but Jack continued, "Look, I know this is important to you guys. But fighting it out here is only going to ruin what we've worked for. Don't let your tempers take over." His tone softened slightly, a hint of understanding weaving through his words.

I watched, captivated, as Jack navigated the tension. His eyes flicked back to me for a fleeting moment, a silent connection passing between us, and for a split second, I thought I saw a flicker of hope in his gaze. He was trying to bridge the gap—not just for the boys but for me, too, inviting me into the fold of this community.

"Why don't we all take a breather?" I suggested, my voice gaining confidence. "How about we grab some of that pie before it's gone? There's plenty to go around, and I hear Ellen makes the best cherry pie in the county." The light-hearted suggestion hung in the air, attempting to diffuse the intensity.

The stocky boy hesitated, his anger flickering like a candle in the wind. "I'm not interested in pie," he shot back, but his voice lacked conviction. I could see the wheels turning in his mind, the conflict between pride and the promise of sugary treats battling it out.

"Suit yourself, but you'll be missing out," I pressed, adding a playful grin to my words. "And I hear Ellen might just toss a slice at you if you're not careful. She has a pretty good aim."

At that, a small chuckle rippled through the crowd, tension beginning to dissolve as the absurdity of the situation lightened the mood. Jack seized the opportunity, stepping closer to the wild-haired boy, his expression earnest.

"Let's go. Grab some food, take a minute. We can sort out the play later," he urged, his voice warm with encouragement. "We're all on the same team here, right? We can't let a little disagreement spoil a good festival."

"Fine," the wild-haired boy conceded, his shoulders dropping as he turned away from the confrontation, his eyes darting to the pie table as if it were a mirage in the desert.

With the tension finally easing, I exhaled a breath I hadn't realized I was holding. The crowd began to disperse, laughter bubbling up again as they returned to the festivities, and I felt the warmth of the moment embrace me. Just as I started to relax, the stocky boy's parting words hung heavy in the air.

"Next time, you won't be so lucky," he muttered under his breath, but loud enough for us to hear. My stomach twisted at the warning, a chill creeping up my spine as I exchanged glances with Jack.

"Let's get some pie," he said, his expression shifting back to playful, though I could see the remnants of the earlier confrontation still lingering in his eyes.

We made our way to the table, a kaleidoscope of baked goods calling to us like sirens. I grabbed a plate and filled it with slices of pie, grateful for the distraction. "So, how many pies do you think Ellen bakes every year? Does she have a pie factory hidden away?" I quipped, trying to lighten the mood.

"Enough to fuel this town's collective sugar rush, for sure," Jack replied, stealing a piece of my pie before I could react. "Hey! That's mine!" I laughed, half-heartedly swatting at his hand.

"You snooze, you lose," he smirked, taking a bite and closing his eyes as if experiencing a moment of pure bliss. "Mmm, the cherry really is divine."

In that moment, the sweetness of the pie was nearly eclipsed by the sweetness of the moment we shared. Laughter danced between us, and I felt my heart lighten as we exchanged playful banter. I had always thought of Jack as a challenge, someone whose playful jabs masked deeper layers of emotion, but now I saw a boy just as uncertain as I was, trying to navigate this crazy life.

As we finished our pie, the festival began to wind down, the sun dipping lower in the sky, casting long shadows across the square. The air was thick with the scent of baked goods and the sounds of laughter that faded as people began to head home. I felt a tug in my chest, a reluctant understanding that the night was slipping away, much like my sense of belonging.

"Hey," Jack said, his voice softer now, a hint of something serious lacing his words. "Can we talk? Away from all this?" His gaze held mine, a mix of sincerity and something deeper that sent a thrill through me.

I hesitated, the weight of the moment settling between us. "Sure," I replied, my heart racing with the possibilities that lay ahead. Just as we turned to leave the fading festivities behind, a commotion erupted at the edge of the square. Shouts rang out, panic rising as someone yelled, "There's been an accident!"

I felt my pulse quicken as we turned toward the sound, the jubilant atmosphere of the festival shattering in an instant, replaced by confusion and dread. The evening, once filled with laughter and dance, now teetered on the brink of something ominous. My heart raced, a drumbeat of uncertainty echoing in my ears as Jack and I exchanged a look of alarm, the promise of a deeper conversation abruptly overshadowed by the sudden chaos.

Chapter 7: Ghosts of the Past

The night air hung heavy with the scent of damp earth and the faint whisper of impending rain. The moon peeked through a veil of clouds, casting a ghostly glow over the courtyard of the old hotel. I stood there, the worn bricks cool beneath my bare feet, lost in the memory of Nana's words that echoed in my mind like a haunting melody. Her journal, tucked away in the attic, seemed to pulse with unspoken secrets, a heartbeat echoing through time. The pages begged for exploration, for discovery, but Jack remained an unyielding wall between me and the truth.

Jack had been distant since the dance, his gaze averted, his presence like a shadow lurking at the edges of my reality. He avoided me, and I couldn't help but feel the tension thrumming in the air whenever we crossed paths. Each interaction felt like stepping into a minefield, every word carefully chosen as if it could detonate something I wasn't prepared to face. I needed answers, but prying them from him was like trying to extract honey from a stone.

"Jack," I finally ventured one evening, desperation coloring my tone. We were standing in the lobby, the grand chandelier flickering above us like a warning light. "What's the deal with Nana's journal? You've been avoiding me since the dance, and I can't shake the feeling that you know something I don't."

He hesitated, his brow furrowing as if weighing the words on his tongue. The silence stretched like a taut wire, and I could almost hear the crickets outside, their chirps a mocking backdrop to our standoff. "You really want to know?" he replied, a hint of irritation threading through his voice.

"Yes, I do," I said, crossing my arms defiantly. "I'm not some fragile flower that will wilt at the first hint of history. If there's something about Nana, about her promises, I deserve to know."

With a heavy sigh, he raked a hand through his tousled hair, the moonlight catching the edges of his jaw, making him look both rugged and vulnerable. "Fine. But don't say I didn't warn you." His tone shifted, softening just enough for me to sense the pain beneath his bravado.

He led me to the cozy sitting room, its deep-blue walls lined with framed photographs of the hotel in its glory days—guests smiling, laughter frozen in time. The fire crackled to life in the hearth, illuminating the dim corners where memories clung like cobwebs. I settled into an armchair, a mix of curiosity and anxiety swirling within me.

"Nana was more than just the heart of this place," he began, his voice low, almost reverent. "She was its guardian. When I was a kid, I used to sneak up here, listening to her stories about the hotel, how it was built on dreams and promises." He paused, as if the memories had weight. "Before she passed, she made me promise to keep it running, to protect it as she had done. This hotel isn't just bricks and mortar; it's family history, a legacy."

"So that's why you've been against my plan to sell," I murmured, piecing together the puzzle. "You think by letting it go, we're losing a part of ourselves?"

Jack nodded, a flicker of pain crossing his face. "It's not just a building to me. It's our past. And the promise I made to her is one I intend to keep. I know it sounds foolish—"

"Foolish? No, it sounds noble," I interrupted, leaning forward, intrigued by the depth of his devotion. "But what about my promise? What does she expect from me?"

The fire crackled as he shifted uncomfortably, the tension thickening. "That's the thing, isn't it? What did she mean by that? Did she want you to take over, to carry the burden?"

The questions hung in the air, sharp and unsettling. I had always seen myself as an extension of Nana's spirit, the granddaughter who could restore the hotel's former glory, but the weight of legacy felt like a shackle tightening around my chest. What if my dreams lay elsewhere, beyond these haunted walls? I had been so caught up in the notion of honoring her memory that I hadn't considered what it meant for my own future.

"I don't want to be a caretaker forever, Jack," I confessed, my voice trembling with the vulnerability I rarely displayed. "I want to forge my own path. But how do I reconcile that with her wishes?"

He met my gaze, his eyes dark and stormy. "Maybe it's not about choosing one over the other. You could find a way to honor her memory while still chasing your own dreams. The hotel doesn't have to be an anchor; it could be a springboard."

A flicker of hope ignited within me, brightening the gloom of uncertainty. Could I navigate the treacherous waters of my inheritance without losing myself in the process? The idea began to take root, but before I could voice my thoughts, the sudden sound of a door creaking open pulled me from my reverie.

Startled, we turned to find the old grandfather clock in the corner chiming, the haunting notes echoing through the stillness. Time had slipped away from us, as if it too were an unwelcome guest. The atmosphere shifted, laden with unspoken words and unresolved tension.

"Jack, what if—" I started, but he cut me off, the urgency in his tone causing my heart to race.

"We can figure this out, but we need to be careful. There are forces at play here, things that even Nana couldn't control." His expression darkened, a flicker of fear crossing his features. "If there's one thing I've learned from the past, it's that some ghosts refuse to be exorcised."

The air crackled with tension, and for a moment, I felt suspended in time, teetering on the edge of something monumental. Jack's words hung between us, heavy and fraught with meaning. He leaned against the mantel, arms crossed tightly over his chest, as if bracing against the weight of his confession. The fire flickered, casting dancing shadows that seemed to animate the very ghosts he spoke of, their whispers curling like smoke in the air.

"What do you mean, forces at play?" I asked, my voice barely more than a whisper. The room felt smaller suddenly, as if the walls were closing in, and I was drowning in a sea of unresolved questions.

Jack's gaze shifted to the crackling flames, his expression hardening. "Nana didn't just run this hotel; she guarded its secrets. I've seen things—things that can't be easily explained. If the hotel's past is intertwined with our futures, we have to tread carefully."

The shadows grew longer, deepening the lines of worry etched on his face. I could see the flicker of memories there, sharp and painful, and I realized this was more than just a promise. It was a burden he had carried, and now it was about to be shared.

"What kind of things?" I pressed, leaning in. The weight of the conversation was palpable, and I craved more, as if the knowledge could cut through the fog enveloping my thoughts.

He hesitated, searching my eyes for understanding. "The hotel has a history of... let's say, strange occurrences. People have come and gone, leaving behind echoes of their lives. Some are harmless; others are... not."

"Are you trying to tell me this place is haunted?" I said, a smirk tugging at the corner of my mouth, partly teasing, partly incredulous.

His expression softened, the corners of his lips lifting in a faint smile, a reminder of the boyish charm that first drew me to him. "In a manner of speaking. There's a reason the locals call it the 'Whispering Hotel.' People say they hear voices, see figures out of the corner of their eyes. I've experienced it myself."

"Like a resident ghost?" I asked, intrigued. The thought of unseen presences gave me a thrill, as if I had stumbled into a novel I hadn't yet finished reading.

"More like memories. Sometimes, they're so vivid it's like the past collides with the present. When I was a kid, I swore I saw Nana talking to someone in the garden, but when I ran out to see, she was alone. She told me it was just the wind. But I knew better."

The flicker of vulnerability in his eyes made me want to reach out, to anchor him to the present. "You're not crazy for believing that, you know," I said gently. "Maybe Nana was holding on to more than just the hotel. Maybe she was protecting something—someone."

Jack's gaze snapped back to mine, the intensity of his blue eyes almost disarming. "And what if whatever she was protecting is still here? What if it's waiting for us to uncover it?"

A shiver ran down my spine, and I couldn't help but glance around the room, half-expecting to see someone watching us from the shadows. The thought made me uneasy, but also exhilarated. "So what do we do?" I asked, my heart racing. "Do we start digging through her things? Find out what she was really trying to shield us from?"

He took a deep breath, and I could see the gears turning in his mind. "That might be part of it. But we need to be careful not to disturb whatever it is she kept hidden. She wouldn't have gone to such lengths if it were harmless."

The fire crackled again, sending a burst of warmth into the room. I pulled my blanket tighter around my shoulders, the fabric soft against my skin. The chill of the night began to seep in, but the heat between us felt like an unspoken agreement, a commitment to unraveling this mystery together.

"I can't just sit back and let the hotel go to waste," I said, my resolve hardening. "If Nana trusted you with her promise, then you're part of this too. We can't back down now, especially if there's a piece of her we haven't uncovered yet."

Jack nodded slowly, the spark of determination lighting his expression. "You're right. But let's do it the right way. We'll go through her journal first. It might have clues—hints about her past and the promise she spoke of. If we can understand what she intended for us, we might make sense of everything."

The mention of the journal sent a thrill through me. "Okay, then. Let's do it." I stood, invigorated by the idea of embarking on this journey with him. The shadows felt less foreboding now, as if they were inviting us to explore their depths.

As we made our way to the attic, the air grew cooler, and I could feel the weight of anticipation settling in my chest. The stairs creaked beneath us, their familiar groans a reminder of the countless times I had climbed them as a child, always feeling Nana's presence guiding me. The attic door loomed ahead, a portal to the past.

Jack hesitated before pushing it open, the rusty hinges protesting as they revealed the dim space beyond. Dust motes danced in the beam of moonlight that streamed through a small window, illuminating the haphazard piles of forgotten treasures. Boxes overflowed with relics of the past—old photographs, vintage hats, and faded linens, each whispering stories I longed to uncover.

"Where do we start?" I asked, glancing around, my heart racing with the thrill of discovery.

"Let's look for the journal first," Jack suggested, scanning the room. "It should be somewhere near her writing desk."

Together, we began to sift through the layers of history, lifting each object with reverence. My fingers brushed over the surfaces, feeling the years of wear, the love embedded in each piece. As I rummaged through a box filled with letters tied with a yellowed ribbon, a pang of nostalgia washed over me. These were more than objects; they were fragments of a life well-lived.

"Here," Jack called, his voice tinged with excitement. He pulled a small, leather-bound book from a nearby shelf, its cover cracked with age. "I think this is it."

I took the journal from him, cradling it in my hands. The weight of it felt substantial, like a vessel of stories waiting to be told. As I opened it, the faint scent of old paper and ink wafted up, enveloping me in memories. The pages were filled with Nana's meticulous handwriting, a neat cursive that flowed like water, each stroke carrying her spirit.

"Let's see what secrets you've been hiding, Nana," I whispered, my heart racing as I began to read. The ink had faded, but the words were clear, each one resonating with the promise of revelation. I felt Jack's presence beside me, his warmth a silent support as we plunged into the depths of her memories, ready to confront whatever awaited us.

And with that, the echoes of the past began to weave into the present, drawing us deeper into a mystery that would intertwine our fates forever.

The musty scent of aged paper enveloped me as I turned the first pages of Nana's journal, each line a fragment of her thoughts, meticulously penned in a flowing script that felt like her voice whispering through time. Jack leaned closer, his shoulder brushing against mine, sending an unexpected thrill racing through me. We were two explorers poised on the brink of discovery, our hearts beating in sync as we delved into the depths of her past.

"January 5, 1968," I read aloud, my voice barely above a whisper. "The winter is harsh this year, but the hotel is full of life. The guests are enjoying the snow, but I fear the winds carry more than just cold." I glanced at Jack, whose expression had shifted from curiosity to concern. "What do you think she meant?"

"Maybe she sensed something," he replied, his voice low and thoughtful. "Nana always had a way of knowing things before they happened."

I flipped through more pages, the journal's spine crackling softly as I uncovered memories steeped in nostalgia. "She talks about the hotel as if it has a heartbeat, like it breathes with the stories of its guests. It's almost poetic."

"Or eerie," Jack interjected with a smirk, lightening the mood. "Maybe the hotel is just a big ol' trap for lost souls."

"Ha! More like a cozy retreat for the weary," I shot back, my heart racing with excitement. "This place is steeped in history, and Nana was its guardian. She had to have known something about the whispers she heard."

I continued reading, the words tumbling from the pages like echoes of laughter. "August 12, 1975: A man arrived today. He carries shadows in his eyes and speaks of things better left unsaid. I do not trust him, but he has a charm that disarms. I will keep my distance." I paused, sensing Jack's tension. "She was warning herself about someone."

"Do you think this man could be related to whatever is haunting the hotel?" Jack asked, his voice barely masking his unease.

"Maybe. Or perhaps he was simply a stranger who left an impression," I mused, flipping to the next entry. "December 2, 1982: The winds howled tonight, bringing with them memories of old. I feel a storm coming, not just in the sky. I fear what this place has witnessed."

The room seemed to grow darker with each revelation, the shadows of the attic becoming more pronounced. Jack shifted closer, the warmth of his body a stark contrast to the chill creeping into my bones. "What if that storm was something more? What if the memories Nana was talking about weren't just her own?"

A heavy silence settled between us as I processed his words. There was something visceral in his gaze, a mixture of fear and determination that sent a shiver down my spine. "You mean... what if the hotel is keeping secrets that even Nana couldn't confront?"

"Exactly. If she was protecting something, it could be the very reason she wanted to keep the hotel running. But what if it's a threat?" His voice dropped, as if afraid the walls themselves might be listening.

I turned the page again, desperate for answers, and my breath caught. "Wait. This one is dated just before her death. She wrote about feeling a presence in the hotel. 'I can feel it lurking just beyond the veil of my understanding, a connection to something darker. I must make sure the promise I made is kept at all costs.'"

"God, that sounds serious," Jack said, concern etched across his features. "What kind of promise could warrant such fear?"

"I don't know," I admitted, frustration bubbling up inside me. "But she didn't just keep secrets for the sake of it. There was something—someone—she feared would be unleashed if the hotel fell into the wrong hands."

Jack ran a hand through his hair, his expression shifting from worry to resolve. "We need to find out who that man was. If he's still connected to this place, it could explain a lot about why the hotel has been so... strange lately."

I nodded, invigorated by the prospect of action. "Let's go through the rest of her entries. Maybe she wrote down names or descriptions that could help us track him down."

As we continued to read, the entries grew darker and more frantic. "March 3, 1990: The echoes of the past are louder now. I can't escape them. The hotel feels alive, but there's something lurking beneath the surface. I must protect my family."

The tension in the air was palpable, thick enough to slice through with a knife. Each entry felt like a piece of a puzzle, leading us deeper into the labyrinth of her memories. I could feel Jack's presence beside me, an anchor in the rising tide of uncertainty.

Then, in a final entry, my heart raced as I read, "I must make a decision tonight. The shadows have a voice, and they want to be heard. If I do not act, I fear the hotel will become a prison, and my family will pay the price. I must keep the promise."

The last line sent chills down my spine, and I could feel Jack's breath hitch beside me. "What promise? What did she mean?" I whispered, my heart pounding in my chest.

Before Jack could respond, a loud crash echoed from downstairs, jolting us from our intense focus. The sound reverberated through the attic like a thunderclap, shaking the very foundations of the hotel.

"What was that?" I exclaimed, my pulse racing.

"Stay here," Jack commanded, his voice tense as he jumped to his feet. "I'll check it out."

"No way," I shot back, adrenaline coursing through my veins. "You think I'm going to sit up here while something goes bump in the night? I'm coming with you."

He hesitated, the weight of the situation hanging in the air. "Fine, but stay close. We don't know what we're dealing with."

Together, we descended the attic stairs, each creak echoing our growing dread. The air felt electric, charged with something unseen. The hotel, once familiar, now felt like a living entity, alive with secrets and the promise of danger. As we reached the ground floor, I could hear hushed voices mingling with the low rumble of something heavy being dragged across the floor.

"What's happening?" I whispered urgently, glancing at Jack, whose eyes narrowed in concentration.

"I don't know," he murmured, moving toward the lobby with caution. "But we're about to find out."

As we stepped into the lobby, the scene before us sent my heart plummeting. A figure loomed in the flickering shadows, their back to us, obscured by the dim light. The atmosphere thickened, a suffocating blanket of tension wrapping around us like a vice.

"Who's there?" Jack called, his voice steady but low.

The figure turned slowly, and I felt my breath catch in my throat. A smile curled on their lips, chillingly familiar. "Well, well, well," the figure drawled, their voice dripping with insidious delight. "I was wondering when you two would stumble upon the truth."

Jack stepped forward, his expression shifting from surprise to anger. "What do you want?"

But before we could react, the figure raised their hand, a glint of something metallic catching the light. "What I want is to see how deep the rabbit hole goes. Are you ready to play?"

And just like that, the world around us plunged into chaos, the promise of danger unfurling like a dark flower in the night. The echoes of the past rose up to engulf us, and as the shadows closed in, I realized that the real game had only just begun.

Chapter 8: The Crack in the Armor

The sun hung low in the sky, casting a warm, golden hue across the dusty wooden beams of the old hotel. Every morning, I woke to the scent of pine and the distant sound of waves crashing against the rocky shore. Yet, despite this picturesque backdrop, I felt an undercurrent of uncertainty, a nagging reminder of the life I had left behind in the city. Jack's confession echoed in my mind, a revelation that changed everything, though the air between us still crackled with unspoken words.

Today, we were tackling the common area, the once vibrant heart of the hotel now dulled by neglect. I stood in the middle of the room, paintbrush in hand, staring at the peeling walls, wondering if they too were mourning the beauty they had once known. Jack stood beside me, a massive figure, clad in paint-stained overalls, his hands rough and calloused from years of hard labor. The sunlight caught the edges of his jawline, highlighting the stubble that often adorned his face, giving him an air of ruggedness that was hard to resist.

"I think the yellow would pop more if we went with a cream," I suggested, gesturing at the bucket of paint. My voice broke the silence, shattering the comfortable quiet that had settled between us.

He looked at me, brow furrowed, as if weighing my suggestion against his own stubborn idea of the color scheme. "Yellow is cheerful. It's supposed to be cheerful. You're just trying to make it too fancy," he replied, his tone teasing but laced with something deeper, a vulnerability that I began to recognize.

"Fancier doesn't mean less cheerful, Jack. It just means we might attract guests who don't have the charm of a dilapidated shack in their preferences," I countered, unable to hide my smile.

He chuckled, a sound that rumbled like distant thunder, and for a moment, I felt the barriers between us begin to dissolve. We stood there, paintbrushes poised, the air thick with paint fumes and something else—a growing connection that seemed to draw us closer with every shared glance and laugh.

As we worked, the conversation flowed easily, drifting from our pasts to our dreams, punctuated by the playful banter that felt as natural as breathing. Jack spoke of the hotel's heyday, of families flocking to its doors, laughter spilling into the halls, and the nights filled with music and dancing. I could almost hear the echoes of those times, the joyous clamor that had long faded into memory.

"And what about you? What brought you here, besides my charming company?" he asked, his eyes glinting with mischief.

I paused, paintbrush hovering above the wall, a swirl of emotions swirling within me. "I needed to escape. The city felt like a cage, all glass and concrete, suffocating me with its noise. I thought the quiet here would be peaceful, a way to find myself again."

"Find yourself, huh?" he mused, tilting his head, studying me like I was a puzzle he was determined to solve. "And have you?"

The question hung between us, heavy and loaded. I could feel my heart racing, not out of fear, but from a burgeoning awareness that perhaps this place—and him—were becoming integral to that journey. "I don't know yet. Some days, it feels like I'm closer than ever, and other days, I just feel lost."

"I get that. Sometimes, I wonder if I'll ever stop being the handyman fixing other people's problems while ignoring my own." His voice dropped, and I caught a glimpse of the man behind the bravado, a vulnerability that tugged at my heart.

The moment stretched, filled with unspoken understanding. There was a depth in his words that resonated with me, a rawness that mirrored my own struggles. I realized how easy it had been to see Jack as just a rugged handyman, a caricature of sorts, when in truth, he was a man navigating his own storm.

As we painted in silence, I noticed his movements—efficient yet careful, every stroke deliberate. It was a dance, one that echoed the rhythm of our conversation, the push and pull of our guarded hearts slowly unfolding. The paint glided over the walls, each brushstroke a testament to our growing rapport, a beautiful mess of colors blending into one another like our lives intertwined.

When we took a break, sitting on the sun-drenched porch overlooking the ocean, I felt a sense of peace that I hadn't known in ages. The salty breeze tousled my hair as I watched the waves crash against the rocks, the sound soothing and rhythmic. It was almost hypnotic, lulling me into a moment of reflection.

"What do you miss about the city?" Jack asked, his gaze locked on mine, piercing and inquisitive.

I hesitated, a flurry of memories colliding in my mind—the bustling streets, the vibrant art scene, the coffee shops where I'd spent countless hours sketching dreams into notebooks. "The energy, I suppose. It's alive in a way that's intoxicating. But then again, it can be overwhelming."

"Like a party where everyone's invited, but you're stuck in the corner feeling like a wallflower?" He quirked an eyebrow, a smirk playing on his lips.

"Exactly!" I laughed, delighted by his understanding. "And here, it's like I can finally breathe. But there's this pull, you know? A feeling that I should be somewhere else, doing something else."

"I think that pull is just the past trying to remind you of what you left behind. Doesn't mean it's where you need to be." His voice was low, as if he were sharing a secret only I could hear, and it sent a shiver of realization coursing through me.

As the sun dipped lower in the sky, painting the horizon in hues of orange and purple, I felt the weight of my own choices pressing down on me. Torn between two worlds, each vibrant in its own right, I was starting to see that perhaps it wasn't about choosing one over the other but finding a way to embrace both. The more time I spent here, the more I recognized the beauty in the quiet, the charm of a life lived simply yet fully.

"Maybe you're right," I finally said, my voice barely a whisper against the roar of the ocean. "Maybe I need to find a way to weave both together."

Jack smiled, that disarming smile that made my heart flutter. "That sounds like a plan worth painting." And as we returned to our work, the warmth of his presence wrapped around me like a comforting blanket, I realized that perhaps, in this moment, I was exactly where I was meant to be.

The following days unfolded in a delightful blur, the rhythm of our work echoing the ebb and flow of the tide just outside the hotel. Jack and I fell into an easy routine, our mornings spent in laughter and lighthearted banter, our afternoons marked by the steady scrape of paint against wood and the occasional clatter of tools. It was during one of these afternoons that the air around us thickened, the palpable tension transforming into something charged and electric.

"Okay, so you think the cream is a better choice," he mused one afternoon, mixing the paint with exaggerated seriousness, "but tell me, what do you think about the new porch furniture? I was thinking of something that says, 'I'm laid-back but still kind of a big deal.'"

I feigned contemplation, tapping my chin. "How about a hammock? It says you've given up on life, but only part-time."

Jack laughed, a genuine sound that rolled over me like a warm wave. "A hammock? So I can fully embrace my lack of ambition? I'd be the laughingstock of the handyman world."

"Or a trendsetter," I retorted, grinning. "I mean, who wouldn't want to lounge like a king on their porch?"

He cocked an eyebrow, his lips twitching into a smirk. "I might just have to steal that idea. If I start seeing hammocks popping up around town, I'll know who to blame."

As the sun began its slow descent, the golden light poured through the cracked windows, painting everything in warm hues. I admired how it caught the dust motes swirling in the air, dancing as if celebrating our shared camaraderie. Each smile exchanged felt like a small victory, a piece of armor chipped away. Yet, beneath the laughter, I sensed a weight lingering in Jack's gaze, something unspoken lurking just below the surface.

"Tell me about your past," I prodded, curiosity bubbling within me. "You must have a fascinating story to tell, right?"

He paused, the playfulness fading as he considered my question, and I could almost see the gears turning in his mind. "Not much to tell, really. Grew up here, left for a bit, then came back. Built this place into what it is—or, well, what it could be again."

"Just like that? What about college? A grand adventure?" I challenged, nudging him with my shoulder.

"More like a cautionary tale," he replied, a shadow flitting across his features. "Let's just say I made some questionable choices and learned the hard way that sometimes, the things you think you want aren't what you need."

"Okay, I can see that the brooding handyman has layers," I said, a playful lilt in my voice. "But if I share my darkest secrets, you'll have to spill the beans, too. Deal?"

He smirked, a hint of mischief creeping back into his demeanor. "Alright, but I reserve the right to choose what I share. I'm not laying all my cards on the table."

"Deal. I'll start, then." I took a deep breath, choosing my words carefully. "I was in the city, working a job that felt more like a cage than a career. I had dreams, but they all felt too far out of reach. I thought I wanted success, but really, I just wanted to be free."

He nodded, and I could see him processing my honesty, perhaps realizing that the weight of vulnerability was a shared burden. "That's brave. You left it all behind for this?"

"Something like that. I thought if I came here, I'd figure it out. But instead, I find myself wondering if I made the right choice."

"Maybe you're too focused on the future," he replied softly, the gentleness of his tone catching me off guard. "Sometimes, the answers we seek are found in the simplest moments."

I considered his words as we resumed painting, the air between us heavy with possibilities. Each stroke on the wall felt like a metaphor for our burgeoning relationship—each layer of paint revealing more of the surface beneath.

As the sun dipped below the horizon, a sudden gust of wind swept through the open windows, sending a flurry of leaves spiraling inside, dancing around us in chaotic harmony. It felt symbolic, like our lives, tangled yet beautifully intertwined.

"I'll show you something," Jack said abruptly, breaking the spell of silence. "You need a break from all this work. Come on."

Before I could respond, he grabbed my hand, his touch warm and steady, guiding me outside. We dashed across the lawn, laughter spilling out between us, invigorated by the unexpected adventure. The world felt alive around us—the ocean roared in the distance, and the sky began to glitter with the first stars.

He led me to a secluded spot just beyond the hotel, a hidden nook where the sound of the waves blended with the soft rustle of trees. "This is my thinking spot," he declared, dropping down onto a large, weathered rock. "A perfect place for introspection or, you know, a nice nap."

"Introspection and napping—what a riveting combination," I quipped, settling beside him. The rock felt cool beneath me, a grounding force against the chaos of my thoughts.

"I'm a complex guy," he said, mock-serious. "You'd be surprised what kind of profound ideas can come to a man while he's catching some Zs."

"I can imagine," I shot back, unable to suppress a grin. "You probably dream about hammocks and home repair."

Jack chuckled, then turned his gaze toward the ocean, the waves shimmering like diamonds under the starry sky. "What about you? What do you dream about?"

I hesitated, the weight of his question sinking in. "I dream about... freedom. Of not being tied down by expectations. And maybe, just maybe, about finding a place where I truly belong."

He turned to me, the earnestness in his eyes stealing my breath. "That's a worthy dream. And I have a feeling you're closer to it than you think."

I swallowed hard, feeling the gravity of his words, the shared vulnerability hanging in the air like an unbreakable thread between us. The night wrapped around us like a blanket, and for the first time, the weight of my city life felt a little lighter, as if Jack's presence was weaving a new tapestry of hope.

"I think I might have just found my place," I murmured, my voice barely above a whisper, and I wasn't entirely sure who I was talking about—the hotel, the town, or the man beside me.

The ocean continued to crash against the shore, a steady reminder of the world around us, yet in that moment, I felt anchored, as if the uncertainty that had shadowed me since I arrived was slowly beginning to dissipate.

The following week brought a cascade of warmth and laughter, as if the hotel itself had come alive, mirroring the burgeoning connection between Jack and me. Each day, we grew more comfortable in our skin, the rhythm of our work now punctuated with shared stories and lingering glances. The walls of the old hotel seemed to echo our newfound camaraderie, creaking and groaning like an ancient being awakening from slumber.

One afternoon, while we were stripping paint from the once-grand staircase, I caught Jack staring into space, his expression distant. I paused, paintbrush poised mid-air, feeling an unexpected urge to reach out. "Penny for your thoughts?" I teased, hoping to coax him from his reverie.

He turned to me, a flicker of surprise in his eyes. "I was just thinking about how this place used to shine. The ballroom was the talk of the town. People would dance until dawn. Now it feels like it's lost its soul."

"There's still time to breathe new life into it," I countered, feeling a surge of optimism. "We can make it beautiful again. Just think—new floors, fresh paint, maybe even a grand reopening. Imagine the couples twirling under the chandeliers once more."

Jack chuckled, shaking his head. "You really have a flair for the dramatic, don't you? I'm not sure we're ready for that kind of fanfare."

"Why not? What's life without a little drama?" I grinned, flicking a paintbrush in his direction, splattering a few drops of color on his cheek.

"Hey! You just declared war," he laughed, the sound deep and genuine, and in that moment, I was acutely aware of how much I craved this connection.

The day continued with our playful bickering, the air around us charged with an unspoken tension, a longing that I felt but couldn't quite articulate. We worked side by side, brushing off old memories and unveiling new possibilities, but beneath the surface, I sensed that Jack's thoughts still lingered in the past, a shadow that tainted the brightness of our present.

That evening, after we had finished for the day, Jack invited me to the local diner, a charming place known for its greasy fries and mouthwatering milkshakes. The neon sign buzzed with life, drawing us in like moths to a flame. As we settled into a booth, the atmosphere was vibrant, filled with the chatter of locals and the clinking of silverware.

"I can't believe I've been living here for weeks and haven't been here yet," I remarked, eyeing the menu as if it held secrets to the universe.

"You've missed out," Jack said, leaning back and crossing his arms. "You haven't truly experienced this town until you've had a milkshake here. It's practically a rite of passage."

"Rite of passage? I like the sound of that. Let's order one of everything!" I declared, excitement bubbling in my chest.

His eyes sparkled with amusement. "I think that might be the worst idea I've ever heard. You'd explode before dessert. Let's stick to two or three flavors."

As we placed our order, the diner's jukebox started playing an old tune, a classic that seemed to encapsulate the very essence of small-town nostalgia. I watched as Jack hummed along, his face softening into a smile that tugged at my heart. There was something undeniably enchanting about these moments, and I savored the way his laughter filled the space between us.

"So, what's the plan after we finish the hotel?" he asked, a more serious note creeping into his tone as our conversation veered toward the future.

"I suppose I'll head back to the city," I replied, forcing a nonchalance that I didn't feel. "I have a job waiting for me. It's not what I envisioned, but it's safe."

"Safe doesn't sound like you," he countered, his brow furrowing slightly. "What do you really want?"

I opened my mouth to respond, but the words lodged themselves in my throat. Did I really know what I wanted? The city felt like a familiar ghost haunting me, urging me to return to the life I had left behind, while this place was a vibrant tapestry still being woven, full of unknown possibilities.

Before I could find my voice, our shakes arrived, tall and frosty, glistening with whipped cream and a cherry on top. "I believe this is the moment we seal our fate with sugar," Jack declared, raising his glass in a mock toast.

"To fate!" I clinked my glass against his, and we both took a sip, the rich sweetness flooding my senses.

"I think I could get used to this," I said, savoring the flavor.

"Yeah? You could be the queen of the diner, holding court with your milkshakes," he teased, his eyes sparkling with mischief.

"Queen of the diner—now that's a title I could wear with pride," I laughed, but a hint of unease crept back in as the conversation turned serious again. "But honestly, Jack, I feel torn. The city calls to me, but I can't shake the feeling that this place is where I'm meant to be. Maybe I'm just scared to make the wrong choice."

He leaned forward, his expression earnest. "Sometimes the right choice isn't about where you go, but who you're with. Maybe it's about finding a place where you feel at home."

Home. The word echoed in my mind, settling over me like a warm blanket, yet its weight felt heavy, full of implications. As the evening wore on, we talked about everything and nothing, the moments flowing effortlessly until the sun dipped beneath the horizon, casting a soft glow over the diner.

As we walked back to the hotel, the air was thick with the scent of impending rain. I felt a thrill at the thought of stormy weather, the excitement of nature's unpredictability mirroring the chaos within me. Just as we reached the door, a sudden flash of lightning illuminated the sky, followed by a booming clap of thunder that rattled the windows.

"Perfect timing," Jack said, grinning. "It's like the universe is conspiring to add some drama to our lives."

"Or maybe it's just trying to tell us to go inside," I quipped, laughing nervously.

But as we stepped into the hotel, the lights flickered ominously, and the air turned electric. "That can't be good," I muttered, glancing toward the darkened hallway.

"Stay close," Jack warned, his voice low. He stepped in front of me, a protective instinct flaring to life. "I'll check the fuse box."

I nodded, my heart racing—not just from the sudden storm but from the intensity of the moment. Watching him move through the shadows, I felt an unsettling mix of admiration and concern. There was a depth to him, an intensity that hinted at battles fought in silence.

Suddenly, a loud crash echoed from the back of the hotel, reverberating through the halls. My heart dropped as Jack spun around, eyes wide. "What was that?"

"I don't know," I whispered, fear curling in my stomach. "It sounded like it came from the old storage room."

"Stay here," he ordered, but I could see the uncertainty flickering in his eyes.

"No way. I'm not hiding while you face whatever that is." My voice held a stubbornness that surprised even me.

We exchanged a glance, the tension thick between us, and in that moment, I realized how much I had come to care for him, how deeply rooted my feelings had grown. But now, with the storm raging outside and danger lurking in the shadows, the warmth of our connection felt fragile, a delicate thread stretched to its limit.

As we approached the storage room, the door creaked ominously, and another crash echoed from within, making my pulse quicken. "Jack, what if—"

"Shh!" he whispered urgently, holding a finger to his lips as we edged closer.

With one swift movement, he flung open the door, revealing a darkness so thick it seemed to swallow the light. "On three," he said, and we both inhaled sharply.

"One... two..."

Before we could reach three, the lights flickered back on, casting eerie shadows on the walls. And in that moment, amidst the chaos, a figure lurched into view, shrouded in darkness, face obscured. The world around us went still as recognition washed over me like ice water, sending chills down my spine.

"Hello, there," the voice came, smooth and unsettling, echoing through the room. I froze, Jack's hand tightening around mine as we stood on the precipice of uncertainty, the weight of unspoken truths and hidden dangers closing in around us.

Chapter 9: The Space Between Us

The mornings at the hotel have settled into a comfortable routine, like the familiar embrace of an old sweater. The air is thick with the scent of salt and pine, and I wake to the soft lullaby of waves crashing against the rocky shore. The sun breaks over the horizon, spilling golden light into my small room, illuminating the peeling wallpaper and the mismatched furniture that I've come to adore. Each day, the world outside beckons with an allure that is both enchanting and perplexing. I still can't shake the weight of my past—the bustling streets, the rush of city life—but here, there's a tranquil rhythm that wraps around me like a warm blanket, coaxing me into the day with its gentle insistence.

Jack is always there, an ever-present figure in my mornings, and it's impossible to ignore how much he's become a part of this new routine. He moves through the hotel with a certain ease, fixing light fixtures, tinkering with the old heating system, or hauling in supplies from his beat-up pickup truck. There's a certain grace to his movements, a rugged charm that transforms the mundane into something extraordinary. When our eyes meet, an unspoken understanding flickers between us, as if we share a secret hidden beneath the surface of our daily exchanges. I pretend not to notice the way his gaze lingers on me, tracing the outline of my silhouette as I stand by the large window, a cup of coffee warming my hands while I watch the waves playfully crash against the shore.

"Careful with that," Jack grumbles one morning, his voice tinged with a teasing sarcasm that always makes me smile. I turn to find him standing there, a toolbox in one hand and a smirk tugging at the corners of his lips. "You might spill it all over the place."

I raise an eyebrow, feigning offense. "And here I thought you were just admiring my artistic approach to morning coffee consumption."

He chuckles, the sound deep and genuine, wrapping around me like the warm breeze filtering through the open window. "Artistic? Is that what we're calling it now? Looks more like a caffeine disaster waiting to happen."

I mockingly clutch my chest as if he's just insulted my honor. "You wound me, Jack. I'll have you know I'm a coffee connoisseur." I take a sip, savoring the bitter warmth, and my heart skips a beat when he takes a step closer, the scent of sawdust and fresh paint mingling with the briny air.

"Connoisseur, huh?" His voice lowers, teasing yet somehow sincere, as if he genuinely appreciates my attempt at sophistication. "Well, if that's the case, you should definitely consider some sort of coffee-spill prevention strategy."

And just like that, the distance between us feels palpable, electrifying. Yet, as quickly as the moment ignites, I feel that familiar wall creeping back in. I clear my throat, glancing away, suddenly overwhelmed by the warmth blooming in my chest. "Right. Because nothing says 'artistic' like a hot cup of coffee splattered all over a vintage armchair." I attempt to laugh it off, but the tension lingers, and my heart races as I shift back to the window, gazing out at the endless ocean.

Each day, the town feels more like a home and less like a temporary refuge. The quaint coffee shop on the corner now knows my order—black coffee, no frills—and the local bookstore has become my sanctuary. I lose myself in novels that transport me away from the mundane realities of life, far from the crushing weight of expectations I left behind. I never thought I'd find solace in a sleepy seaside town, and yet here I am, wandering its streets with a newfound appreciation for the beauty of stillness.

Yet, for every moment of clarity, there are echoes of my past, whispers of a life I once thought I would always return to. In quiet moments, I find myself staring at the horizon, envisioning the skyscrapers of my former life, the bustling energy of the city—a vibrant pulse that is now just a distant memory. But as I linger in this picturesque setting, the waves crashing rhythmically against the shore seem to drown out those thoughts, wrapping me in their embrace. Here, I am free to rediscover myself, to breathe without the suffocating weight of obligations and expectations.

But then there's Jack, with his knowing glances and playful banter. He represents an allure I can't quite place, an invitation to bridge the gap between our worlds. Yet, there's something unspoken between us, a hesitance that hangs in the air, thick like the fog that sometimes rolls in from the sea. It's as if we both understand the fragility of this connection, and neither of us dares to disrupt it, fearing that once we acknowledge it, everything will change.

"Hey, I'm thinking of heading out to the cliffs later. Care to join?" he asks one afternoon, his eyes bright with a hint of mischief. The invitation hangs between us, tantalizing and terrifying in equal measure. I want to say yes, to dive headfirst into this adventure with him, but the thought of stepping into that unknown space sends a chill down my spine.

"Cliffs?" I ask, feigning casualness as I run a hand through my hair. "Sounds... dangerous."

He steps closer, his eyes narrowing playfully. "You're telling me you're afraid of a little height? I thought you were a coffee connoisseur, not a coward." His voice drips with mock challenge, and I feel the weight of his words settle in my chest.

"Oh please," I retort, crossing my arms defiantly. "I'm afraid of more than just heights. Like getting caught in a storm or having my coffee go cold. Those are very real fears."

Jack laughs, the sound rich and infectious. "I promise I won't let anything happen to you. Just a little adventure. What do you say?"

In that moment, with his infectious laughter and that charming smirk, the space between us feels both thrilling and intimidating.

There's a fleeting thought of what it would be like to take that leap, to step closer to him and let him pull me into his world. But the safety of my walls feels like a fortress I'm not quite ready to breach.

The cliffs loom ahead, jagged and majestic against the bright blue sky, and as Jack leads the way, I can't help but feel a twinge of excitement mixed with an all-too-familiar apprehension. The salty breeze tangles my hair, whipping it around my face like a playful child, and I tuck it behind my ears, stealing glances at Jack as he navigates the rocky path with a confidence that makes me both admire and envy him. Each step we take brings the vibrant sea closer, a shimmering expanse of turquoise and emerald that dances under the sun, as if trying to beckon us closer.

"Just watch your step," he calls over his shoulder, glancing back with that trademark smirk, his eyes glinting with mischief. "Wouldn't want to become part of the local wildlife."

I roll my eyes, pretending to be unimpressed by his bravado, but my heart races as I approach the edge. "You mean I wouldn't want to be mistaken for a beach rock?" I retort, trying to inject some levity into my nerves. "I hear they have a terrible reputation for being dull."

"Dull?" He raises an eyebrow, his tone feigning outrage. "You've clearly never met a rock in this town. They've got layers of history, like you. It's all about perspective."

"Layers of history, huh?" I laugh, shaking my head. "That sounds like a terrible first date story."

"Only if you let it be," he replies, and there's something in his gaze, a spark that ignites the air between us, making it almost electric. I'm acutely aware of how easily our banter flows, and it both comforts and unnerves me.

As we reach the summit, I take a moment to breathe in the breathtaking view. The cliffs drop sharply to the sea below, waves crashing against the rocks with a fierce intensity that mirrors the conflict brewing within me. Here, at the edge of this new world, the horizon stretches infinitely, and I can't help but feel a sense of freedom mingling with the salt in the air. Yet, that freedom comes with a heaviness, a realization that this moment could change everything. Jack steps closer, and I can see the thrill in his eyes, the way he thrives in this rugged beauty.

"Isn't it amazing?" he asks, his voice barely above a whisper, as if he's afraid the magic of the moment will dissipate with too much noise.

"It's... breathtaking," I admit, my gaze fixed on the water. "It feels like the edge of the world."

He nods, and for a moment, we stand in companionable silence, the roar of the ocean filling the spaces between us. But then he shifts, his presence suddenly heavier, charged with a tension that begs to be addressed. "You know," he starts, hesitating for just a beat, "I think you're more than you let on. There's this fire in you that's just waiting to be kindled."

I turn to him, my heart racing at his words. The way he looks at me, like he sees right through the layers I've wrapped around myself, unnerves me. "You don't even know me," I reply, trying to inject some levity into my voice. "I could be a criminal mastermind or a secret agent. You should probably be worried."

He laughs, a deep, throaty sound that vibrates in my chest, and I find myself smiling despite the weight of his observation. "Yeah, right. You can barely handle a coffee without spilling it all over yourself. I don't think the world needs to worry about your grand plans of villainy."

I nudge him playfully, but the moment is fragile, hanging in the air like the sea mist. His laughter dies down, replaced by a serious look that makes my pulse quicken. "But really," he continues, "you're not just running from something, are you? You're trying to find something too."

The question hangs in the air, heavy and daunting. I want to answer him, to peel back the layers I've hidden behind, but the truth feels like a loaded gun I'm not ready to fire. "I'm just... figuring things out," I manage, my voice almost too quiet against the crashing waves.

Jack takes a step closer, and I can feel the warmth radiating from him. "You know you don't have to do that alone, right?"

The sincerity in his voice stirs something within me—a longing, a fear, and a desperate hope. I take a breath, steadying myself against the onslaught of emotions, but my heart still races with uncertainty. I think of the city, of the chaos I left behind, and how the comfort of routine now feels like a gilded cage. "It's just... complicated," I finally say, my voice wavering. "I'm not exactly the poster child for stability right now."

Jack tilts his head, an understanding gleam in his eyes. "Complicated doesn't scare me. It's the simple things that do. They're the ones that sneak up on you when you least expect it."

I can't help but smile at his honesty, a rare trait that feels refreshing in this tangled web of uncertainty. "Is that your way of saying you're afraid of falling in love with a coffee-spilling, cliff-hugging weirdo?"

"Maybe," he says with a playful grin, his tone light, but his eyes betray a deeper understanding. "But I'm also afraid of letting someone like you slip away because you're too scared to leap."

The air crackles between us, and in that moment, I realize how close we stand, the abyss of the ocean and the complexities of our lives swirling beneath our feet. I want to lean in, to bridge the distance that feels both tantalizing and terrifying, but the fear of what might happen next sends a shiver down my spine.

"Leaps can be dangerous," I reply, my voice a whisper as I look away, breaking the spell. "And I'm not sure I'm ready to take one yet."

Jack's expression softens, and for a heartbeat, I see something vulnerable in him—a glimpse of his own fears laid bare. "You don't have to leap blindly. Just take it one step at a time."

With a gentle hand, he reaches out, brushing his fingertips against mine, and the warmth of his touch sends a shockwave through me. The space that once felt so secure now seems fragile, like the edge of the cliff itself, and my heart races with both desire and fear.

Just then, a sudden gust of wind sweeps across the cliff, sending a spray of salty mist our way, dousing our moment in cool droplets. I laugh, surprised, but Jack doesn't pull away. Instead, he holds my gaze, a challenge and an invitation all at once.

"See?" he says, his voice laced with warmth. "Even the wind agrees—there's a thrill in the unknown. We're not meant to stand still, you know."

I let out a soft laugh, the tension between us easing just a bit. "I didn't realize I was being lectured by the local handyman."

"Guilty as charged," he replies, his grin widening. "But I'm not just a handyman. I'm also a professional cliff tour guide, and I assure you, the view gets better from here."

His lightheartedness breaks through the heaviness that has settled in my heart, and I can't help but chuckle at the absurdity of it all. "So what's next? Are we going to scale the entire cliff and then bungee jump off?"

Jack leans in closer, his eyes twinkling with mischief. "Now you're talking. Or we could just enjoy the view a little longer."

As the sun begins its descent, casting a warm golden hue over everything, I realize that perhaps the leap doesn't have to be about fear or recklessness. Maybe it's simply about taking a step forward, one heartbeat at a time, and letting the tide of change pull me closer to something beautiful, something worth risking the fall.

As the sun dipped lower in the sky, casting a golden glow over the cliffs, I felt the thrill of possibility weaving through the air. Jack and I stood side by side, our shoulders almost brushing as we surveyed the vast ocean. The rhythmic crashing of waves below became a soothing soundtrack, a reminder of the ever-present motion in life. Jack turned to me, his expression suddenly serious, the teasing glint in his eyes replaced with something deeper, something vulnerable.

"Do you ever think about what you really want?" he asked, his voice barely rising above the whisper of the wind. The question settled heavily between us, as if daring me to explore the depths of my desires.

I opened my mouth to respond, but no words came. Instead, I stared at the horizon, the setting sun casting a fiery reflection on the water, blurring the line between sky and sea. What did I want? I had traded the bustling streets of the city for this quiet town, yet even now, when life felt simpler, I couldn't shake the lingering shadows of my past. "I think I want... freedom," I finally managed, feeling the weight of my own honesty. "But freedom comes with a cost."

Jack studied me, his brow furrowing slightly, and I wondered if he could see through my carefully constructed walls. "Freedom often feels like an escape," he said thoughtfully. "But it's really about finding where you belong."

His words hung in the air, sparking a flicker of hope amidst the chaos of my thoughts. I had started to feel a connection to this place, to the gentle rhythm of the ocean, and, more importantly, to him. The tension between us felt charged with unspoken words and emotions that danced like the waves below.

"Do you think we can belong anywhere?" I asked, turning to meet his gaze. "I mean, truly belong?"

Jack's eyes softened, and he stepped closer, the space between us diminishing further. "I think belonging is about finding the right people. It's about building something together. Like a good coffee blend—you take different flavors, mix them just right, and create something unique."

I couldn't help but laugh at the metaphor, but beneath the humor lay a truth that resonated within me. "So, are we a coffee blend now?" I teased, nudging him lightly. "What flavor do I bring to the table?"

He grinned, his expression playful. "You're definitely the bold roast. You've got that fiery kick that surprises people. Me? I'm more of a smooth, mellow blend. Good for a lazy afternoon but lacking the punch."

"Ah, so I'm the one who keeps things interesting?" I shot back, my heart racing at the playful banter.

"Exactly," he replied, his voice warm. "But sometimes, bold needs a mellow to balance it out."

I felt a flutter of something deep within me, the way he spoke igniting a spark of excitement. Maybe this was the moment I needed to let go, to take a leap into the unknown, but the weight of my fears held me back. "And what if we mix too well? What if the blend turns out to be a disaster?"

Jack's expression turned serious again. "Life is a series of risks. We never know how it will turn out. But isn't it better to try?"

His eyes held mine, and in that moment, I felt as though he could see right through my defenses. The connection between us was undeniable, and I wanted to leap into it with both feet, but the specter of my past loomed, a lingering shadow that refused to let go.

"Maybe," I said, my voice barely above a whisper. "But I'm not ready to tumble headfirst into something I can't control."

"I get that," he replied, his voice low and steady. "But sometimes you have to let go of the reins a little. Just trust the process."

The silence enveloped us, filled only by the sound of the waves crashing against the rocks. As I turned to look back at the ocean, the horizon blurring with shades of pink and orange, I felt a swell of conflicting emotions. Could I really trust him?

Then, without warning, the tranquility shattered. A loud rumble echoed through the air, a deep growl that seemed to come from the very heart of the cliffs. Jack stiffened beside me, his expression shifting to concern as the ground beneath our feet trembled slightly.

"What was that?" I asked, my heart racing as I glanced around, searching for the source of the noise.

"Not sure," he replied, a frown creasing his forehead. "It sounded like it came from further down the cliffs."

As if on cue, a flock of seabirds erupted from their resting places, their wings beating wildly against the wind. The atmosphere shifted, charged with an electric energy that set my senses on high alert.

"Should we check it out?" I suggested, the thrill of adrenaline pulsing through my veins despite the apprehension gnawing at my gut.

Jack nodded, his jaw set in determination. "We should be careful, though. It might not be safe."

We moved closer to the edge, the ground giving way to a steep drop where the waves crashed violently below. As we peered down, I could see a thick plume of dust rising from a narrow ledge several feet below us, where the rock face had shifted ominously.

"What could've caused that?" I asked, my voice shaky as I gripped the edge of the cliff tighter, my heart pounding.

"Could be a rockslide," Jack speculated, squinting into the distance. "But it seems a little more intense than that."

My stomach churned with unease as the reality of our precarious position sunk in. "Are you thinking what I'm thinking?"

"Depends. Are you thinking we should get the hell out of here?" he quipped, but his smile didn't reach his eyes.

"Not exactly," I said, anxiety creeping into my voice. "What if someone's in trouble?"

Jack's expression shifted, determination flickering to life in his gaze. "Then we can't just stand here. We should investigate. Stay close."

With that, he carefully made his way down the rocky path, each step calculated, as if he were testing the ground beneath him. My heart raced as I followed, the thrill of adventure battling against the instinct to turn back.

As we descended, the air felt charged with anticipation, and I couldn't shake the feeling that we were stepping into something larger than ourselves—an adventure that would test not just our resolve but also the fragile bond that had begun to grow between us.

When we reached the narrow ledge, the dust had settled to reveal a gaping fissure in the rock face, ominously dark and foreboding. Jack peered into the abyss, his face set in grim determination. "I can't believe we're doing this," he muttered, glancing back at me.

"Neither can I," I replied, my voice trembling slightly. "But what if someone really needs our help?"

Just as he nodded, a sudden crashing sound erupted from the darkness below, sending a cascade of rocks tumbling down the cliffside. My heart dropped, panic rising within me like the tide. "Jack, we need to go back! This is too dangerous!"

He hesitated, caught between the desire to leap into action and the reality of our precarious situation. "Wait. Let me just—"

But before he could finish, a shadowy figure emerged from the fissure, stumbling into the fading light. It was a woman, her clothes torn and dirty, eyes wide with fear. "Help me!" she cried, reaching out as the ground shook once more beneath us.

Time slowed, my heart hammering in my chest as I realized we were on the brink of something we couldn't have anticipated. Jack moved forward instinctively, but I grabbed his arm, a rush of instinctive fear coursing through me. "Jack, no!"

But it was too late. The ground beneath our feet groaned ominously, and suddenly, the world tilted. The cliffs shuddered violently, and I could feel the earth slipping away. "Hold on!" Jack shouted, his grip tightening around mine.

The last thing I saw before the world crumbled into chaos was that terrified woman's face, her scream piercing through the air as everything plunged into darkness.

Chapter 10: A Bridge Too Far

The letter lay nestled between the yellowed pages of a faded paperback, its ink as crisp as the day it was penned. My fingers trembled slightly as I pried it from its resting place, the scent of old paper mingling with the salt of the sea air. I recognized my grandmother's meticulous handwriting immediately, each loop and curve speaking of her patience and care, traits I often wished I had inherited. It felt surreal to read her words again, a voice echoing across time, and my heart raced with anticipation, like a child unwrapping a long-desired gift.

"Dear Amelia," it began, and just like that, I was swept into a moment suspended between past and present. She spoke of a bridge, one that I had no memory of, spanning the bay and leading to a small island cloaked in mystery and allure. My heart sank a little at the thought of yet another piece of my childhood lost to the fog of memory. But as I continued reading, a warmth spread through me, woven into her descriptions of the sanctuary where we had spent lazy summer afternoons. I could almost hear the whispers of the ocean breeze, feel the soft, cool grass under my bare feet, and see the sunlight dancing on the water's surface, a million diamonds glimmering in the afternoon light.

Jack's shadow fell across the page, a solid presence that somehow grounded me. He leaned in closer, his curiosity piqued. "What's that?" he asked, his voice low and gentle, as if he feared disturbing the fragile moment. I looked up at him, caught between the urge to share and the instinct to protect my secret. His dark hair fell into his eyes, and I could see the hints of worry etched into his brow.

"It's a letter from Nana," I replied, my voice barely above a whisper. "She talks about a bridge to an island." I held it out for him to see, but he shook his head, his expression shifting as though he understood instinctively that this was something I needed to hold onto alone, a fragment of my past that was not meant to be dissected or analyzed.

"Do you want to go there?" His question hung in the air, heavy with unspoken implications. The bridge, a mere thread connecting me to a version of my childhood that I longed to reclaim, beckoned like an enchanted path through the woods. But as I stared out at the glittering bay, the weight of grief settled over my shoulders like a well-worn coat. The island felt like a double-edged sword, offering beauty yet shadowed by loss.

"Maybe," I said, my voice barely more than a breath. "I just don't know if I can handle it." My thoughts spiraled, drawing me back to memories of laughter, the scent of my grandmother's garden, and the soft melody of her voice guiding me through the stories that had once enveloped me in warmth. The island represented everything I had lost—Nana, my childhood innocence, the sense of belonging I had clung to like a lifeline.

Jack shifted, as if sensing my turmoil. "You don't have to go alone," he offered softly. "I can take you." There was a sincerity in his tone that made my heart flutter unexpectedly. It was a simple suggestion, yet it felt like a promise—a promise that he would stand by me as I ventured into the heart of my memories, a shield against the storm of emotions that threatened to engulf me.

The decision hung between us like a fragile thread, and for a moment, I weighed the options. Could I face the ghosts of my past? The thought of walking the bridge, the sound of the water lapping against the wooden posts, the sensation of the wind tugging at my hair, both terrified and thrilled me. I nodded slowly, an unspoken agreement passing between us, his quiet strength fortifying my resolve.

We set off toward the bridge, the sun dipping lower in the sky, casting a golden hue across the landscape. Each step felt like a small victory against the tide of hesitation that threatened to pull me under. As we reached the bridge's edge, the wooden planks creaked beneath our weight, a familiar yet eerie sound that stirred a blend of nostalgia and apprehension within me.

"Here goes nothing," I murmured, my voice steady despite the tremor in my heart. I took a deep breath, the salty air filling my lungs and mingling with the warmth of Jack's presence beside me. With every step, the memories began to rise, vivid and alive. I could see myself as a child, running barefoot across the grass, laughter spilling from my lips as Nana watched from a weathered bench, her eyes twinkling with love.

The bridge swayed gently beneath us, the rhythm of the water lapping against its supports resonating like a heartbeat, a reminder of the life that pulsed around us. I glanced sideways at Jack, who walked with an ease that belied the undercurrent of tension we both felt. His expression was a mix of concentration and something deeper, a connection that tied us together in this moment of shared vulnerability.

"Do you think we'll find anything there?" I asked, trying to shake off the creeping dread. The thought of unearthing old memories sent shivers down my spine, yet the idea of discovery was tantalizing. The bridge was not just a passageway; it was a portal, a chance to reclaim pieces of myself I feared were lost forever.

"I think you'll find what you need," Jack replied, his voice steady as we approached the island's shore. I marveled at his confidence, the way he seemed to hold a certainty I desperately craved. As we stepped onto the soft, sandy beach, the world around us burst into life. The island, untouched by time, welcomed us with open arms, its lush greenery a striking contrast against the cerulean sky.

I felt the weight of the past begin to lift, if only slightly. Together, we wandered deeper into the island's heart, the beauty surrounding us whispering promises of healing and hope. The air was thick with the scent of wildflowers and the distant call of seabirds echoed above, guiding us toward the unknown. As we ventured further, I realized that this was more than just a journey to an island; it was a pilgrimage to the very essence of who I was, a chance to reclaim the joy I thought was lost forever.

The sandy beach stretched out like a welcoming mat, inviting us to explore its hidden treasures. Each step sank into the soft grains, sending a soft sigh into the air as if the island itself were exhaling, inviting us deeper into its embrace. I felt the sunlight warm my skin, a gentle reminder of the world's beauty that coexisted alongside my heartache. Jack walked beside me, his presence a steady anchor against the tide of memories crashing around me.

"Look at that," he said, pointing toward a cluster of vibrant wildflowers dancing in the breeze. The blooms were a riot of colors—purple, yellow, and orange—each petal glowing like a jewel under the sun's gaze. I had forgotten how alive this place could feel, how nature wrapped its arms around you, whispering secrets only the wind understood. "I bet they bloom every year, just waiting for someone to notice." His eyes sparkled with a hint of mischief, and I couldn't help but smile, the tension in my chest easing just a fraction.

"Let's not get too attached," I teased, nudging him playfully with my shoulder. "I mean, they might be hiding a dark secret. Ever seen a flower that wasn't secretly plotting world domination?"

Jack laughed, a sound that bubbled up like champagne, brightening the atmosphere between us. "I think these ones are harmless, but we could always interrogate them just to be safe."

Our banter filled the air, mingling with the sounds of the waves lapping at the shore. For a moment, the island felt like a sanctuary of laughter and light. I was surprised at how easy it was to slip back into a rhythm of connection, even amidst the emotional weight I still carried. But as we ventured further into the island, the laughter began to fade, replaced by an uneasy silence that settled like a fog.

A trail wound through the greenery, its edges overgrown yet enticing, like a secret path waiting to be discovered. As we walked, the trees loomed overhead, their branches intertwining to form a natural archway that felt both inviting and foreboding. The sunlight filtered through the leaves, casting a mosaic of shadows on the ground, a stark contrast to the vibrant blooms we had just admired.

"Do you ever get the feeling that places hold memories?" I mused aloud, my voice barely breaking the silence that enveloped us. "Like the walls could tell stories if they had tongues?"

Jack nodded, his expression thoughtful. "Absolutely. Every inch of this island is probably saturated with echoes of laughter, whispered secrets, and maybe even a few arguments."

I chuckled at the thought, but the laughter felt hollow as I remembered my own past—the laughter that had filled this space once before, now replaced by the chilling absence of my grandmother's presence. "Nana and I had our share of adventures here. I remember one time, she tried to teach me how to catch crabs. I ended up chasing them around in circles while she laughed so hard, I thought she might burst."

"Catching crabs? That sounds like a fine way to spend a summer afternoon," he replied, a smile tugging at the corners of his mouth. "I can picture it. You, the fearless crab hunter, and her laughing until she cried."

"More like the crab's worst nightmare," I countered, warming to the memory despite the ache it brought. "I think they all conspired against me, plotting my demise."

The lighthearted exchange lightened the air between us, but just as quickly, the laughter evaporated, swallowed by the thickening silence. I halted mid-step, my gaze drawn to a shadow creeping into the corners of the island's charm. There, partially hidden among the bushes, stood an old wooden gazebo, its once-white paint peeling away like the fragile layers of time. It was a relic from the past, a ghost of memories waiting to be exhumed.

"Do you think anyone else comes here?" I asked, almost hesitantly. The thought of sharing this sacred space with anyone else felt foreign.

"Hard to say," Jack replied, stepping closer, his curiosity piqued. "It looks like it hasn't been used in ages."

A shiver crawled down my spine as I approached the gazebo, each step feeling heavier than the last. I could almost hear Nana's voice in my head, urging me forward, reassuring me that this place still held fragments of joy, even if they were buried under layers of dust and neglect. As I reached the threshold, I hesitated, my heart pounding in my chest.

"I don't know if I can go in," I admitted, my voice trembling slightly. "What if it's too much?"

"Then we'll leave. But you won't know until you try," Jack encouraged, his voice a soothing balm against my rising panic. "And I'll be right here with you."

With a deep breath, I stepped into the gazebo, the floor creaking underfoot as though it hadn't felt the weight of a visitor in years. The air inside was thick with nostalgia, a blend of sunlight and shadows that wrapped around me like an old blanket. Dust motes floated lazily in the beams of light filtering through the cracks in the wooden slats, creating a dreamlike quality that tugged at my heartstrings.

"See?" Jack whispered, stepping in behind me. "It's just us and the ghosts."

I couldn't help but laugh, the sound ringing out like a bell, shattering the silence. "Great, I've always wanted to be haunted by my childhood."

"I hear they're friendly ghosts. Besides, think of all the stories they could tell." He leaned against a support beam, arms crossed, a playful smirk on his face. "You could have your own little ghost tour."

His lighthearted demeanor made me feel lighter, as if the weight of the past were lifting, even if just a little. "Right, and I'll charge admission. Ghosts always have the best stories. It'll be a hit!"

As I surveyed the gazebo, memories flitted through my mind like fireflies on a warm summer evening. I could almost see Nana sitting on the old swing, her laughter echoing through the trees, her presence imbuing the space with warmth and life. "We used to come here to escape," I murmured, my voice thick with emotion. "Nana said this was our little hideaway, a place where the world couldn't reach us."

"And now you're reclaiming it," Jack said softly, the weight of his words hanging in the air.

I met his gaze, finding strength in his eyes. The island, once a bittersweet reminder of loss, was now a canvas for healing. Perhaps this place was not just a bridge to the past, but a pathway to rediscovery—a chance to connect with who I was beneath the layers of grief.

Just as the thought began to settle, a soft rustling echoed from the nearby bushes, drawing my attention. "Did you hear that?" I asked, my voice laced with a sudden thread of anxiety.

"Probably just a squirrel," Jack replied, though he, too, turned to look, his body tense.

But before I could respond, a figure emerged from the foliage, stepping into the clearing with an unexpected swagger. A tall man with tousled hair and a cocky grin stood before us, an uninvited guest in our sanctuary. My heart dropped, caught between surprise and the nagging discomfort that tinged the air.

The figure stepped into the sunlight, and for a fleeting moment, I wondered if I'd conjured him from my own imagination. He was tall, with an easy swagger that suggested confidence bordering on arrogance, the kind that made you roll your eyes and begrudgingly admire him at the same time. His tousled hair glinted like spun gold in the light, and his grin held an unmistakable charm—one that felt like a double-edged sword, equally likely to charm or disarm.

"Ah, a lovely day for a little adventure, isn't it?" he said, his voice smooth as silk, as if he'd been born for the role of charming interloper. He leaned against the gazebo's support post, a picture of casual nonchalance, as if he owned the island rather than just stumbling upon it.

Jack stiffened beside me, the warmth of our moment shattered. "Who are you?" he asked, his tone clipped, protective. The air around us thickened with tension, a palpable current that crackled as I struggled to process this unexpected disruption.

The newcomer straightened, his expression unfazed by Jack's hostility. "Name's Leo. I'm just out for a walk, enjoying the sunshine and, apparently, a bit of a family reunion," he replied, casting a sweeping glance over our little sanctuary. "I didn't think I'd find anyone else here. This place has been my little secret for ages."

"Must be a pretty small secret if you're just barging in uninvited," I shot back, surprised at my own sharpness. It felt good to reclaim some semblance of control, to push back against the intrusion.

Leo raised his hands in mock surrender, a twinkle in his eye. "I get it, trust issues and all that. But come on, lighten up! I'm not a monster. Just a guy trying to enjoy a day on a hidden island."

Jack's jaw tightened as he moved slightly closer to me, a protective barrier I was grateful for. "We were here first," he asserted, his gaze unwavering. "If you're looking for a picnic spot, I suggest you try the beach. It's quite nice there."

I appreciated Jack's defiance, but there was something in Leo's demeanor that intrigued me. Beneath his bravado lay an unmistakable undercurrent of mischief. "Okay, okay," Leo said, feigning defeat. "I'll head down to the beach. But you two should really consider the advantages of sharing this little piece of paradise. Who knows? Maybe I could show you around."

"Thanks, but we're good," I replied, feeling a surprising warmth at the thought of rejecting his offer. The gazebo, with its peeling paint and memories, was mine to reclaim. The idea of sharing it with someone so casual about its magic felt wrong, like allowing a stranger to rummage through my grandmother's things.

Leo's grin faltered for a moment, but then it returned, accompanied by a roguish spark in his eye. "Suit yourselves. But if you change your mind, I'm always up for a good story or two. I've got plenty of my own."

As he turned to leave, I felt an unexpected pang of curiosity. "Wait," I called out, halting him in his tracks. "What do you mean by stories? What brings you here?"

He glanced over his shoulder, his expression suddenly serious. "Let's just say, I've had my share of adventures on this island—ghostly tales included. You might find my insights fascinating."

"Fascinating, huh?" I couldn't help but arch an eyebrow, skepticism creeping into my voice. "And how exactly did you discover this place?"

Leo leaned back against the gazebo, arms crossed as if he was weighing his options. "A friend of a friend told me about it, a little gem hidden from the world. You wouldn't believe the secrets it holds."

"What kind of secrets?" Jack interjected, his protective stance softening slightly, the curiosity in his eyes betraying his wariness.

"Secrets that might interest someone like you," Leo replied, a knowing smile playing at the corners of his mouth. "I've seen things on this island—things you can't explain, things that could put a spark in your heart or a chill in your bones."

"What do you mean?" I pressed, feeling a mixture of intrigue and caution.

"Legends," he replied, his voice dropping to a conspiratorial whisper. "There's a reason this place is so secluded. Some say it's because it's a portal of sorts, a meeting place for spirits and those who dare to tread lightly."

"Now you sound like a character from a cheesy horror novel," I scoffed, though my heart raced at the thought of the island being anything more than just a beautiful piece of land.

"Maybe, but you'd be surprised what kind of truths hide behind those stories. You just have to know where to look," Leo challenged, his eyes sparkling with a mix of mischief and sincerity.

"Yeah? And what would that truth be?" Jack challenged back, clearly not ready to let his guard down.

"Sometimes the past isn't just something we remember," Leo said, his tone shifting, becoming oddly serious. "Sometimes it's something we confront. This island holds pieces of lost time, and if you're willing to dive deeper, you might just find something worth uncovering."

A tense silence hung in the air, each of us caught in the web of Leo's words. My heart thudded in my chest as I exchanged glances with Jack. I could see his skepticism mirrored in my own expression, yet there was an undeniable allure in the idea of uncovering hidden truths.

"Look, I didn't come here to ruin your day," Leo continued, sensing the shift in our mood. "Just wanted to let you know that if you ever want to dig deeper, I'll be around." He pushed off the gazebo and began to stroll away, but I found myself calling out again.

"Wait! What's your deal?"

Leo paused, turning back to face us. "Just a guy looking for stories. But I can see you're both holding onto some of your own."

With that cryptic remark, he sauntered away toward the beach, leaving us in a thick silence punctuated only by the distant sound of waves crashing against the shore. I felt the tension settle back around us, heavy and palpable.

"I don't trust him," Jack said, his voice low, as if Leo might somehow hear him from across the sand.

"Neither do I," I replied, glancing back toward the retreating figure. There was something magnetic about him, even if he was an enigma wrapped in charm and arrogance. "But what if he knows something? About the island, about the past?"

"Or he's just a guy who likes to tell tall tales to impress people," Jack countered, his expression torn between frustration and concern.

"Maybe," I conceded, feeling a flicker of doubt gnaw at the edges of my certainty. "But isn't it worth asking? If there's a chance he knows something about Nana or..." My voice trailed off, caught in the weight of unspoken memories.

"Or what?" Jack pressed, his eyes narrowing as if sensing a darker thread woven into my thoughts.

"Or maybe there's something more to this place than we understand," I said, my voice barely a whisper. "Something beyond just memories."

Jack opened his mouth to respond, but before he could, a sudden rustle from the bushes caught both of our attention, our heads snapping toward the source of the noise. A flash of movement darted through the foliage, quick and agile, before it disappeared just as fast.

"What was that?" I asked, my heart racing again, the earlier banter forgotten.

"Just a rabbit, I'm sure," Jack replied, but I could hear the uncertainty in his voice.

"No," I insisted, my intuition flaring. "That felt... different. It felt deliberate."

As if in response, the underbrush rustled again, more forcefully this time, the sound echoing with a sense of urgency that sent a chill down my spine. My pulse quickened, and I felt a wave of dread wash over me.

"Amelia..." Jack began, but before he could finish, a figure stepped out from behind the bushes—a shadow materializing into form.

My breath hitched in my throat as I faced the newcomer, a woman with a familiar face and piercing blue eyes, a haunting echo from my past. "You shouldn't be here," she said, her voice an eerie whisper that chilled me to the bone, carrying a warning I couldn't ignore.

And just like that, the echoes of my childhood were no longer mere whispers; they stood before me, threatening to unravel everything I thought I understood.

Chapter 11: Collateral Damage

The scent of damp wood and the faint musk of mildew hung heavy in the air, clinging to the faded wallpaper like an unwelcome guest. I stood in the middle of the lobby, taking in the sight of cracked tiles and disheveled furniture as if they were remnants of a time long forgotten. A chandelier, once grand, now lay awkwardly on the floor, its glass shards glinting like tiny stars fallen from the sky. The hotel, a once-vibrant haven for weary travelers, was now a shell of its former self, and the weight of its decay pressed down on me, stifling.

"Just hold it steady, would you?" Jack's voice broke through my reverie, sharp as the hammer he wielded with unnerving ease. He was crouched over a stubborn door hinge, his brow furrowed in concentration, yet his tone held a trace of exasperation. I rolled my eyes, not that he could see. I was supposed to be helping, but every attempt I made felt more like a disservice to the cause. I grabbed the other side of the door, my fingers slipping slightly on the wood, and grimaced.

"Steady? This entire place is about as steady as a drunk at a wedding," I shot back, trying to keep my frustration at bay. My words had a bite, but I didn't care. The peeling paint, the dusty corners, the broken promises of this hotel mirrored the chaos of my own life.

"Then maybe stop daydreaming and pay attention," he snapped, the tension in his voice crackling like static in the air. I didn't respond, but the tension hung between us, thick and electric.

The sun slanted through the tall, grimy windows, casting slivers of light that danced across the debris, illuminating our shared space but doing nothing to illuminate the chasm growing between us. I had come here to escape—to find solace in the familiar chaos that was Nana's legacy. Instead, I felt like an intruder, wandering through the ruins of a life I barely understood. Jack, with his sturdy frame and calloused hands, was as much a part of this place as the wallpaper. He belonged here; I was an interloper.

Jack set the hammer down with a decisive thud and stood, wiping his forehead with the back of his hand. "You're not here to fix it all at once. It's going to take time."

"Time? You mean more like a lifetime," I replied, sarcasm dripping from my words like the drab paint from the ceiling. "You're stuck in this endless loop of repairs and renovations, and for what? To keep something alive that's already dead?"

His eyes flared, and I could see the hurt lurking beneath the anger. "Maybe you're the one who's stuck. You left everything behind, and now you want to waltz back in like you own the place?"

We stared at each other, the air thick with unresolved emotions. I could feel the heat rising in my cheeks, the truth of his words hitting home like an unwelcomed revelation. I wasn't just running from my past; I was running from him, from the life I had walked away from so decisively. But the more he pressed, the more I bristled.

"I'm not the one clinging to a wreck," I shot back, my voice rising in pitch. "I came back to help, but all you see is a stranger trying to take your precious hotel away from you."

"Your precious hotel?" Jack's incredulous laugh echoed through the hollow space, but it wasn't joyful. It was bitter, tinged with the weight of truth that hung over us. "This place is a burden, Mia. It's a reminder of everything that went wrong."

And suddenly, I was there again—standing in that sterile hospital room, my mother's frail form swallowed by the sheets, the smell of antiseptic sharp in my nostrils. I could feel my heart stutter at the memory, a wound that hadn't yet healed, one I didn't want to share with Jack.

"I'm not the one holding onto the past, Jack," I said, quieter now. "I came back because I thought it might be different. That maybe this place could mean something again."

His expression softened for a moment, and I could see the conflict in his eyes. "It's not just about the hotel. It's about you, too. You think fixing this will fix everything else?"

"Maybe it's not about fixing at all. Maybe it's just about finding a way to live with the broken pieces," I said, my voice low, threading sincerity through my anger.

Silence stretched between us, taut as a bowstring, and for a heartbeat, I thought he might let it go. But instead, he stepped closer, his gaze piercing into me. "So what's next, Mia? Are you going to help me put this place back together, or are you going to run away again when it gets too hard?"

I wanted to tell him I was here to stay, that the pieces of my heart were scattered but not lost, that somehow, together, we could find a way to make this work. But the words slipped away like sand through my fingers. Instead, I turned away, crossing my arms against the chill that crept into the space. The gulf between us felt insurmountable, as though the walls of the hotel were slowly closing in, tightening around our shared pain.

And as I stared out at the crumbling façade of what had once been a home, I realized that perhaps fixing this hotel was just the beginning. It was time to confront the wreckage of my own life. But the question lingered in the air, heavy and unresolved—was I brave enough to face it?

The sun dipped low in the sky, casting long shadows that crept across the battered lobby like reluctant memories. The quiet hum of the settling dust filled the air, punctuated by the occasional creak of the floorboards, reminding me that this place was still alive in its own peculiar way. I leaned against the worn reception desk, its surface marred by countless scratches and stains, remnants of the laughter and tears that had echoed here over the years. The weight of our argument clung to me, wrapping around my chest like a vise, and I felt the urge to escape that suffocating tension.

Jack had gone quiet after our heated exchange, busily tossing aside debris with a fervor that suggested he was trying to exorcise the ghosts of our confrontation rather than the physical remnants of the hotel. Each thud of a fallen piece of wood against the floor was like a heartbeat in the stillness, marking the rhythm of his frustration. I felt a pang of regret twist in my gut.

"Look, I know I'm not exactly cut out for this," I said finally, breaking the silence that had settled like a heavy fog. "But I didn't come here to make things worse. I thought we could make this place work again."

He paused, turning to face me, his brow slightly furrowed. "It's not just about fixing the hotel, Mia. It's about fixing everything that's broken—between us, too." His voice was softer now, edged with a vulnerability that caught me off guard.

"Everything's broken?" I echoed, the weight of his words hanging between us like a fragile thread. "Maybe everything just needs a fresh coat of paint."

A flicker of a smile crossed his lips, but it vanished as quickly as it appeared. "Fresh paint won't cover the cracks, you know. You have to dig deeper."

There it was again, the underlying issue that had always simmered beneath our surface—a fear of confronting the truths we both avoided. I stepped closer, the scent of sawdust mingling with the lingering perfume of something sweeter from the bakery down the street. "Maybe it's not just about digging. Maybe it's about knowing when to let go."

"Let go?" His tone shifted, a mixture of disbelief and challenge. "Is that what you're doing? Letting go of everything that mattered?"

I crossed my arms defensively, feeling the tension coil tighter. "I'm trying to find my own way, Jack. But every time I think I've got a grip, I find myself slipping back into the past."

"You can't slip back into the past if you don't try to hold onto it," he shot back, the fire returning to his voice. "You want to leave, but you can't keep dragging it along with you like a suitcase full of memories."

His words struck a nerve, echoing the very battle I fought within myself. I had come here to reconcile my past, yet I felt as if I were carrying an entire suitcase factory on my back. The memories of my mother's illness, my father's absence—they were all wrapped up in this dilapidated hotel. The walls echoed with their laughter and sorrow, and I couldn't help but feel that this place was a bittersweet reminder of everything I had lost.

"Maybe I don't want to keep it all," I said quietly, my voice trembling with the weight of unshed tears. "Maybe I want to let go of some of it, even if it hurts."

Jack's expression softened, and for a moment, I thought I saw a flicker of understanding. "You're not alone in this, Mia. You never were. I'm here, too."

Before I could respond, a sharp knock echoed from the front door, pulling us from our charged moment. I turned, my heart racing as I wondered who might venture into this chaotic shell of a hotel. Jack frowned, glancing toward the sound, his expression a mix of curiosity and caution.

"Expecting someone?" I asked, trying to shake off the heaviness that lingered in the air.

"Not a soul," he replied, and we exchanged a glance that screamed caution. I stepped toward the door, hesitating just a moment before pulling it open.

Standing there was a stranger, an older man dressed in a tattered leather jacket and a broad-brimmed hat that cast a shadow over his eyes. He looked like he had weathered more storms than I could imagine. "You're the ones running this place?" he asked, his voice gravelly, yet it carried an odd warmth.

"Depends on your definition of 'running,'" I replied, trying to keep my tone light despite the unease crawling up my spine.

He chuckled, revealing a grin that split his weathered face. "You might want to reconsider that definition. This place has seen better days, but it still holds potential. I've been keeping an eye on it for a while now."

Jack stepped up beside me, his posture shifting to one of guarded interest. "And you are?"

"Name's Gus." He extended a hand, his grip firm and surprisingly warm. "I used to come here years ago when it was a proper hotel. Thought I might check in on the place." He let out a soft chuckle, then leaned against the doorframe, assessing us. "I see it needs a little love."

"More than a little," Jack muttered, his skepticism palpable.

Gus studied us both for a moment, his gaze flickering between our expressions. "You two look like you've been through a battle zone. Fitting, I suppose, for a hotel in ruins." He gestured to the debris strewn about the lobby. "But I've got some ideas that might breathe life back into this place. It's got character, you know?"

"Character?" I echoed, a sarcastic edge creeping into my voice. "More like a death wish."

"Ah, but there's beauty in brokenness, lass," Gus said, a twinkle in his eye. "You just have to know where to look."

I exchanged a glance with Jack, uncertainty mirrored in his expression. This stranger, with his tales of the past and the glimmer of hope he offered, held a strange magnetism. It was as if he understood the layers of history this place had wrapped around itself, much like the layers of hurt I was trying to shed.

"What kind of ideas?" Jack asked, leaning in just slightly, the skepticism softening a touch.

"Think of it as a revival," Gus replied, leaning closer as if sharing a secret. "Get the community involved. Host events. Give people a reason to come back and remember why this place was loved."

"Revival," I mused aloud, the word hanging in the air, tantalizingly sweet. Perhaps it was what I needed too—a chance to resurrect not only the hotel but the pieces of myself I had tucked away.

"Count me in," I said, my voice steady, igniting a flicker of possibility in the air between us. Jack shot me a look of surprise, but I held my ground. Maybe this time, instead of running away, I could stand firm and fight for something—this hotel, this moment, and perhaps even Jack.

Gus grinned, and it felt as if he had just handed me a key to unlock the door to my own buried aspirations. The shadows around us receded just a bit, leaving room for the light to seep back in, illuminating the cracks that still needed mending.

The atmosphere crackled with a fresh tension, sparked not just by our heated exchanges but by Gus's unexpected arrival, which felt like a bolt of lightning illuminating a darkened sky. His enthusiasm was infectious, and I could sense the simmering energy in Jack, who was visibly torn between skepticism and curiosity. As we stood there, surrounded by remnants of a place that had once been vibrant, it was impossible not to feel the pull of possibility.

Gus leaned against the doorframe, the warm light filtering through the broken glass creating a halo effect around him. "You have to understand, this hotel is more than just bricks and mortar. It's a story waiting to be rewritten." His voice held a gravelly charm, each word weighted with experience.

"And what story would that be?" Jack interjected, his brow still furrowed with caution. "Last I checked, this place was on life support."

"Ah, but life support can turn into a revival with a little creativity. Picture it: a community fair in the courtyard, local artists showcasing their work, live music echoing through the halls—bringing back the laughter, the life." Gus's eyes sparkled with vision, and I felt a flicker of hope ignite within me, kindling my imagination.

"Community fair?" I mused, tapping my chin as I considered the possibilities. "You mean like a town gathering? Would anyone actually show up?"

"Show up? Honey, they'd be clawing at the doors to get in. You'd be surprised how many people long for a taste of nostalgia," Gus replied, a smirk playing on his lips. "Just need to give them a reason to remember why they loved this place in the first place."

I glanced at Jack, who was now studying Gus with newfound interest. There was something compelling about the way Gus spoke, as if he could conjure up the ghosts of this hotel's past and breathe life back into them. "What do you think?" I asked Jack, my voice softer, more vulnerable. "Could we really make this happen?"

"Maybe," he replied slowly, his gaze still on Gus, assessing him like a wary dog examining a potential intruder. "But it's going to take more than just a few banners and a potluck dinner. This place needs serious repairs."

"And that's where you come in," Gus replied, his grin widening. "You and your lovely assistant." He pointed a finger at me, his enthusiasm undeterred. "But you can't fix it in isolation. You need the community. You need them to care again."

Jack hesitated, clearly weighing the options. "And if they don't care?"

"Then we make them care," I interjected, the words tumbling out before I could think. "What if we started small? A bake sale? A storytelling night? Just something to bring people through those doors. To remind them that this place can still be a part of their lives."

"Now you're talking," Gus said, a twinkle in his eye. "You bring in the heart, and I'll bring in the soul."

Jack finally cracked a smile, albeit a cautious one. "All right, I'm in. But we need to be practical. This isn't just about throwing a party; we need a plan."

"A plan, yes! A blueprint for a revival," Gus declared, straightening up, the light catching his hair and making it glint like a wild mane. "We can meet tomorrow, brainstorm some ideas, get the word out. We'll spread the word faster than gossip at a family reunion."

I could feel the excitement bubbling up within me, and despite the shambles around us, the possibilities felt like a sweet breeze blowing through a window long left shut. "I can reach out to the local shops, see if they'd be interested in collaborating. We could set up some promotional events."

"Fantastic idea," Gus replied, nodding enthusiastically. "I'll get some flyers printed up. We'll hit the farmers' market and start spreading the word like butter on warm toast."

Jack chuckled, and I felt a surge of warmth at the sound. It was the first hint of levity we'd shared since my arrival. "Okay, then. Let's do it. Let's bring this place back to life."

As we continued to brainstorm ideas, the air around us began to change. The weight of unspoken fears started to lift, replaced by an eagerness that felt almost electric. Yet, a tiny seed of doubt still lingered at the back of my mind. Could we really pull this off?

Just as I began to embrace the optimism swirling within, a sudden commotion erupted outside. A cacophony of voices mixed with the sound of footsteps thudding against the pavement drew my attention. Jack and I exchanged a quick glance before rushing toward the entrance, curiosity piqued.

As we stepped outside, a group of townspeople gathered near the entrance, their animated chatter filled the air with an air of urgency. I squinted into the fading light, trying to discern what was happening. Then I saw it—a familiar face in the crowd. My heart skipped a beat as I recognized Marlene, my childhood friend, her expression torn between excitement and concern.

"Mia!" she shouted, her voice cutting through the noise. "You need to come quick! It's... it's about your mom!"

Time seemed to freeze around me, a hushed silence enveloping the world. The warmth that had ignited in my chest extinguished, replaced by a cold grip of dread. I felt Jack's hand on my arm, steady and reassuring, but it didn't quell the rising panic within me. "What do you mean?" I managed to choke out, the words barely forming.

"She's in the hospital. There's been an accident," Marlene said, breathless and wide-eyed.

The world around me spun, the laughter and plans for the hotel fading into the background as fear clawed at my throat. "What kind of accident? Is she okay?" My voice trembled, each word laced with urgency and disbelief.

"She's... they're saying she's stable, but you need to come. Now!"

With each word, the weight of my past crashed back down, heavy and relentless. I felt the ground shift beneath me as if the very foundations of my life were crumbling once again. Jack's grip tightened on my arm, grounding me in the chaos, but my heart raced toward the storm that lay ahead.

"We need to go," I said, urgency dripping from my words. I barely heard Jack's reply as I turned, ready to leave the fragments of the hotel behind, the plans for revival replaced by an all-consuming dread.

And just as I reached the edge of the crowd, a voice rose above the commotion, sharp and accusatory. "You think you can just waltz back in here and fix everything? You don't even know what you're doing!"

I turned, my stomach dropping as I recognized the owner of that familiar voice. It was Kelly, my mother's longtime friend, her face contorted in a mixture of anger and despair. "You left, Mia. You abandoned her when she needed you the most!"

Her words hit me like a slap, raw and unrelenting, as the crowd's eyes turned toward me. In that moment, I felt exposed, like a raw nerve laid bare for all to see. The shadows of my past stretched long and dark, mingling with the fading light as I stood on the precipice of uncertainty, the weight of my choices crashing down upon me.

And in that instant, everything shifted. The plans for the hotel, the hope for revival, all hung in the balance, eclipsed by the daunting question of whether I could truly face what awaited me.

Chapter 12: The Turning Point

The shadows stretched across the porch, clinging to the old wood like ghosts reluctant to depart. The warm glow from the few porch lights cast flickering patterns, creating an atmosphere thick with unspoken words and shared history. I found Jack hunched over, his strong hands deftly maneuvering a hammer against a stubborn nail that seemed determined to resist his every attempt. The rhythmic sound echoed in the stillness, a heartbeat that matched my own tumultuous thoughts. He didn't look up as I approached, the weight of my presence unacknowledged, but I could see the tension in his shoulders, a coiled spring ready to snap.

I held a chilled bottle of beer, its condensation slick against my palm, a simple offering that felt monumental in this moment of fracture. "Thought you might need this," I said, my voice light, a facade for the heaviness that hung between us. The silence stretched, taut like the string of a bow, ready to release the tension that had built up since our last confrontation.

Jack paused, glancing up just long enough for me to catch a glimpse of the storm brewing in his blue eyes, so often calm and inviting. "Thanks," he replied, taking the bottle without meeting my gaze. There was a world of distance wrapped in that one word, a quiet acknowledgment of all the things left unsaid. He took a long swig, his throat working as he swallowed, and I watched, entranced by the simple act, the way the coolness seemed to ground him in this moment of turmoil.

We sat in silence, the faint sound of crickets chirping in the background, a familiar song that had accompanied countless evenings spent together. The porch creaked under our weight, a reminder of its age, just as the hotel bore the scars of time. I let my eyes wander over the peeling paint, the way the wood was warped in places, echoing the struggles we both faced. This place had seen better days, and so had we. It was an unsettling mirror reflecting our insecurities and fears.

"I didn't mean what I said," I finally broke the silence, the words spilling out before I could cage them. It felt necessary, though whether it would bridge the chasm between us or deepen it, I had no idea. "About selling the hotel. It was an emotional reaction."

Jack turned his head slightly, and the look he gave me was a blend of surprise and hurt. "You were just being honest," he said, his voice low, almost gravelly. "You've always been straight with me. If it's what you want, then—"

"No," I interrupted, the word bursting forth with urgency. "That's not what I meant. I've been so focused on my future, my escape, that I never really considered what staying would mean—not just for me, but for this town, for you." The admission hung in the air, heavy with implication.

He leaned back against the railing, the wood warm against his skin, as if he needed the heat to dispel the chill that had settled in his heart. "This town is a dead end for some," he said, staring into the darkness beyond, where the trees loomed like sentinels. "But for me, it's home. It's where I buried my father, where I watched friends grow up and grow old. You can't just walk away from that."

The weight of his words sank deep, twisting in my chest. I'd thought I was running toward something better, a life filled with possibilities, but what if I was leaving behind something beautiful, something worth fighting for? I took a deep breath, steadying myself against the realization. "You've stayed through everything, haven't you? Through the losses, the disappointments. Why?"

He paused, his brow furrowing in thought, as if he were unraveling a complex puzzle. "Because sometimes, it's easier to stay than to leave," he said finally, his voice barely above a whisper. "It's familiar. It's painful, but it's home. And home... well, it has its own kind of beauty, doesn't it?"

I felt a flicker of understanding ignite within me. My own home was not just a place to flee but a canvas painted with memories, laughter, and love. The hotel, with all its quirks and flaws, was a part of me, and perhaps I had been too quick to dismiss its worth. The ghosts of my past and the hope of my future intertwined, revealing a tapestry I had yet to fully appreciate.

"Tell me about your father," I urged gently, the question hanging delicately between us like a whisper.

Jack shifted, a shadow passing over his features as he weighed the words. "He was a dreamer, you know. Always talking about the next big thing, the next adventure. He had plans to expand the hotel, to make it a destination, not just for locals but for travelers. But then... life happened." His voice faltered, a crack appearing in his facade. "He lost his fight to the bottle, and I watched him slip away. It wasn't just the man I lost; it was the dream he had for this place."

I felt my heart clench. "I'm so sorry, Jack. I can't imagine how hard that was."

"It was like losing two people," he continued, his gaze still far away, as if he were revisiting that time. "The father I wanted to know and the man he became. But I stayed. I couldn't leave him behind in a place that had once been filled with so much life."

The depth of his pain wrapped around me, a warm shroud that made my heart ache for him. "And what about you?" he asked, suddenly turning the focus back to me, his eyes searching mine. "What's your dream?"

For a moment, I hesitated. My dreams had felt so elusive, fluttering just out of reach like autumn leaves in the wind. "I thought I wanted to escape, to find something bigger and better," I said softly. "But now... now I wonder if maybe I've been running from the very thing I needed all along."

Jack nodded slowly, the understanding in his eyes warming me like the setting sun. The evening air shifted, a cool breeze wrapping around us, and I realized that, in that moment, we were no longer just two wounded souls sharing silence. We were two people beginning to understand the weight of their choices, the significance of staying.

The evening air wrapped around us like a familiar blanket, comfortable yet charged with a tension I could feel prickling at the edges. As I sat next to Jack, the quiet between us was no longer suffocating; it was contemplative, a fragile bridge across the space we'd created since our fight. The distant sounds of the town wound their way through the dark, a comforting symphony of life continuing without us, yet right here, everything felt suspended.

Jack took a deep breath, as if gathering the courage to continue sharing pieces of himself. "My dad was a good man," he said, his voice steadying as he focused on the wood grain of the porch, running his fingers over the splintered edges. "He wanted to build something lasting, something that would matter. When he passed, I felt like I had two choices: I could walk away, or I could try to honor what he started."

"That's a heavy burden," I murmured, my heart aching for him. "Didn't it feel impossible at times?"

He finally looked at me, a ghost of a smile touching his lips, though it didn't quite reach his eyes. "Every single day. But then I'd think of all the people who stopped by, all the memories wrapped up in this place. I couldn't just let it slip away. So, I stayed. Even when it would have been easier to go."

His words hung in the air, mingling with the faint scent of honeysuckle from the garden. The moonlight painted his features in silver, and for the first time, I truly saw him—not just Jack the handyman or the local hero, but Jack the dreamer, the keeper of his father's legacy. It resonated within me, igniting a flicker of purpose I hadn't realized I'd lost in my quest for escape.

"Maybe," I ventured, feeling emboldened by his openness, "maybe it's not about running away or staying, but finding a way to make this place matter to us."

"Exactly," he said, his enthusiasm rising. "What if we could breathe new life into the hotel? Not just as a business, but as a community hub? A place where people gather, where memories are made?"

The idea blossomed in my mind, rich and vibrant. I could almost hear the laughter of guests, the clinking of glasses, the aroma of freshly baked bread wafting through the halls. "You mean like a revival?" I asked, my voice laced with excitement. "We could host events, maybe a local art fair or music nights?"

Jack's eyes lit up, a spark of passion igniting within him. "Yes! We could turn that old ballroom into a venue. I've seen some amazing talent in this town. With the right support, we could create something special."

I felt my heart race, caught up in the vision. "And what about the community? I mean, they've always been so invested in the hotel. What if we engaged them? We could do workshops, invite local artisans to showcase their crafts."

He nodded enthusiastically, his smile growing. "Exactly! Let's draw them in, make them feel part of this dream. It's not just about saving the hotel; it's about reviving the spirit of the town."

I couldn't help but grin at him, the idea weaving its way through my thoughts like a melody. "And maybe we could throw in a few surprises. You know, like a murder mystery dinner or a themed weekend? I've always wanted to host something a bit offbeat."

"Count me in!" Jack chuckled, and the warmth in his laughter sent a ripple of hope through me. It felt good to plan, to dream about a future that was no longer clouded by fear. The tension that had woven itself into our conversations began to dissipate, replaced by a shared vision, a partnership that felt more meaningful than any I had imagined.

We spent the next hour bouncing ideas off one another, our laughter mingling with the rustling leaves and the distant hum of the town. With each suggestion, the atmosphere shifted from heavy to buoyant, filling the void between us with a new energy, like the dawn breaking after a long night.

As the stars began to twinkle above, I felt a shift in my heart. The whispers of doubt that had plagued me were fading, replaced by a burgeoning sense of belonging. I could envision the hotel filled with life again, a tapestry of stories woven together by the townsfolk. This place was not just a building; it was a vessel for dreams, both shared and individual.

"Jack," I said, catching his eye as we stood to leave, "thank you for believing in this. In us."

He shrugged, a lightness in his demeanor. "It's easy to believe when I see the fire in your eyes. You bring something to this place that's been missing for a long time."

A warm blush crept up my cheeks, and I brushed it off with a playful roll of my eyes. "You're not too bad yourself. Though I can't promise I'll keep my hammer skills to the same standards."

He laughed, a sound so genuine it warmed the chill of the evening air. "We'll figure it out together. You handle the ideas; I'll handle the hammers. Teamwork, right?"

I nodded, a feeling of camaraderie blossoming between us, and for the first time, it felt like more than just a shared goal. There was an undercurrent of something deeper, a connection woven through our laughter and dreams. As we stepped back into the flickering light of the porch, the world around us seemed to pulse with possibility.

Just as I turned to leave, I paused, catching sight of the old oak tree that stood sentinel at the edge of the property, its gnarled branches reaching out like an embrace. "You know, this place might just surprise us," I said, the thought tumbling from my lips. "Maybe we'll end up building something even more beautiful than either of us imagined."

Jack smiled softly, a look of quiet determination in his eyes. "Maybe we will."

In that moment, I felt the weight of my past begin to lift, replaced by the promise of what lay ahead. Together, we could carve out a future filled with laughter, community, and the kind of love that thrives in the face of adversity. The hotel was not merely a structure; it was a dream waiting to unfold, and I could hardly wait to see where it would lead us.

As the days turned into a blur of planning and excited conversations, the town of Maplewood began to feel alive again, pulsating with a rhythm that echoed my own renewed spirit. Each morning, I woke with a sense of purpose, the faint scent of pine and coffee mingling in the air as I stepped out onto the porch, ready to embrace whatever the day had to offer. Jack and I had become a formidable duo, brainstorming ideas for revitalizing the hotel, and with every passing moment, the distance between us diminished.

One bright Saturday, as we set up for our first community meeting, I couldn't help but marvel at the transformation around me. The once-dilapidated ballroom sparkled under the strings of fairy lights we had draped across the ceiling, casting a warm glow over the polished wood floor. The smell of freshly baked pastries wafted in from the kitchen, where I'd enlisted the help of Mrs. Gentry, our local baker and a fount of knowledge about the town's history. Her laughter filled the room as she shared stories of weddings held under this very roof, each tale a thread in the intricate tapestry of Maplewood's past.

"Are you sure you're ready for this?" Jack leaned against the doorframe, arms crossed, his expression a mix of excitement and skepticism. He had always been the practical one, grounded by a caution that often kept him from dreaming too far. I caught the glint of doubt in his eyes, even as he couldn't hide his smile.

"Absolutely," I replied, the determination in my voice almost tangible. "This place is about to become the heartbeat of the community again. Just wait until the townsfolk see what we've done."

He chuckled, shaking his head as he pushed off the doorframe and stepped inside. "You always did have a knack for optimism, didn't you? What's next? A fireworks show?"

"Hey, don't knock it until you try it!" I shot back, unable to suppress a grin. "And it could very well be in the works. You never know what kind of wild ideas might come to life tonight."

As people began to trickle in, I felt the familiar flutter of nerves twist in my stomach. The room filled with familiar faces, friends and neighbors whose lives were woven into the fabric of the hotel's history. They were curious and apprehensive, whispering among themselves as they took in the new decorations and the lively buzz of possibility that seemed to hang in the air.

When Mrs. Gentry set a platter of her famous cinnamon rolls on the table, I watched as eyes lit up, and suddenly the chatter grew louder, enveloping the room in a warm cocoon of comfort and nostalgia. This was it; this was the spark I had hoped to ignite.

I took a deep breath, stepping forward to address the crowd. "Thank you all for coming! I know change can be daunting, but together, we have the chance to create something extraordinary here at the hotel."

A soft murmur of agreement rippled through the crowd, bolstering my confidence. "We're looking to breathe new life into this place—not just as a business, but as a gathering spot for our community. We want your input, your ideas. What do you want to see happen here?"

"I want to see the ballroom packed with dancing!" shouted Henry, a sprightly old man with a shock of white hair. The crowd erupted in laughter, the tension melting away like snow in the sun.

"And I want a pie-eating contest!" chimed in Alice, a local shop owner, her eyes twinkling with mischief.

"Consider it done!" I replied, buoyed by their enthusiasm. As we tossed around ideas, it felt like the hotel was awakening from a long slumber, its heartbeats in sync with those of the townsfolk.

But as the night unfolded, I noticed a familiar face lingering at the back of the room. Laura, my childhood rival, stood with her arms crossed, an expression of skepticism etched on her face. She had always been the town's golden girl, and I couldn't shake the feeling that she was here to undermine my efforts.

I tried to brush off the feeling, focusing on the warmth of the room, but as the meeting progressed, she continued to cast glances my way, her sharp gaze an icy reminder that not everyone was ready to embrace change. Just as I was wrapping up the evening, she stepped forward, arms still crossed defiantly.

"So, let me get this straight," she began, her tone dripping with sarcasm. "You think you can just waltz in here, throw a few parties, and suddenly this place will be bustling again? Sounds a bit too good to be true, don't you think?"

I felt the room's energy shift, a collective breath held in anticipation of my response. Jack's presence beside me was a reassuring anchor, but I knew I had to stand my ground. "It won't happen overnight, but it's a start. This hotel has been a part of our lives for generations. Don't you want to see it thrive?"

Her smile twisted into something more akin to a sneer. "I guess I'd just like to know how much of a role you plan to play once the novelty wears off. People are fickle. They'll forget you once you sell out."

A hush fell over the crowd, and I could feel the tension thickening, almost suffocating. My heart raced as I searched for a way to address her jibe without revealing the self-doubt that began to creep in. "I'm not going anywhere," I stated, my voice steadier than I felt. "This is my home too, and I believe in this place."

Jack stepped forward, his voice low but firm. "We're committed to this project. It's not about selling out; it's about investing in the community. We want to build something that lasts."

Laura's eyes narrowed, but she didn't press further, the spark of challenge still simmering beneath her surface. "We'll see," she said, turning away with a dismissive flick of her hair.

As the crowd began to disperse, I couldn't shake the feeling of unease that settled like a stone in my stomach. The excitement from earlier dimmed slightly, overshadowed by Laura's insinuations.

"Hey, you handled that like a pro," Jack said, his voice low and reassuring as we began to clean up the remnants of the evening. "Don't let her get to you. She's just afraid of change."

"I know," I sighed, feeling the weight of the night's events pressing down on me. "But what if she's right? What if people do forget?"

Jack paused, a thoughtful look crossing his face. "Then we give them something unforgettable. We can't control how others feel, but we can control what we put into this place."

His words grounded me, but as I glanced around the ballroom, something caught my eye—a small envelope had slipped from the table, its edges worn as if it had been there for years. Curiosity piqued, I bent down to pick it up, my fingers brushing against the aged paper.

As I opened it, my heart raced. The contents were handwritten, a letter that smelled faintly of cedar and time. My pulse quickened as I read the first few lines, the words blurring together, twisting into an unexpected revelation.

"Dear whoever finds this letter," it began, and I could feel the weight of the past pressing in around me.

Before I could digest what I was reading, the door swung open with a creak, and a shadow fell across the threshold, freezing my breath in my chest. I looked up, my heart pounding as I realized who stood there. Jack's expression shifted, his smile faltering as he took in the figure in the doorway.

"Mom?" Jack's voice was barely above a whisper, filled with disbelief.

My heart sank, the words on the page slipping from my fingers as I watched the woman I had only heard about from him, the one who had left years ago, step into the light of the ballroom. The revelation spun around me, like a whirlwind of possibilities and consequences I hadn't anticipated. In that moment, everything shifted, and the vibrant dreams we had woven together hung in the balance.

Chapter 13: An Unexpected Offer

The sun dipped low in the sky, casting a golden hue over the quaint town of Maplewood, its familiar streets adorned with the fading colors of autumn. The air was crisp, infused with the sweet aroma of cider simmering on the stove and the sharp bite of fallen leaves crunching underfoot. I stood on the hotel's weathered porch, a fortress of memories rising behind me, its peeling paint telling stories of laughter, love, and the occasional heartbreak. It was a haven I had nurtured back to life, and now, just when I thought I had finally found my place within its walls, a tempest brewed on the horizon.

The email had come through just as I was arranging the wilting daisies for the lobby's centerpiece, the screen flashing like a warning light on a stormy day. It was from a high-powered developer, one with an impressive portfolio of transforming charming locales into sprawling luxury resorts. He offered an eye-watering sum, enough to erase my financial woes and pave my way back to the glittering streets of New York. The thought was intoxicating—no more late nights spent fretting over repairs, no more scrambling to keep the hotel afloat during the off-season, and the tantalizing promise of a new beginning. I could almost feel the weight of my carefully curated dreams unfurling in my chest.

But with each word I read, a knot tightened in my stomach. The hotel—this beautiful, creaky old structure—was more than a building to me. It was a tapestry woven from the lives that had passed through its doors, each guest leaving a thread of their story, making it richer, more vibrant. The thought of tearing it down, of exchanging its soul for glistening marble and overpriced spa treatments, felt like sacrilege.

Just then, Jack stormed onto the porch, his expression a mix of disbelief and fury. "You can't seriously be considering this," he blurted, his voice tinged with a gravelly urgency that set my nerves on edge.

"I'm not," I replied, though the words felt slippery on my tongue. "I just got the offer today. It's tempting, isn't it?"

"Tempting? It's a nightmare! This place is the heart of Maplewood, and you're thinking of selling it off like some old relic?" His brow furrowed, and for a moment, I could see the hurt etched in the lines of his face. Jack had become my closest ally, the one who stood by me through sleepless nights and the inevitable hurdles of running this hotel.

"It's more than just a building, Jack," I said, my voice steadying. "But I can't deny that the money would change everything."

"Change everything for who?" he shot back, his hands balled into fists at his sides. "For you? For the town? You think those resorts care about the soul of Maplewood? They'll wipe it out for their profits, and you'll be left with a fat bank account and a hollow victory."

I took a step back, the weight of his words pressing down on me. "It's not that simple. What if I could finally pay off my debts, start fresh? I could..." The words trailed off, and I felt the flicker of hope dimming against the storm of his objections.

Jack sighed, running a hand through his tousled hair. "You think starting over means leaving? You've built something incredible here, Clara. You've brought life back to this place. What about all those families who depend on this hotel for their livelihoods?"

"Don't you think I know that?" I snapped, the frustration spilling over. "I care about them as much as you do, but I can't keep drowning in this sea of uncertainty. What happens when I can't pay the staff? When the bills pile up so high that even I can't ignore them?"

"Then we figure it out," he said, his voice softening. "Together. This town thrives because of people like you—people who care enough to fight for it. Selling out isn't the solution; it's the easy way out."

As he spoke, I could see the passion igniting in his eyes, a flame that mirrored the one I had buried deep inside me. It was impossible to ignore the bond that had formed between us, one forged through late-night talks and shared dreams over coffee and pie at the diner down the street. Yet, my heart was caught in a tempest of uncertainty, torn between the promise of a new life and the undeniable connection I felt to this town and to him.

"I don't want to be the villain here," I confessed, my voice barely above a whisper. "I love this place. I love what it's become. But I also feel trapped, Jack."

"Then let's figure it out," he insisted, his intensity burning through the haze of my doubts. "Don't let this offer pull you into a decision you'll regret. We can make a plan—bring in more guests, revamp the marketing, maybe even host local events to draw in crowds. You're not alone in this."

His words hung in the air, a lifeline thrown amidst the swirling chaos of my thoughts. The idea of fighting back, of refusing to bow to the pressures that threatened to dismantle my dream, ignited a spark within me. Maybe I didn't have to choose between two worlds; perhaps I could carve out a new path, one that honored both my aspirations and the legacy of this hotel.

"Alright," I said, the resolve solidifying in my chest. "Let's fight for it, together."

Jack's expression shifted from anger to something softer, a hint of relief mingling with a flicker of admiration. "That's the spirit. We'll show them that Maplewood isn't just another stop on the map. It's home."

As the last rays of sun slipped beneath the horizon, painting the sky in shades of lavender and gold, I realized that maybe, just maybe, I wasn't ready to say goodbye to the life I had built here. There was still so much to fight for, and for the first time in a long while, I felt the thrill of possibility coursing through my veins.

The following morning, the air was thick with the scent of fresh coffee and the sweet notes of cinnamon wafting through the hotel's dining room, mingling with the soft chatter of early guests. I busied myself behind the counter, arranging a display of pastries that glistened with glaze, each one a small work of art that beckoned patrons like sirens to sailors. The sunlight poured through the tall windows, illuminating the room with a warm glow that somehow felt like a hug, wrapping around me just as I desperately needed the comfort.

I moved through the space with a practiced grace, but beneath the surface, my thoughts churned like a stormy sea. Jack's impassioned plea echoed in my mind, mixing with the image of the email I had read a dozen times. Each glance at the offer felt like a betrayal of everything I had worked for, yet the siren call of a fresh start tugged at my heart. What was I really afraid of? Change? Or was it something deeper—a fear of losing the very essence of what made Maplewood feel like home?

"Morning, Clara!" called Marlene, the town's self-appointed breakfast enthusiast, as she swept into the dining room, her vibrant scarf dancing in the breeze of the open door. "What's on today's agenda? More delightful pastries, I hope?"

"Of course! You know me, always chasing that elusive pastry perfection," I replied with a grin, even as my insides knotted. Marlene settled at her usual table by the window, where the sunlight highlighted her silver-streaked hair and twinkling eyes. She was like a walking embodiment of warmth, the kind of person who could make you feel at ease with just a smile.

Marlene leaned over her coffee cup, a conspiratorial look in her eyes. "You've been awfully pensive lately. Something on your mind?"

"Oh, just the usual hotel drama," I said, waving a hand dismissively, though the tension in my chest betrayed me. "You know how it is."

Her brow arched, the kind of expression that signaled she wasn't buying my feigned nonchalance. "Darling, you're as transparent as a freshly washed window. Spill it. You know I'm not just a pretty face and a penchant for baked goods."

I hesitated, glancing around the room to see if anyone else was listening. The last thing I wanted was to gossip about my predicament, but the urge to share my burden was almost overwhelming. "There's been an offer on the hotel. A developer wants to buy it and turn it into a resort."

Marlene's eyes widened, and she leaned back as if I had slapped her. "A resort? In Maplewood? They really think they can just bulldoze history for some shiny facade?"

I sighed, nodding. "That's the gist of it. The money would solve everything for me, but at what cost? This place is a part of the town—its spirit, its charm. I can't just sell it off like some old car."

"And what do you plan to do, then?" she asked, her voice gentle but firm, like a mother prompting her child to face the truth.

"I don't know," I admitted, the weight of my uncertainty heavy in the air. "Jack thinks I should fight for it, maybe do some renovations to attract more guests. But I feel like I'm standing at a crossroads, and every path has its pitfalls."

"Ah, the classic dilemma," Marlene mused, stirring her coffee slowly. "Weighing security against passion. You could be free of your burdens in one fell swoop, but would you be free of regret?"

I met her gaze, the wisdom in her expression grounding me. "What if I regret not taking the chance? Going back to New York could mean finally living the life I thought I wanted."

"Or it could mean losing something precious that you've already built," she countered, her voice steady. "You've brought this place back to life, Clara. What's the point of running away from that?"

"Running away?" I echoed, the phrase reverberating in my mind. Was I truly running, or was I simply looking for a way to breathe again? The panic I had felt moments before began to lift, replaced by a sense of clarity, however fleeting.

Marlene patted my hand, her touch warm and reassuring. "Trust your heart, my dear. It knows where to guide you, even if your head is filled with doubt."

As she spoke, Jack appeared in the doorway, his silhouette framed by the light behind him. His eyes scanned the room, landing on me before he strode over with purpose. "I heard the pastries were exceptional today," he said, his tone playful, though I could sense an undercurrent of seriousness lurking just beneath the surface.

"Only the best for our guests," I quipped, trying to keep things light even as the weight of our earlier conversation loomed large. "Care for a cinnamon roll?"

He grinned, the tension in his shoulders easing just a fraction. "You know I can never resist a cinnamon roll."

As I handed him a pastry, our fingers brushed, sending an unexpected jolt of warmth through me. It was a simple touch, yet it stirred something deeper—a connection forged over late nights, laughter, and shared goals. But there was more to it now, a delicate tension simmering beneath the surface that felt both thrilling and terrifying.

"So, what's the plan for today?" he asked, biting into the pastry with unrestrained delight. "You seem more... contemplative than usual."

I exchanged a glance with Marlene, who gave me a nod of encouragement. "Just trying to figure out the future of this place," I admitted, the words tumbling out before I could stop them. "You know about the offer."

His expression hardened, the familiar resolve returning. "Clara, you can't seriously be considering it. We need to fight for this hotel, for Maplewood. You've built something incredible here, and it deserves a chance."

"I know, Jack," I replied, feeling the familiar tug of frustration. "But what if this is my chance to finally break free? What if—"

"What if you lose yourself in the process?" he interrupted, his voice rising just a notch. "You've come so far; it would be a shame to throw it all away for a shiny new life that may not even be what you want."

I opened my mouth to respond, but the words caught in my throat as I grappled with the truth of his statement. Jack was right, in many ways. The thought of packing up and leaving felt like trading my soul for a promise, a gamble on a future that might not even exist.

As the morning light streamed in, illuminating the diner and casting long shadows across the tables, I realized that my battle wasn't just with the offer but with myself. In the silence that followed, I could feel the weight of my choices pressing down on me, demanding to be acknowledged.

"Let's make a plan," I finally said, my voice steadying. "A real plan. I want to fight for this hotel, but I need your help. Together, we can show everyone what Maplewood truly means."

Jack's expression softened, a flicker of relief crossing his face. "That's the spirit. We'll get the town involved, reach out to locals, and revitalize this place into something even more beautiful."

And as he spoke, I felt a surge of hope ignite within me. Maybe the path forward wasn't about running away or clinging desperately to the past; perhaps it was about redefining what it meant to call Maplewood home. With each idea exchanged, a spark of determination ignited in my heart, reminding me that the fight was only just beginning.

The plan to revitalize the hotel hung in the air like a banner of hope, bright and buoyant against the encroaching clouds of uncertainty. Over the next few days, Jack and I poured our energy into brainstorming sessions that felt electric with possibility. We created lists filled with ideas, scribbling them down on napkins and scrap paper, their edges fraying under the weight of our ambition. It was invigorating, a shared purpose that ignited something deep within me—a flicker of belief that perhaps Maplewood could flourish without sacrificing its heart.

Jack's enthusiasm was contagious. Each morning, he arrived at the hotel with a stack of brochures for local businesses, each one more charming than the last. "Look at this," he'd say, waving a vibrant flyer in the air. "The bakery's hosting a pie-eating contest next weekend. We should partner with them and offer a special 'Maplewood Pie Weekend' package! Guests can stay here and gorge themselves on homemade goodness."

"Brilliant!" I'd reply, my heart racing with excitement. "And we can showcase local artisans—maybe host a craft fair on the lawn to draw in foot traffic. People love a good festival!"

As we brainstormed, the hotel began to transform. We organized a team of locals, a motley crew of artists, bakers, and craftsmen, all eager to lend their talents. Every afternoon, the lobby buzzed with energy as our small group painted signs, hung fairy lights, and crafted unique decorations. The hotel was coming alive in a way I hadn't expected, morphing into a vibrant tapestry of the community's spirit. Laughter and chatter filled the air, along with the tantalizing scents of Jack's cooking wafting in from the kitchen as he tested new recipes for our upcoming events.

Still, beneath the surface of our collective enthusiasm, doubts lingered. The developer's looming offer sat heavy on my mind, a specter that refused to fade away. It loomed like a thundercloud, waiting to unleash its storm. Each time I glanced at my phone, my heart raced, fearing a message that might suggest I'd wasted my chance.

On a particularly crisp morning, as leaves danced down from their branches like confetti, I decided to take a walk through town to clear my head. The sun shone brightly, illuminating the quaint storefronts that lined Main Street, each one bursting with seasonal decorations. I waved at Mrs. Thompson, the elderly woman who ran the floral shop, her eyes sparkling with warmth. "You know, Clara," she called, arranging a bouquet of golden chrysanthemums, "you've brought a lot of joy back to this town. We all see it. Don't let anyone take that away from you."

Her words struck a chord, echoing in my mind long after I left the shop. I wandered into the local park, the heart of Maplewood, where children played and families gathered, laughter ringing like a melody. This was what I wanted to preserve, the essence of community that thrived around me. It was intoxicating, filling me with purpose.

When I returned to the hotel, I found Jack in the garden, kneeling among the wildflowers, his shirt slightly rumpled, his hands dirty with soil. "I thought we agreed on the lavender for the garden," I teased, standing with my arms crossed, a smile breaking through my earlier tension.

He looked up, feigning innocence. "This was a special find! I figured we could add some color. Besides, who doesn't love a little spontaneity?" His grin was infectious, and I felt the tightness in my chest ease.

"Spontaneity, huh? Well, I hope you're prepared to explain that to the florist," I laughed, but the sound quickly faded as I noticed his expression shift, a shadow of concern clouding his eyes.

"What is it?" I asked, stepping closer.

Jack hesitated, glancing at the soil as if it held the answers to his unspoken worries. "I saw the developer's truck parked down the street earlier. They're still interested, Clara. I think we should be prepared for them to come sniffing around again."

The weight of his words settled heavily between us, casting a pall over our earlier exuberance. "You think they'll try to push the offer again?"

"Maybe. Or maybe they'll try to undermine everything we're doing here. Developers can be... persuasive." His voice dropped, carrying an edge of warning.

I inhaled sharply, the delicious scent of the flowers now tainted by the thought of what lay ahead. "We need to solidify our plans. Show them we're not going down without a fight."

Jack nodded, determination flashing in his eyes. "We'll need more than just a few events. We should gather the townsfolk—make it clear we're all in this together. We can rally everyone to speak out against their plans."

The next few days flew by in a flurry of preparation. Posters went up around town, and we organized a community meeting at the local library, inviting everyone to share their thoughts and ideas on how to preserve Maplewood's charm. The response was overwhelming; the townsfolk rallied with enthusiasm, eager to share their memories and visions for the future.

As the evening of the meeting approached, I felt a mixture of excitement and dread knotting in my stomach. What if no one showed up? What if our plans fell flat? But as I stood in the library, the room filled with familiar faces, I was buoyed by the shared energy of our community. Jack stood beside me, his presence a steadying force, and as we addressed the crowd, I felt a fire igniting within me.

"This is our town," I declared, my voice rising with fervor. "We've all invested so much into making Maplewood what it is today. Let's stand together to protect it!"

The room erupted with applause, a wave of support washing over us, filling my heart with hope. I exchanged glances with Jack, and his smile reflected the same exhilaration I felt coursing through me. Maybe we really could make a difference.

But as the meeting wrapped up and people began to disperse, I noticed a figure lingering in the shadows, a tall silhouette cloaked in uncertainty. I squinted, my heart sinking when I recognized the familiar face. It was the developer, his expression inscrutable as he observed us, a calculating glint in his eye.

"Clara," he called, his voice smooth and disarming. "I've been looking for you."

I felt the weight of the room shift, the air thickening as everyone turned to watch. Jack stepped closer, a protective stance forming as I met the developer's gaze. "What do you want?" I asked, my voice steady despite the turmoil inside.

"Just a chat," he replied, his tone casual, but the glimmer of ambition danced at the edges of his words. "I think it's time we discussed your future—and the hotel's."

The tension in the room was palpable as I exchanged a look with Jack, whose expression darkened. The air crackled with the potential for conflict, and I realized this was just the beginning of the battle for our beloved Maplewood. As the developer stepped forward, a storm brewing behind his poised demeanor, I braced myself, ready to fight for everything that mattered to me. Little did I know, the real battle had only just begun.

Chapter 14: The Kiss That Changes Everything

The kitchen hummed with the low drone of the refrigerator, a stark contrast to the storm brewing between Jack and me. The scent of sautéed garlic lingered in the air, the remnants of dinner barely cleared from the table, which was littered with dishes we both ignored as we circled each other like wary animals, each of us too stubborn to retreat. The summer heat clung to my skin, the day's labor etched in the lines of my brow and the ache in my muscles. We'd spent hours side by side, arguing over details like paint colors and furniture placements, all the while pretending that everything was fine. But it wasn't fine—not for me. Not for him.

"Maybe if you actually listened instead of throwing your weight around," I shot, my voice tinged with exhaustion, frustration spilling over. The words left my mouth sharper than I intended, laced with the unspoken tension that had been building for weeks.

Jack leaned against the counter, his arms crossed tightly over his chest. His blue eyes sparkled with indignation, a storm brewing behind their surface. "And maybe if you weren't so hell-bent on doing everything your way, we could actually make some progress," he retorted, a fire igniting in his tone.

I bristled at his accusation, my heart racing in protest. We both knew I was stubborn, but wasn't he too? The very air between us crackled, the heat escalating as the walls we'd constructed began to feel not just protective but suffocating. "You think I'm the only one holding on to my vision here? You've had your own ideas, Jack," I countered, taking a step closer, my voice lowering to a challenge.

His gaze held mine, unwavering and intense, and in that moment, I saw something else beneath the fury—a longing, an intensity that both terrified and exhilarated me. "You know what?

Maybe I'm just tired of pretending," he said, his voice dropping to a low growl.

Pretending. The word hung in the air, heavy with all the things we had avoided acknowledging. My breath caught in my throat, an electric charge thrumming between us, as if the universe had shifted and revealed a truth neither of us had dared to voice. The rhythm of the evening felt out of sync, as if the world outside had come to a standstill, leaving only the two of us suspended in this charged moment.

Before I could form a response, he surged forward, closing the distance between us in an instant. His hand gripped my wrist, pulling me toward him with an urgency that stole my breath. The kitchen, once familiar and mundane, faded into the background as he tilted my chin upward, his gaze piercing through the chaos of my thoughts. Then, without warning, he kissed me.

It wasn't a kiss born of sweetness or romance; it was raw, urgent, filled with everything we had left unsaid. His lips were warm and demanding against mine, igniting a fire that spread through me like wildfire. I melted into him, all the tension and anger dissolving, replaced by a dizzying rush of exhilaration. This was more than just a physical connection; it was a catharsis, a release of weeks' worth of pent-up emotions. I could feel the walls crumbling, the careful constructs of our friendship collapsing under the weight of this one, earth-shattering moment.

But as quickly as it began, doubt crept in. I pulled back slightly, breathless, my heart racing as I searched his eyes for clarity. "What was that?" I asked, my voice barely a whisper, the vulnerability of the moment washing over me.

Jack ran a hand through his hair, clearly wrestling with his own tumult of emotions. "I... I don't know," he admitted, his brow furrowing. "I just couldn't take it anymore. You make everything so complicated, and I'm sick of pretending we don't feel something more."

More. The word echoed in my mind, ricocheting off the walls of my carefully constructed barriers. I was acutely aware of the shift in our dynamic, the delicate balance we had maintained now tipping precariously into uncharted territory. What did it mean for us, for the project, for everything we had built together?

The kitchen felt too small, the air too thick with unsaid promises and the weight of expectations. I stepped back, creating space, my thoughts racing. "But we can't just—" I started, trying to grasp the reality of what had just happened, but Jack cut me off.

"Why not?" His voice rose, passion igniting in his eyes. "You want to build a life here, and so do I. Why shouldn't it include each other?"

His words hit me like a wave, pulling me under, dragging me into depths I wasn't sure I was ready to explore. I had come to this town hoping to find a fresh start, a sanctuary from my past, but somewhere along the way, Jack had become more than just a colleague. He was the compass that had guided me through uncertainty, and now, with this kiss, everything was at risk of changing.

"I don't know if I'm ready for that," I confessed, my voice trembling. "It's one thing to work together, to dream together. But this? It's messy. It's complicated."

"Life is messy. And complicated." He stepped closer, his eyes searching mine, willing me to understand. "But it can also be beautiful. We can't keep pretending there isn't something here. It'll eat us alive if we do."

His words lingered in the air, resonating with the truth I had tried to ignore. As I stood there, caught in the whirlwind of my thoughts, I felt the pull of something deeper than just the project or the town. It was about connection, about vulnerability, and the fear of what it meant to truly open my heart to someone again. The risk was daunting, but beneath it all lay a spark of hope, a glimmer of possibility that begged me to take a chance.

With the weight of our unspoken truths hanging between us, I had a choice to make. But in that moment, all I could do was breathe, caught in the delicate balance of fear and desire, unsure of where this kiss would lead us.

The moment lingered in the air like the last rays of sunset clinging to the horizon, vibrant yet fragile. I could feel the shift beneath my skin, a fluttering uncertainty that danced around the edges of what had just happened. Jack's hand still grazed my arm, his thumb brushing against my skin as if he, too, were hesitant to break the spell. A myriad of emotions swirled within me—excitement, fear, longing—and I struggled to find the words to match the whirlwind in my chest.

"Jack," I began, forcing myself to meet his gaze, the weight of everything unsaid suddenly suffocating. "This changes... everything."

He smiled, a mixture of hope and challenge. "Does it? Or does it just make it more interesting?" His tone was light, but there was a seriousness underlying his words that pierced through the humor.

I wanted to laugh, to push back against the heaviness that threatened to settle in, but the truth was, I wasn't sure if I could handle the shift. "Interesting? It feels like we've opened a Pandora's box, and now the whole world is in chaos."

Jack stepped back, the playful lightness fading from his expression. "Or maybe we've just been pretending too long," he replied, the intensity of his gaze piercing through my defenses. "What we have is more than just a partnership, and you know it."

The reality of his words settled around us like a thick fog. There was a vulnerability in the way he spoke, an honesty that stirred something deep within me. I had fought so hard to keep my heart shielded, to focus on the renovation, the hotel, the town—everything but this undeniable connection. Yet here we were, standing at the precipice of something entirely new and terrifying.

"I can't just jump in headfirst, Jack," I said, trying to rein in the chaos brewing within. "There's too much at stake. We've worked so hard to create this space together."

He sighed, rubbing the back of his neck as he paced the small kitchen. "And I want to keep working on it, but what's the point if we're both tiptoeing around our feelings? We're building a future here, and I don't want it to be a future built on half-truths and what-ifs."

His words struck a chord, a painful yet exhilarating reminder of all the possibilities that lay ahead. I thought of the plans we had drawn up, the dreams we'd shared, and now this new, intoxicating element threatening to derail it all. "I didn't plan for this," I confessed, my voice softening as I fought to maintain my composure.

"Neither did I," he admitted, his tone gentle now, coaxing rather than confrontational. "But maybe that's what makes it worth exploring. We could be so much more than just a project team."

His earnestness tugged at my heartstrings, a mix of affection and fear washing over me. I was drawn to him, but the last thing I wanted was to complicate our professional lives with personal feelings. "What if we lose everything? What if this doesn't work out?"

Jack took a step closer, his eyes searching mine. "What if it does? We can't let fear dictate our choices. Isn't that why you came here? To take risks?"

A flicker of something like hope ignited in my chest. He was right, of course. I had left everything behind in search of something more—something real. But could I really take this leap with him, knowing how precarious our situation was? The hotel was our shared dream, a beautiful yet fragile vision built on trust and collaboration. To throw my heart into the mix felt reckless, like tossing a match into a powder keg.

Just then, the doorbell rang, shattering the moment like glass falling to the floor. We both froze, eyes darting toward the front of the house, the weight of what had just happened hanging heavily in the air. "Who could that be?" I wondered aloud, the spell of intimacy shattered.

"Maybe it's your fan club," he quipped, a teasing smile creeping back onto his face, but I could see the tension lingering beneath the surface.

"I don't have a fan club," I shot back, trying to inject some levity into the situation. "If I did, they'd likely want to know why I can't keep my life straight."

Jack chuckled softly, but the laughter didn't quite reach his eyes. I moved to the front door, the uncertainty swirling in my stomach a potent reminder of how delicate the situation was. Opening the door, I was greeted by a sight I hadn't anticipated—Maggie, my next-door neighbor, stood there with a bright smile and a basket of freshly baked cookies.

"Hey there! I thought I'd drop by and share some treats. You know, to celebrate your new venture!" she chirped, her energy as effervescent as the summer breeze.

"Um, thanks, Maggie!" I replied, stepping aside to let her in. "That's really sweet of you."

As she breezed into the kitchen, her cheerful demeanor seemed to suck the tension out of the room, though Jack remained slightly aloof, leaning against the counter with an air of quiet contemplation. "What's the occasion?" Maggie asked, her eyes sparkling with curiosity as she glanced between us, sensing something amiss.

"Oh, just a little... renovation stress," I explained, forcing a smile. "You know how it is."

"Renovation stress? Pfft. You two are going to be the envy of the town once you finish! And maybe even a little more, if you play your cards right." She winked, clearly unaware of the emotional earthquake that had just rocked my world.

Jack shot me a sidelong glance, a knowing look passing between us, and I could feel the heat rising in my cheeks.

Maggie placed the cookie basket on the table and settled in, her bright chatter filling the room with warmth and laughter. As she regaled us with stories of her latest escapades, I couldn't help but feel the weight of the moment slipping through my fingers. Every lighthearted comment made by Maggie felt like a thread pulling me back from the precipice I had been teetering on moments before.

"Isn't it funny how life throws these unexpected curveballs?" Maggie mused, casually leaning back against the counter, glancing between us. "One minute, you're planning out your future, and the next, it feels like everything's up for grabs."

Her words resonated deeply, a reminder that life was often unpredictable, and maybe that was what made it worth living. As I caught Jack's eye, I saw the flicker of understanding there—an unspoken agreement that, whatever happened next, we'd navigate it together.

Maggie continued to chatter away, blissfully unaware of the undercurrents of emotion swirling around us. I joined in her laughter, the sound mingling with the memories of the kiss, the uncertainty, and the possibilities stretching out before me like an open road. With each passing moment, I felt the resolve within me shifting, expanding, as if I were finally ready to embrace the chaos of life and love.

As the evening wore on and the cookies disappeared, I realized that perhaps this was where I was meant to be—navigating the unpredictable with Jack by my side, ready to explore the messy beauty of it all, no matter what came next.

The evening wore on with Maggie's laughter echoing through the kitchen, a stark contrast to the tumult of emotions swirling inside me. I leaned against the counter, trying to balance the carefree banter with the reality of what had just unfolded between Jack and me. Each time I caught Jack's eye, that spark of something unnameable flickered again, igniting the heat I had felt moments before the doorbell rang. It was a dance of distractions, laughter, and cookies, all while the real tension simmered just beneath the surface.

Maggie dove into another story about her disastrous date with a local artist who, apparently, had spent the entire evening discussing his "unique vision" of abstract pancake art. "I mean, who does that?" she laughed, her infectious joy brightening the room. "You'd think I'd learned my lesson after the last guy who claimed he could communicate with trees. But hey, at least he wasn't boring."

Jack leaned against the counter, arms crossed, an amused smirk playing on his lips. "Did he at least get you a pancake in the shape of something interesting? Like a unicorn?"

Maggie rolled her eyes, still chuckling. "No, just a burnt circle that looked suspiciously like a hockey puck. Clearly, he wasn't an artist in the kitchen."

"Maybe he was just saving the creativity for his canvas," Jack replied, the playful banter easing the lingering tension, yet I could feel the weight of his earlier words still hanging between us.

But as Maggie launched into her next tale, I felt my mind drifting, caught between the warmth of friendship and the raw energy that had ignited in that stolen moment with Jack. Was I really ready to shift the boundaries of our relationship? Every instinct told me that crossing that line could either be the best decision I'd ever made or a catastrophic mistake.

"Do you think you'll have the hotel finished in time for the summer season?" Maggie asked, her gaze shifting to me, her curiosity piqued.

I hesitated, caught off guard by the question, the possibilities spinning like the whirring blades of a fan. "We're getting there, slowly but surely," I replied, trying to keep my tone light. "It's been a bit chaotic, but I think we're making progress."

Jack nodded in agreement. "Chaos is kind of our thing at this point, right? We thrive in it." He gave me a teasing look, a playful challenge that sent my heart racing once more.

"Only because someone insists on micromanaging every little detail," I shot back, unable to suppress a grin.

"Oh please, if you didn't have me to keep you in line, who knows what kind of color scheme we'd end up with? Neon pink walls and yellow polka dots?"

"Honestly, it might work," I laughed, my heart swelling at the banter that felt so natural, so easy. Yet the laughter faded, and I caught a glimpse of Jack's serious side again, the fire behind his eyes reminding me of the deeper conversation still waiting to be had.

Maggie, seemingly oblivious to the shift, continued chatting, but I could sense Jack's tension coiling again, a low hum of unspoken words swirling around us like a summer storm waiting to break. The clock on the wall ticked steadily, the minutes passing with a slow inevitability that made the air feel thick, almost electric.

As Maggie started another story, I excused myself, needing a moment to gather my thoughts. I stepped outside onto the small porch, the night wrapping around me like a cool, comforting blanket. The moon hung low, casting silvery light over the quiet street, while the sound of laughter floated from inside, a reminder of the warmth and camaraderie we had built.

Taking a deep breath, I tried to shake off the doubt clinging to me like a wet towel. This was my chance to embrace change, to lean into the possibilities that lay ahead. But could I really risk everything for a feeling that seemed both exhilarating and terrifying?

As I leaned against the railing, the soft creaking of the wood beneath me reminded me of the old hotel, the history that had seeped into its walls, much like the memories I was trying to forge here. Just then, Jack stepped outside, the door clicking shut behind him, and for a moment, we stood in silence, each lost in our thoughts.

"Did you need a break from the pancake artist saga?" he asked, a hint of humor dancing in his voice.

"Something like that," I replied, crossing my arms against the cool night air. "I just needed to breathe for a second."

Jack moved closer, the space between us narrowing, the intimacy of the moment palpable. "I know things got a bit intense back there," he said softly, his voice a low rumble that sent shivers up my spine. "But I meant what I said. I don't want to keep pretending."

I turned to face him fully, the vulnerability in his expression making my heart ache. "It's not that simple, Jack. There's so much at stake. What if this doesn't work out? What if we ruin everything?"

"We could also make it everything we've ever wanted," he countered, a fierce determination in his gaze. "You said you wanted to build something real, and I want that too. With you."

His words wrapped around me, warm and heavy, but just as I opened my mouth to respond, the unmistakable sound of footsteps echoed in the stillness. We both turned to see a shadow moving down the street, a figure shrouded in darkness.

"Is that...?" I squinted into the night, my heart racing as recognition struck.

"Wait," Jack said, his voice suddenly taut with tension. "That can't be—"

Before we could fully comprehend what we were seeing, the figure stepped into the light, revealing an all-too-familiar face. A face I thought I'd left behind for good.

"Surprise!" she exclaimed, a sly smile creeping across her lips as she approached, her eyes glinting with mischief and something more. "Did you really think you could start fresh without me?"

As the reality of her words sunk in, my heart dropped. The world around us felt like it was tilting on its axis, every possibility I had just begun to embrace now swirling into uncertainty. I glanced at Jack, his expression a mix of confusion and anger, mirroring the chaos erupting within me. The night, once filled with promise, now hung heavy with the weight of past mistakes, old fears, and a future I had thought was finally within reach.

Chapter 15: The Road Back

The morning sun spilled golden light across the cobblestone streets, illuminating the quaint shopfronts and sleepy corners of my little town. The air was rich with the smell of fresh coffee mingling with the faint sweetness of baked goods wafting from Lydia's bakery down the block. I paused outside her shop, watching as the door swung open and the warmth spilled out like an invitation. Inside, Lydia was already arranging a tray of blueberry muffins, their tops glistening like jewels under the bakery's soft lights. I thought about stepping in, sharing a laugh over her infamous "muffin magic," but today felt different. Today, my heart was a jumbled mess of emotions, tangled and twisted since that kiss with Jack.

As I strolled further, each step seemed heavier than the last. I watched the townsfolk greet each other, their voices carrying the comfortable cadence of familiarity. They laughed, shared stories, and went about their day, while I felt like a solitary island amidst a sea of connection. My thoughts drifted back to that moment by the lake, the intensity of Jack's gaze, the warmth of his lips against mine. It was like a spell had been cast, one that now made the mundane feel achingly dull. I needed to shake this off, to find clarity.

"Hey there! You look like you've seen a ghost!" called out Sam, the town's mechanic, as I passed by his garage. He wiped grease from his hands and flashed a toothy grin, his blue coveralls a stark contrast to the cheerful yellow of the daisies in the garden behind him.

"More like a very confused person," I replied, forcing a smile. "Just trying to sort through some... feelings."

He chuckled, leaning against the open hood of a vintage Mustang. "Ah, the classic conundrum. You should just take a drive and clear your head. Nothing like the open road, you know?"

"Or the closed road if you're stuck in town with a stubborn man," I quipped back, hoping to steer the conversation toward something lighter.

"Stubborn? You mean Jack?" Sam raised an eyebrow, clearly intrigued. "You two had a thing going, huh?"

I felt my cheeks warm. "Just a moment. But now it feels like we've entered a new dimension of awkward." The admission slipped out before I could rein it in, and I felt a wave of vulnerability wash over me.

"Welcome to the club," he said with a laugh, holding up a wrench. "Everyone's got their stories. Just remember, it's a small town. You can't hide forever." His grin softened, turning sincere. "But if you need a distraction, I'm always up for a chat."

"Thanks, Sam. I appreciate it," I said, offering him a genuine smile before moving on, the weight of the conversation lingering in the air like the scent of motor oil.

As I wandered further, I couldn't shake the feeling that the townspeople were watching me, whispering about the kiss, about Jack's sudden withdrawal. It was like living under a magnifying glass, every thought and every decision scrutinized. I rounded the corner towards the park, a serene place where I often sought solace. The path was lined with trees, their leaves a vibrant tapestry of autumn colors. I inhaled deeply, letting the earthy scent of fallen leaves fill my lungs. Nature always had a way of grounding me, of reminding me of life's simplicity amidst chaos.

The park was relatively quiet, save for the occasional laugh of children playing nearby. I settled onto a bench, the wood warm against my skin, and watched the world unfold around me. The laughter of children felt like a balm to my soul, a reminder of joy untainted by adult complications. Yet, as much as I tried to immerse myself in the moment, my mind spiraled back to Jack.

What was he thinking? Did he regret that kiss? Was he as torn between staying and leaving as I was? It felt like we were dancing on the edge of something profound, something worth exploring, yet fear held us captive, tying our tongues and fueling our doubts. I could still feel the heat of his touch lingering on my skin, a reminder that we had ventured into uncharted territory.

Just as I was lost in thought, a familiar voice broke through my reverie. "There you are," Jack said, stepping into view, his posture tense and guarded. My heart skipped a beat, a mix of exhilaration and apprehension flooding my senses. "I've been looking for you."

"Is that a good thing or a bad thing?" I asked, tilting my head slightly, attempting to mask the tremor in my voice.

"Depends on how you define 'good,' I guess." He shoved his hands into his pockets, his expression inscrutable. "You seemed... distant. I wanted to check in."

"I've been trying to figure things out," I admitted, my pulse racing. "About us. About this... situation."

Jack nodded, his gaze flickering to the ground as if searching for answers in the scattered leaves. "I don't want to make this harder for you. I know you're facing a big decision."

I leaned forward, my heart pounding. "What if I don't want to go back? What if I want to stay?"

His eyes met mine, a flash of surprise igniting within their depths. "Then why do you look so torn?"

The question hung between us, thick with tension and unspoken words. My breath caught in my throat, as I realized that perhaps the biggest obstacle we faced was not our circumstances but our own fears. The warmth of the sun enveloped us, but in that moment, the air felt charged, electric with possibility and uncertainty.

The moment stretched between us like an elastic band, taut and quivering with unspoken words. I could see the gears turning in Jack's mind, each thought a potential pitfall. The autumn sunlight filtered through the leaves, dappling his face with a warm glow, but it did little to thaw the ice that had formed around our conversation. I wasn't sure whether to fill the silence with laughter or plunge into the deep end of our awkwardness. Instead, I took a breath, the crisp air filling my lungs, an attempt to summon courage from the very atmosphere.

"I don't want to regret this," I finally blurted, the truth spilling out before I could reel it back. "I don't want to regret not saying what I feel because we're scared of what might happen next."

Jack's brow furrowed, and he looked down, his jaw tightening. "And what exactly is it that you feel?" The words came out like a challenge, as if he were testing the waters before plunging in himself.

"What I feel?" I echoed, biting back a grin at the absurdity of the moment. "Isn't it obvious? You've turned my world upside down with one kiss, Jack. And now I'm wondering if I've been living in a dream—or a nightmare."

"Great, so now I'm both a dream and a nightmare. Quite the honor," he replied, a wry smile tugging at his lips, but it didn't reach his eyes. The tension was still thick enough to cut with a knife.

I crossed my arms, shivering slightly despite the warmth of the sun. "Look, I get it. You're built like a brick wall, but I'm not asking for much. Just... talk to me. I need to know if this is real or if we're just pretending."

Jack ran a hand through his hair, frustration mingling with something else—vulnerability, perhaps. "What if I told you I'm scared too? I'm not ready to lose what we have, even if it feels like we're walking a tightrope."

The admission hung in the air, a softening of his defenses that felt monumental. "And what if I don't want to lose it either?" My heart raced at the possibility of our conversation pivoting toward something brighter, a shared understanding where fear transformed into connection.

"Then we're both in a tricky spot, aren't we?" he said, his tone lightening just a fraction, enough for me to sense a shift. "So, what's the plan? Flip a coin to decide whether we keep avoiding each other or go for it?"

I laughed, the sound escaping me like a breath I hadn't realized I was holding. "A coin toss? Really? I thought you'd have something more... profound in mind."

Jack leaned against the bench, a hint of mischief sparkling in his eyes. "Well, I'm more of a 'make decisions on the fly' kind of guy. But I could be persuaded to put some thought into it." He raised an eyebrow, an invitation to explore the layers of this precarious moment.

"Okay, let's brainstorm then," I said, my heart fluttering at the shift in his demeanor. "What if we don't think of it as an ultimatum? Let's say we take it slow, like a dance. One step at a time, no pressure."

"I'm good at following leads," he replied, tilting his head as if weighing my suggestion. "But if we're dancing, I don't want to trip over my own feet."

I chuckled, the tension dissipating slightly as we shared this light-hearted moment. "Just don't step on my toes. I can't handle another injury after that last trip to the hospital."

He laughed, the sound deep and genuine. "You know, you might be the most accident-prone person I've ever met."

"Guilty as charged. But it gives me character, right?" I nudged him playfully, enjoying the ease of our banter. "So, shall we try this dance? See where the rhythm takes us?"

Jack looked contemplative for a moment, and I could almost see the gears turning in his mind. "Alright. But don't expect me to lead; I have two left feet when it comes to matters of the heart."

"Then we're in perfect sync," I replied, my smile infectious. "I've never been good at leading anyway."

As we began to move from the bench, a new sense of hope blossomed within me. Maybe this wouldn't be as painful as I feared. Maybe, just maybe, Jack and I could carve out a path that embraced both our vulnerabilities without fear of losing ourselves in the process.

We ambled through the park, the crunch of leaves beneath our feet adding to the rhythm of our conversation. I pointed out little details—an unusually shaped acorn, a cluster of wildflowers defiantly blooming at the edge of the path. "You know, this place has a kind of magic to it," I said, my eyes sparkling as I gestured toward a patch of sunlight filtering through the trees.

Jack nodded, his expression softening as he observed the world around us. "You're right. It's like nature is trying to remind us that beauty thrives even in the most unexpected places."

"Exactly! It's like this town has its own heartbeat," I said, growing animated. "Every corner holds a story, every person carries a piece of history. It's vibrant and alive, just like us."

He stopped, turning to face me. "And what story do you want to write here?"

I hesitated, the weight of his question settling over me. The truth was, I wasn't entirely sure. "One where I get to decide what happiness looks like. Maybe it involves this hotel, or maybe it's something else entirely. But I want to feel like I have a choice."

Jack's gaze intensified, a flicker of understanding igniting in his eyes. "Then let's not rush into anything. Let's take our time and figure it out together."

I nodded, the thrill of possibility buzzing through me like electricity. In that moment, as we stood beneath the vibrant canopy of autumn leaves, it felt as if we were crafting something new, something worthy of the unpredictability of life. We might stumble, we might falter, but we would do so together, and that felt like the most liberating choice I could make.

As we continued to walk, a light breeze stirred the air, rustling the leaves above us, and with it came the exhilarating sense that perhaps we had crossed a threshold—one that might lead us somewhere beautiful, filled with the untamed potential of a shared future.

The crisp air wrapped around us like a well-worn blanket, infusing the atmosphere with a hint of cinnamon and nutmeg from a nearby café. Jack's presence beside me felt both comforting and unnerving; he was a riddle wrapped in a mystery, and today, I was determined to unravel some of those layers. As we walked, I couldn't help but steal glances at him, noting the way his brow furrowed in thought, the way he occasionally let his gaze drift to the ground as if searching for answers in the gravel. I marveled at the man standing beside me, the man who had turned my life upside down with a single kiss, and I felt a new resolve forming within me.

"So, how do we tackle this?" I asked, breaking the tranquil silence that had settled over us. "How do we avoid the dance of awkwardness while we figure out what we want?"

Jack chuckled softly, shaking his head as if trying to clear away the fog of uncertainty. "I'm not exactly known for my dance skills. But I do know that if we're going to figure this out, we might as well be honest about it."

"Honesty is good," I replied, grinning. "But I'm also a big fan of chocolate. Maybe we should sweeten the deal with some dessert?"

He raised an eyebrow, a teasing smile dancing on his lips. "Are you suggesting we bribe our way through this?"

"Why not? Nothing like sugar to ease the heart's tension," I shot back, my spirit lifting as we veered toward the café. I could already smell the rich aroma of freshly baked goods wafting from the entrance, a warm invitation that felt almost like a hug.

Inside, the café was bustling with locals, their laughter and chatter creating a comforting hum. I felt at home here, surrounded by familiar faces and the intoxicating scent of coffee mingling with something sweet. As we approached the counter, a vibrant display of pastries caught my eye, each one more tempting than the last.

"Two of your finest pastries, please," I said to the barista, a bright young woman with an infectious smile. She nodded enthusiastically, as if I'd just requested the moon.

Jack leaned closer, a mock-serious expression on his face. "Do you think we'll be able to focus on the conversation with all this deliciousness around?"

I smirked, handing over a few bills. "You underestimate my multitasking skills. I can handle deep philosophical discussions while devouring a chocolate croissant."

After placing our order, we settled into a cozy corner, a small round table adorned with a vase of wildflowers, their colors as vibrant as our conversation. As the barista returned with our treats, I couldn't help but admire Jack, who seemed a little less guarded, a little more open than he had been just hours before.

"Alright, Mr. Philosopher," I said, taking a generous bite of my croissant. "Tell me your thoughts on this whole us situation."

Jack took a moment, his gaze drifting toward the window where the autumn leaves danced in the breeze. "I guess my thoughts are like these pastries—layered, messy, and occasionally sticky. I didn't plan on feeling this way about you. I came to help, not to get caught up in whatever this is."

"Whatever this is," I echoed, feeling the weight of his words settle between us. "It's not exactly a small thing, is it?"

"No, it's not." His eyes met mine, earnest and intense. "And I don't want to mess it up, but the thought of walking away feels just as terrifying."

I set my croissant down, sensing the gravity of the moment. "What if we decided to stop trying to control everything? We could just... be. See where that takes us."

Jack's brow furrowed slightly as he processed my suggestion. "You really think it could work?"

"Why not? If life has taught me anything, it's that the unexpected often leads to the best stories. Maybe we're just beginning ours."

He took a long sip of his coffee, contemplative, and I could see the wheels turning in his mind. "Okay, I'm in. Let's be us, whatever that looks like."

Just then, the door swung open with a jingle, and the café's ambiance shifted as a chill gust of wind swept through. I glanced over, and my heart skipped a beat. A tall figure stepped in, shaking off the cold like a wet dog. It was Emily, my childhood friend, but the look on her face sent a ripple of unease through me.

"Sorry to interrupt," she said, her tone sharp, her eyes scanning the room before landing on me. "I need to talk to you. Now."

I exchanged a confused glance with Jack, who looked equally perplexed. "Is everything alright?" I asked, concern threading through my voice.

Emily hesitated, biting her lip as if weighing her words carefully. "Not really. Can we step outside?"

The urgency in her request sent alarm bells ringing in my mind. I nodded, the sweetness of the moment with Jack dissipating like steam from a cup of coffee. "Yeah, of course. Give me a second."

I stood up, my heart racing as I caught Jack's worried expression. "I'll be right back," I promised, but I felt the weight of his gaze lingering on me as I followed Emily outside, into the brisk air that felt suddenly colder.

Once outside, the wind tousled my hair, the sun still shining down but feeling more distant now. "What's going on?" I asked, my voice low but urgent.

Emily took a deep breath, her eyes darting around as if searching for someone or something. "I don't want to alarm you, but I think someone's been following me. I saw them when I left the diner yesterday. At first, I thought I was just being paranoid, but it's been happening ever since."

Panic clawed at my throat. "What do you mean 'following you'? Like, stalking you?"

She nodded, her expression serious. "I can't shake the feeling that someone is watching me, and I think it might have something to do with the hotel."

My stomach dropped at the mention of the hotel, and I felt an overwhelming urge to return to Jack, to share this burden and find safety in numbers. "We need to tell Jack," I said, my mind racing. "He can help us figure this out."

"Not yet," Emily insisted, her eyes glistening with anxiety. "Just promise me you'll keep this between us for now. I don't want to scare him off. You know how he can be."

I hesitated, my heart aching at the thought of shutting Jack out again. But looking at Emily, I saw the fear etched on her face, and I nodded. "Okay. But we have to keep an eye out. If you see anything else..."

"Trust me, I will." She gave me a shaky smile, but the tension hung thick between us.

Just then, I caught a movement in the corner of my eye. A shadow flitted across the street, too quick to identify, but the instinctive jolt of fear that surged through me was unmistakable. "Emily," I whispered, pointing toward the direction of the shadow. "Did you see that?"

Before she could respond, a figure stepped into view, a familiar silhouette that sent my heart racing. Jack stood just outside the café, his expression a mixture of concern and curiosity. He had overheard, and the worry etched across his face made my stomach twist with dread.

"Are you two alright?" he called out, but I could sense something more behind his words, a protective instinct kicking in.

I opened my mouth to respond, but as I turned to Emily, I realized her expression had shifted from anxiety to something deeper—something I couldn't quite decipher. "Jack!" I shouted, but before I could explain, a loud crash echoed from inside the café, followed by a scream.

In that split second, the world around us shifted, and I could only hope we weren't too late to unravel whatever darkness was closing in.

Chapter 16: A Leap of Faith

The air was thick with the scent of pine and the distant sound of waves lapping at the shore. The sky, a mosaic of pink and gold, hinted at a sunset that felt like a promise. I stood on the weathered deck of the old beach house, my fingers tracing the smooth wood grain, each groove a story waiting to be told. I had come here searching for solace, a retreat from the relentless pace of life back in the city, but what I found instead was a tempest of emotions I hadn't anticipated.

Jack leaned against the railing beside me, his posture casual yet tense, like a coiled spring ready to release. He had always been a man of few words, but in the silence that stretched between us, unspoken thoughts crackled like electricity in the air. Our kiss, a moment that had ignited everything, hung over us like a fog, palpable and stifling. It was a reminder of the connection we shared—a connection that felt both exhilarating and terrifying.

"Penny for your thoughts?" he asked, his voice a low rumble that sent a shiver down my spine.

I turned to him, searching for the right words to encapsulate the chaos swirling inside me. "Just trying to figure out if I'm brave enough to take a leap of faith," I replied, my voice steady but my heart racing. I had spent so long chasing after a future that was neatly outlined, following the predictable path laid out before me. But here, amidst the unpredictable rhythm of the ocean and the vibrant colors of the sunset, I was questioning everything.

"Leap of faith? You mean the offer from the developer?" Jack asked, his gaze sharp, as if he were peeling back the layers of my thoughts. "You can't seriously be considering it."

His words hit me like a splash of cold water. I knew he was right. The offer was a golden ticket back to a life of comfort and certainty, one I had clawed my way into through years of hard work. But in that process, I had buried my dreams beneath the weight of expectations.

The thought of leaving this place—the sun, the sea, the laughter that echoed in the wind—made my heart ache.

"I don't know what I'm considering," I admitted, glancing back at the horizon. "It's not just about the money, Jack. It's about what I want."

"And what do you want?" he challenged, his brow furrowing. "To leave this paradise behind? To return to a life that almost crushed you?"

His words were a dagger wrapped in concern, and I could feel the sting. But there was an underlying current in his voice, an urgency that made my heart race. He wanted me to stay. I could see it in the way he held my gaze, how his body angled toward mine, as if drawing me into his orbit. The realization left me breathless.

"I want..." The words hung in the air, tangled with uncertainty. "I want to know if I can create something that's truly mine. Something real."

"Real?" he echoed, incredulous. "This place, these people—they're real. You're just afraid to embrace it."

His accusation stung, but beneath the layers of his challenge was a flicker of hope. Jack had always seen me more clearly than I saw myself. The warmth of his voice wrapped around me like a comforting embrace, yet the weight of his expectations pressed down harder than I could bear.

"I'm not afraid," I replied, perhaps too quickly. "I just don't want to make a mistake. I don't want to hurt you—or myself."

"Sometimes, mistakes are what lead us to the right path," he said softly, his eyes searching mine for understanding. "What if you take the leap and find something beautiful waiting for you on the other side?"

His words hung in the air like the last note of a song, and I could feel my pulse quicken. What if? It was the question that had lingered since I first set foot in this town, a whisper urging me to embrace the chaos, to shed the skin of my old life. The thought terrified me.

"What if I fail?" I asked, my voice cracking, betraying the vulnerability I tried so hard to mask.

Jack stepped closer, the warmth radiating from him wrapping around me like a lifeline. "What if you fly?"

His eyes held a depth of sincerity that ignited a spark of courage within me. I thought of the little things I had come to love in this place—the way the sun cast golden rays over the water at dawn, the laughter of children playing on the beach, the quiet moments with Jack where words were unnecessary.

As the sun dipped lower in the sky, casting a tapestry of colors across the horizon, I felt the weight of my decision bearing down on me. The developer's offer lingered in my mind, a siren call to safety and predictability. Yet here, standing beside Jack, I was being offered something far more precious—an opportunity to choose my own path, to carve out a life that resonated with my soul.

The tension between us crackled like the last firework in a brilliant display. Jack took a step closer, the warmth of his body almost magnetic. "You don't have to decide right now," he murmured, his voice soothing yet insistent. "But whatever you choose, know that I'll support you. Just don't forget to choose yourself."

His words, a promise and a challenge intertwined, ignited a flame of resolve within me. I knew that the road ahead would be fraught with uncertainties, but standing here with Jack, I felt a surge of possibility. The horizon held countless paths, each one cloaked in mystery. I could run back to the familiar, to a life scripted in neat little boxes, or I could embrace the wildness of my heart.

In that moment, as the last rays of sunlight dipped below the waves, I understood what I had to do. It was time to leap, to embrace the unknown, and to trust that I would land where I was meant to be.

The morning light filtered through the curtains, casting soft shadows across the room, a gentle reminder of the new day unfolding outside. I lay in bed, the sheets tangled around my legs, replaying the events of last night in my mind. The kiss with Jack, electric and full of promise, had shifted something deep within me, like the earth cracking open to reveal the rich soil underneath. The weight of the developer's offer loomed large, but amidst the turmoil of emotions, I felt a stirring of clarity—a rare and beautiful feeling that was foreign yet intoxicating.

As I threw back the covers, the cool air sent a shiver up my spine, grounding me in the reality of my situation. I took a deep breath, inhaling the salty breeze wafting through the open window. The beach was waking up; I could hear the distant calls of gulls and the gentle thud of waves meeting the shore. The world outside was alive, vibrant, and full of possibility. I felt a pull, a longing to dive headfirst into that life, but the specter of my past weighed heavily on my shoulders.

In the kitchen, the aroma of freshly brewed coffee mingled with the sweetness of cinnamon from the breakfast pastries I had left out the night before. I fumbled with the lid of the coffee pot, my hands a little shaky as I poured myself a cup. Just then, the door swung open, and Jack stepped inside, the morning light illuminating his tousled hair and the slight smile that always made my heart skip a beat.

"Good morning, sunshine," he said, leaning against the doorframe, his arms crossed casually over his chest. He was the epitome of easy confidence, yet I could sense the tension beneath his relaxed facade.

"Morning," I replied, my voice a little breathless. "I was just about to make breakfast. Want some?"

He stepped further into the room, the scent of the ocean clinging to him, and took a seat at the small, rustic table. "I thought you'd never ask. You do have a way with pastries." His smile was teasing, but there was an edge to it, a hint of vulnerability that made my stomach flutter.

As I scrambled eggs and buttered the pastries, we fell into a comfortable rhythm, the kind that comes from shared moments and unspoken connections. But beneath the surface, a storm brewed. I could feel his gaze on me, and it sent shivers through my skin. The question loomed large between us, begging for an answer.

"So," he said, breaking the silence, "have you thought more about the developer's offer?"

I paused, the spatula hovering over the frying pan. I turned to face him, the gravity of the question settling heavily in the air. "Yeah, I've thought about it," I replied, my heart racing. "I just... I don't know. It feels like an easy way out."

Jack raised an eyebrow, a playful smirk tugging at his lips. "Well, running away has always been your specialty, hasn't it?"

His jab caught me off guard, and I shot him a look, half-amused, half-annoyed. "Thanks for the reminder, Jack. I was hoping to forget my past for a moment."

"It's not about forgetting," he replied, his tone softening. "It's about facing it head-on. You can't let your past dictate your future. This is your chance to start fresh, to build something real here."

His words resonated, striking a chord deep within me. But the fear was still there, coiled tightly in my gut. "What if I fail? What if I'm not cut out for this?"

Jack leaned forward, his expression earnest, those deep-set eyes boring into mine. "What if you soar? You won't know unless you try. You can't let fear of failure hold you back. You have to take that leap."

I wanted to believe him, to embrace that wild, reckless notion of pursuing my dreams. But doubt crept in like a thief in the night.

"And what if I end up regretting it? What if I can't do this without you?"

His silence hung heavily in the air, a reminder of the unspoken feelings swirling between us. "I'll always be here, whether you decide to stay or go," he finally said, the weight of his words settling like a warm blanket around my shoulders.

His honesty was both comforting and daunting. I had never been one to rely on anyone else, to trust in the stability of someone else's heart. But here, in this moment, Jack was offering me something I had never dared to ask for: support without conditions.

I turned back to the stove, my heart racing as I wrestled with my thoughts. "You make it sound so simple," I said, trying to keep my voice light. "Just jump off the cliff and hope for the best?"

He chuckled, the sound warm and inviting. "Well, the best part about cliffs is that you can always find a way back up if you fall. It's about the adventure along the way."

"Adventure," I repeated, mulling over the word like a fine wine. "Isn't that just a euphemism for chaos?"

"Chaos is where the magic happens," he countered, a mischievous glint in his eyes. "Besides, who said anything about not enjoying the ride? Think of the stories we could tell."

His words ignited a flicker of excitement within me, battling against the tendrils of fear that wrapped around my heart. Maybe it was time to step out of my carefully constructed bubble and embrace the unpredictability of life.

As breakfast finished cooking, I felt a shift in the atmosphere, an electric charge that made the air feel thicker. Jack stood to help set the table, and as he moved, I caught a glimpse of something deeper in his expression. There was longing, but there was also determination. A silent promise that whatever happened next, we would face it together.

After breakfast, we ventured outside. The salty breeze tousled my hair, and I inhaled deeply, the ocean air filling my lungs with a sense of freedom. The beach stretched before us, the waves shimmering in the sunlight like a dance of diamonds on the surface.

"Let's walk," Jack suggested, gesturing toward the shoreline. The idea sparked something within me—a sense of liberation I hadn't felt in years. As we walked side by side, our footsteps leaving temporary imprints in the sand, I could feel the rhythm of the waves echoing the tumult in my heart.

"So, what's your plan?" he asked, glancing sideways at me, curiosity evident in his eyes.

I considered his question, letting the weight of my dreams settle comfortably within me. "I think I want to stay and see what happens. I want to build something meaningful, something that feels like home."

His expression brightened, and for a moment, the tension between us eased. "You're going to love it here," he said, his voice filled with an enthusiasm that ignited a spark of hope within me. "And who knows? You might even find that you're not alone in this after all."

The promise in his words hung between us, a tether connecting our fates. I felt the weight of the decision begin to lift, replaced by a burgeoning excitement for what lay ahead. The sea was a vast, untamed expanse, but I was ready to dive in—ready to embrace the chaos, the adventure, and the possibility of finding myself along the way.

The sun was climbing higher in the sky, spilling warm light across the beach, and with it came a renewed sense of purpose. As Jack and I walked along the shore, the cool, foamy waves lapped at our feet, drawing me into a rhythm that felt both comforting and exhilarating. The salty breeze tangled my hair, but I welcomed it, each gust invigorating the part of me that had felt so dormant for so long.

"Are you really sure about this?" Jack asked, breaking the comfortable silence that had settled between us. His tone was soft, but there was a steeliness beneath it, an urgency that spoke to the weight of my choice. "I mean, staying here means taking a risk—a big one."

I paused, the sun warming my back, and turned to him, searching his face for any sign of doubt. Instead, I found only concern mixed with admiration, as if he were watching me unravel a mystery he was desperate to solve. "Jack, for once, I don't want to play it safe. I want to find out what happens if I actually lean into what I want instead of running away."

He looked at me, his expression shifting from worry to something that resembled pride, which sent a rush of warmth through me. "Then I guess we'd better make the most of it."

The words hung between us, a challenge wrapped in possibility. I felt my heart quicken as we continued down the sandy path, the reality of my decision sinking in. I would stay. I would embrace the uncertainty, and maybe, just maybe, I would forge a new path that didn't feel like a straightjacket.

As we walked, we spotted a group of locals setting up for an afternoon festival along the beachfront. Colorful banners fluttered in the breeze, and the sound of laughter mixed with the distant strumming of guitars. My heart leaped; this was the kind of life I had craved but never dared to claim.

"Let's check it out," I suggested, my eyes shining with excitement.

Jack raised an eyebrow, his smile playful. "What, and miss the chance to talk about our feelings? I thought that was the main attraction here."

"Very funny," I shot back, playfully nudging his shoulder. "Maybe the real attraction is living life for once."

He chuckled, a sound that sent a wave of warmth washing over me, and together we made our way toward the festivities. The atmosphere was electric, a blend of energy and joy that felt contagious. Children darted between stalls, their laughter ringing out like music, while adults gathered to chat, the camaraderie palpable.

As we wandered through the crowd, a sense of belonging enveloped me, a feeling I hadn't experienced in a long time. Here, with the ocean as our backdrop, everything felt right, as if the pieces of my life were finally aligning. I watched as Jack interacted with the locals, his charm effortless, drawing smiles and laughter. It was a side of him I had always admired—open, genuine, and unguarded.

"Looks like you're a hit," I teased, nudging him again.

"It's not my fault they're drawn to good looks and charisma," he shot back with mock arrogance, the glint in his eyes telling me he was joking.

"Ah, yes, the two traits you possess in abundance," I replied with a grin, feeling a weight lift off my shoulders with every lighthearted exchange.

As the afternoon wore on, I found myself enveloped in a whirlwind of activity. I sampled local delicacies, watched a dance troupe perform with vibrant enthusiasm, and even joined a friendly game of beach volleyball, my laughter mingling with the chorus of happy voices around me. It was liberating, a rush of freedom that I hadn't allowed myself to feel in years.

But even amidst the joy, a flicker of uncertainty nagged at the back of my mind. The developer's offer was still there, an anchor tethered to my old life. A reminder that I could always retreat back to safety if things became too overwhelming. Yet every time I caught Jack's eye, the laughter shared between us felt like a secret promise, a hint of a future that could be—if I chose to stay.

After an exhilarating game that left me breathless and sandy, I wandered over to the edge of the festival. The sunset was beginning to paint the sky in hues of orange and purple, an artist's palette that made the world seem surreal. I leaned against the railing, taking a moment to breathe in the beauty surrounding me, letting the vibrant colors soak into my skin.

Jack joined me, his presence as warm as the fading sun. "You did great out there," he said, a genuine smile lighting up his face. "I'm surprised you didn't knock anyone over with your enthusiasm."

"I was too busy enjoying the moment," I replied, grinning. "Who knew I could actually have fun instead of worrying about the future?"

"Welcome to the club," he teased, nudging my shoulder again.

As we stood there, the festival buzzing around us, I felt a shift in the air. The world felt electric, as if something was about to happen. And then, just as I was about to speak, a commotion erupted from the center of the gathering.

"Hey, what's going on?" I asked, leaning forward to catch a glimpse.

The crowd began to part, and my heart sank as I saw a familiar figure being escorted through the throng—Ryan, the slick developer from the city. The very man whose offer had thrown my life into disarray. He looked out of place amid the vibrant joy of the festival, his crisp suit stark against the casual beach attire of the locals.

"Penny!" he called, his voice carrying over the din. "There you are! I've been looking for you."

"Great," I muttered under my breath, a mixture of annoyance and dread bubbling inside me. "Just when I thought I was free of him."

Jack's expression darkened as he watched Ryan approach. "What does he want?"

"Probably to remind me about the life I'm trying to escape," I replied, crossing my arms defensively.

Ryan reached us, his smile slick and rehearsed. "Penny, there you are! We need to talk about your decision. This is an opportunity you can't afford to miss."

My heart raced as I shot a glance at Jack, whose jaw had tightened. The tension between us had shifted, replaced by a new current that crackled with uncertainty. "I'm busy right now," I said, trying to keep my voice steady.

"Oh, I don't think this can wait," Ryan said, his tone condescending, like he was brushing away my concerns with a wave of his hand. "This is about your future. You know you'll be unhappy here in the long run."

I could feel Jack's presence beside me, a quiet force that emboldened me. "I think I've got a pretty good idea of what I want, Ryan," I said, my voice gaining strength. "And it doesn't involve your development plans."

Ryan's smile faltered for a moment, revealing a flash of irritation. "You're making a mistake, Penny. You know that, right?"

I took a breath, steadying myself. "Maybe it's not a mistake at all. Maybe I'm finally ready to fight for something that matters to me."

Just as the words left my lips, a loud crash echoed through the festival, drawing everyone's attention. My heart raced as I turned to see one of the large festival tents collapsing under the weight of something—what looked like a series of heavy crates. People screamed, and chaos erupted as festival-goers scrambled to move out of the way.

"Jack!" I shouted, panic surging through me as I turned to him. "We have to help!"

But as I moved toward the chaos, I felt a sharp tug on my arm—Ryan. "Penny, wait!"

"Let go of me!" I snapped, wrenching free and rushing into the crowd. The world blurred around me, the sounds of shouting and confusion ringing in my ears. The decision I had thought was so clear moments before now felt like a fragile thread, ready to snap at any moment.

Just as I reached the edge of the fallen tent, a shadow loomed above me. I looked up, my breath hitching in my throat, and saw one of the crates teetering dangerously, ready to fall. Time seemed to slow as I realized I had mere seconds to react.

And then, everything went black.

Chapter 17: The Weight of Goodbye

The decision I made wasn't supposed to feel like this—so final, so heavy. The developer's papers lie untouched on the kitchen table, but I can't bring myself to sign them. Jack has barely spoken to me since that night, and I keep telling myself that it's for the best. That whatever spark flickered between us is fleeting, just a product of proximity, of shared responsibilities and long nights in a town that moves too slow for my liking. But the ache in my chest tells a different story. The town watches me, waiting for my decision, but none of them can see the real reason I'm hesitating. It's not about the hotel anymore. It's about Jack. And if I sell, I know I'm leaving more than just a building behind.

The sun hangs low in the sky, casting a warm golden hue across the worn wooden floorboards of my kitchen. It feels like a postcard moment, the kind of picture that captures idyllic rural life, yet I can't shake the sense of impending loss that looms over me. I glance out the window at the sprawling fields beyond the hotel, a patchwork of greens and golds that sway gently in the evening breeze, and I wonder how it will all change once I'm gone. The thought of those fields under new ownership, reshaped into something that could fit into a developer's vision, twists in my stomach like a knot that refuses to loosen.

I pour myself a cup of coffee, the rich aroma filling the air, yet it does little to soothe my restless thoughts. With each sip, I try to convince myself that this is what I want: a new beginning somewhere else, far from the whispers of this town that have grown into a constant hum in my ears. But what if the only thing waiting for me out there is an echo of regret? I let out a soft sigh, leaning against the counter, watching as a stray cat wanders past the porch. She pauses, glancing back at me with emerald eyes that seem to see right through my indecision, before continuing on her way.

In moments like these, I wish I could be more like that cat—unencumbered, roaming wherever the day leads her. Instead, I'm tethered to this decision, the weight of it pressing down on me. Just yesterday, I saw Jack at the diner, standing at the counter with that same disheveled charm that used to make my heart skip a beat. He was laughing with the waitress, his easy smile lighting up the small space, but when I walked in, his gaze shifted, falling away as if he had suddenly remembered something important that needed his attention. The churning in my stomach twisted tighter.

"What'll it be today, Lucy?" asked Ben, the owner, flashing me his signature grin as he poured coffee into my cup.

"Just the usual," I murmured, not bothering to look at the menu. It always felt like a waste of time, each item blurring into another under the weight of my thoughts. I could have ordered anything, yet I found myself drawn to the comforting familiarity of a blueberry muffin and a strong coffee.

"Coming right up!" he chirped, before glancing at Jack over his shoulder. "You should talk to him, you know."

I shot him a look that could curdle milk. "What do you mean?"

He shrugged, glancing at Jack again, who was now engrossed in conversation with a couple of regulars. "I mean, you both look like you're carrying a weight. Might as well drop it on each other, right?"

"Thanks for the advice, Dr. Phil." My voice dripped with sarcasm, but deep down, I knew he had a point. The tension was palpable, hanging in the air like thick fog, and here I was, refusing to acknowledge it, much like the papers back home.

When my muffin arrived, the blueberries glistened like tiny jewels, each one promising a burst of sweetness. But even as I took my first bite, I couldn't escape the bitter aftertaste of uncertainty. I'd grown so accustomed to the hotel and the rhythm of my life here, where every creaky floorboard and faded wallpaper held memories I couldn't bear to leave behind. Yet, every day that passed felt like another link in the chain binding me to a future I wasn't ready to embrace.

Later that evening, the sun dipped beneath the horizon, painting the sky in hues of orange and pink, igniting a fire within the clouds that mirrored the turmoil inside me. I found myself standing in the hotel lobby, the musty scent of old wood and dust wrapping around me like a familiar embrace. The flickering light from the antique chandelier above danced across the walls, illuminating the faded photographs that captured laughter and love from years gone by. I ran my fingers over the worn banister, tracing the memories embedded within its grain.

"Lucy?" The sound of Jack's voice sent a jolt through me, and I turned to find him standing there, hands shoved deep in his pockets, a hint of uncertainty shadowing his features. My heart raced, the familiar warmth flooding through me, battling with the cold reality of our situation.

"Hey," I managed, my voice barely above a whisper.

He stepped closer, the air thick with unspoken words. "I, uh, was just... passing by."

"Right," I said, forcing a casual tone that felt anything but. "This is my hotel, you know."

A half-smile broke through his guarded demeanor, and for a moment, the tension ebbed. "And it's beautiful. It's like stepping back in time."

"Or a time trap," I replied, a nervous laugh escaping my lips. "I'm starting to feel like I'm stuck in one."

"Maybe you are." His gaze locked onto mine, a flicker of something deeper passing between us. It was a reminder of those late nights filled with laughter, the comfort we found in one another, and the shared dreams that had begun to intertwine.

I swallowed hard, trying to catch my breath. "Jack, I—"

But before I could finish, the sound of a car engine rumbled outside, drawing both our attention. I caught a glimpse of a sleek, unfamiliar vehicle pulling into the driveway, the kind that hinted at wealth and ambition. My heart sank. Another potential buyer? The thought sent a wave of panic through me, drowning out the moment we were just beginning to share.

"Looks like I'm not the only one who's been thinking about this place," I muttered, the weight of that realization pressing down on me even harder than before.

The car parked outside glimmered under the fading sunlight, a pristine contrast to the weathered charm of my hotel. My heart raced as I watched the driver step out, a tall figure in a tailored suit, exuding a polished confidence that felt alien in our little town. A flurry of questions erupted in my mind. Was this the buyer the developer had hinted at, or just another passerby drawn to the peculiar allure of our crumbling establishment?

"Looks like you've got company," Jack said, his voice low, laced with a hint of protectiveness that made my heart flutter, even amidst the uncertainty. I turned to him, searching his expression for something, anything that would help me make sense of the swirling chaos in my thoughts.

"Yeah," I replied, unable to hide the edge of frustration in my voice. "Just what I need right now. Another reminder that my decision is about to become very real."

Jack crossed his arms, the muscles in his forearms tensing, a testament to his undeniable strength. "You don't have to do this, you know. Selling the hotel, I mean."

His words hung in the air, palpable and charged. Did he really mean it, or was this just another fleeting moment of bravado? I searched his eyes, desperate for clarity, but all I found was the same storm of emotions reflected back at me—confusion, hope, fear. "What if I don't?" I asked, my voice barely above a whisper. "What if

I stay and everything falls apart? What if I'm not enough to keep it going?"

"Then we figure it out together." He stepped closer, invading the space that had felt so charged just moments before. "You've done it before. You've put everything into this place. Don't you want to see what else could come from it?"

Before I could answer, the stranger ambled up the front steps, his polished shoes echoing against the wood like a tolling bell. I straightened, suddenly feeling vulnerable under the weight of his scrutiny. He paused, taking in the grandeur of the hotel's exterior with an expression that blended curiosity with mild contempt, as if assessing the value of a piece of art that had seen better days.

"Good evening," he said, his voice smooth and practiced. "I'm looking for the owner."

"I'm Lucy," I said, forcing a smile that felt a little too tight around the edges. "What brings you to our lovely little corner of the world?"

"Elliot Kane." He extended a hand, and I took it, surprised by the firmness of his grip. "I represent a development group interested in revitalizing this area."

Jack shifted beside me, his jaw tightening. I could almost hear the gears turning in his head, the protective instincts flaring as he assessed the man in front of us. "You mean gentrifying it," he replied, a wry edge to his tone.

Elliot raised an eyebrow, unfazed. "Call it what you will. The point is that this hotel has a lot of potential, and we believe it could serve a greater purpose than merely standing idle."

"Idle?" I echoed, feeling a spark of indignation flare up inside me. "This place has been a home, a refuge for people. It's not just bricks and mortar."

"Of course," he replied, a disarming smile plastered on his face. "But isn't it time to think bigger? To bring in something that can really make this town thrive?"

The air between us crackled with tension, and I felt Jack's presence beside me, a solid anchor in the maelstrom of my thoughts. I glanced at him, his expression unreadable but with a protective fire that told me he wouldn't let this stranger steamroll us.

"What are you proposing?" I asked, pushing my irritation aside to maintain a sense of professionalism.

Elliot took a step closer, his voice lowering conspiratorially. "We envision a boutique hotel, perhaps with a restaurant that showcases local cuisine. A place that draws tourists, not just from the nearby cities but from across the country."

"A restaurant?" I repeated, feeling the idea roll around my mind like a marble in a tin can. "And what happens to the people who already call this place home? What happens to the essence of what it is?"

"Change can be good, Lucy." He leaned back slightly, as if assessing my reaction. "You could benefit financially, and with your background, you'd have a pivotal role in its transformation."

"Financial benefit?" Jack scoffed, a mix of disdain and skepticism in his voice. "That sounds a lot like a hollow promise."

"Look," I interjected, feeling the need to assert myself. "I've spent my life building this place, and I'm not about to hand it over to someone who sees it as a stepping stone for profit."

Elliot's smile faltered for a brief moment, replaced by a flicker of annoyance. "Then perhaps we're wasting each other's time," he said, turning slightly on his heel.

"Wait," I called out, surprising myself with the urgency in my voice. "I'm not saying I'm not interested; I just need to think about it."

Jack's gaze swung to me, a mix of surprise and concern etched across his face. I could see the cogs in his mind turning as he processed my words.

"Perhaps I should have set up a more formal meeting," Elliot said, regaining his composure. "But I'll leave my card. Think it over, Lucy." He slid a sleek card from his pocket and placed it on the counter before making his way back to the exit.

As the door swung shut behind him, I turned to Jack, the adrenaline still pumping through my veins. "What just happened?"

"You just opened Pandora's box," he said, a hint of sarcasm in his voice. "You know how development works in this town. It's never as simple as they make it sound."

"I know," I replied, running a hand through my hair. "But what if it is a good opportunity? What if this could breathe new life into everything we've been fighting to save?"

Jack took a deep breath, his expression softening. "What if it's a trap? What if it pulls you away from what really matters?"

His words struck a chord within me, resonating with the very fears I had tried to bury. But the thrill of possibility had ignited something deep inside, and I couldn't help but feel that perhaps this was the pivotal moment I had been waiting for.

"Maybe it is both," I said, contemplating the complexities of my decision. "But I have to find out for myself."

Jack's eyes held mine, a mixture of understanding and concern dancing behind them. "Just don't lose yourself in the process."

I nodded, feeling the weight of his words settle over me like a gentle shroud, warm yet suffocating. I wasn't ready to make a choice just yet, but I knew one thing: I was teetering on the edge of something monumental, and the fall—whether it led to ruin or resurrection—was mine to face.

The air was thick with anticipation, each passing second feeling like a countdown to an explosion. I turned back to the lobby, my mind racing. The prospect of revitalization that Elliot had dangled before me hung like a tantalizing carrot, but it also felt like a baited trap. The quiet hum of the hotel around me, the creak of the floorboards, the faint rustle of wind against the windows—everything seemed to pulse with the weight of my decision.

"What are you going to do?" Jack asked, his voice low but edged with urgency, pulling me from my thoughts.

"I don't know yet," I admitted, rubbing the back of my neck as I paced the faded Persian rug that had seen better days. "There's a part of me that wants to take the risk. To breathe new life into this place."

"And what about the other part?" His gaze followed me, fierce and steady. "The part that's been doing just fine on its own?"

I halted, suddenly aware of the struggle reflected in his eyes, a depth that went beyond the conversation we were having. "That part is tired, Jack. Tired of scrubbing floors and patching up walls, tired of fighting for something that feels like it's slipping away from me. I thought if I sold, I could find something more."

"More of what? Stress? Uncertainty?"

"More of a future," I snapped, the sharpness in my voice surprising even me. "Or maybe just the courage to embrace change."

"Change is not always the answer." He stepped closer, the space between us shrinking. "You're chasing something you can't even define. What if what you need is right here?"

"Right here?" I gestured around the hotel, the familiar walls closing in on me like a cage. "You mean a place that feels like it's crumbling?"

Jack sighed, his frustration simmering just beneath the surface. "I mean the community, the people who care about you. Not every opportunity comes dressed in a business suit with a shiny car."

His words struck me, not just with their truth but with the raw emotion woven through them. "You care, don't you?" I asked, my tone softening. "About this place? About me?"

He opened his mouth to respond, but before he could find the words, the front door swung open again, and a gust of wind swept through, carrying with it a cascade of leaves that swirled around our feet like confetti.

In stepped an older woman, her frame slightly hunched yet dignified, with a vibrant scarf wrapped around her neck and a confident air that belied her age. "Lucy! There you are!"

"Mrs. Thompson," I exclaimed, rushing forward to embrace her. She was the heart of our community, a living library of stories and memories. "What a surprise! I wasn't expecting you today."

"Of course, you weren't," she said, her voice a rich tapestry of warmth and mischief. "But I've got news that can't wait."

I glanced at Jack, who looked equally intrigued and wary. "What is it?"

She leaned closer, lowering her voice conspiratorially. "You remember the town meeting last week? The one about the future of the hotel?"

I nodded, the tension in my stomach tightening. "What about it?"

"Well, some folks aren't thrilled about the idea of a fancy boutique hotel taking over."

Jack shifted slightly, his posture relaxing just a fraction, as if Mrs. Thompson had become a tether back to sanity. "I can't imagine why," he said, sarcasm threading through his words.

"Exactly! We don't need outsiders telling us how to live. We've built something special here, and they want to change it all for profit."

My heart raced. "What do you mean?"

She straightened, her expression turning serious. "I heard whispers that Elliot Kane isn't just interested in the hotel. He's got plans for the whole town—new roads, new buildings, and a complete overhaul of our beloved Main Street."

"What?" I couldn't help but blurt out. "That's outrageous!"

"Outrageous and very much in the works," she said, her voice dropping to a whisper. "They're trying to get rid of the old to make way for the new, and they think we're too small to fight back."

Jack stepped forward, his expression fierce. "We can't let that happen."

Mrs. Thompson nodded, her gaze shifting between us. "I came here to rally support. If we stand together, we can push back against this change."

"And how do you propose we do that?" I asked, feeling a spark of hope flicker to life.

"Organize a town hall meeting," she said, determination etched on her face. "We need to voice our concerns, get people involved. If we don't stand up now, it'll be too late."

The energy in the room shifted, a current of possibility flowing between us. I could feel the heaviness of my earlier decision lifting, replaced by a sense of purpose that ignited my spirit. "I'll help," I said, the words spilling out before I fully understood the weight of what I was committing to. "I'll reach out to everyone."

Jack looked at me, his eyes a mix of admiration and surprise. "You really want to do this?"

"I have to." I felt a wave of certainty wash over me, grounding my earlier fears. "This hotel is more than just a building; it's a piece of history. And if we lose it, we lose a part of ourselves."

Mrs. Thompson beamed, her eyes shining with pride. "That's the spirit, dear! But we need to act fast. I'll gather some of the townsfolk tonight. Let's meet at the diner at six."

"Sounds good," I replied, my heart racing at the thought of mobilizing the community.

As she turned to leave, a noise outside caught my attention—a commotion, sharp and jarring, cutting through the stillness. My pulse quickened, a knot tightening in my stomach. "What's happening out there?"

Jack moved to the window, peering out. "Looks like a crowd is gathering."

"Maybe they heard about the development plans," I suggested, anxiety bubbling in my chest.

"Or maybe they heard about you," he replied, turning to face me, his expression unreadable.

Just then, the front door swung open again, and a group of townsfolk burst in, voices raised, eyes wide with urgency. "Lucy! You have to come see this!"

"What is it?" I asked, my heart pounding.

One of the men, Sam, gestured wildly. "There's a protest forming down by the square! People are rallying against the development, and they're calling for you to lead them!"

A wave of disbelief washed over me. "Me?"

"Yes! They want your voice, your vision. This is your chance to take a stand!"

The gravity of the situation crashed down around me, a whirlwind of emotion swirling within. I exchanged a glance with Jack, and I could see the fear mirrored in his eyes, but there was also a spark of something else—determination.

With the sound of chanting growing louder from the streets, I felt the pull of fate, drawing me toward the unknown. "Alright," I said, my voice steadying. "Let's go. But this time, we're not just fighting for the hotel; we're fighting for our home."

As I stepped into the lobby, the momentum surged through me, a powerful tide that threatened to sweep everything in its path. The faces of my friends and neighbors flickered through my mind, their hopes and dreams woven into the fabric of this place. I could hear the murmur of their voices, the echo of their laughter, and suddenly, I felt larger than life, as if the weight of goodbye had transformed into the promise of a bold new beginning.

But just as I stepped outside, ready to embrace the chaos, my heart froze. There, at the edge of the square, was Elliot, watching with a smirk that sent a chill racing down my spine. He raised a hand, and in that moment, I understood that the battle was far from over. The real fight was just beginning.

Chapter 18: The Confession

Sunlight dripped through the leaves like molten gold, warming my shoulders as I knelt among the chaos of weeds that had taken up residence in my garden. The air was rich with the scent of damp earth and fresh blooms, a fragrant promise of spring that belied the turmoil swirling in my mind. My fingers dug into the soil, wrestling with stubborn roots that refused to yield. This garden had always been my sanctuary, a patch of beauty amidst the whirlwind of my life, but today it felt more like a battleground.

As I tugged at the stubborn tendrils, frustration bubbled inside me, an unwelcome companion. I had returned to this quaint little town with hopes of reclaiming a piece of my past, but every step I took seemed to tangle me further in memories I thought I had left behind. Just as I was about to give in to my exasperation and leave the weeds to their own devices, I heard the soft crunch of gravel beneath a heavy foot. I looked up, and my heart lurched.

Jack stood there, framed by the vibrant greens of my garden, his dark hair tousled by the gentle breeze. There was something magnetic about him, a pull I couldn't quite name. His expression was carefully composed, a mask of neutrality that sent my mind racing. Hadn't we already gone through this dance of feelings and uncertainties? What more could he possibly say?

The moment stretched, thick with unspoken words and unresolved tension. My pulse quickened as I gauged his expression, trying to decipher the riddle of his silence. He took a step forward, his shoulders relaxing slightly, as if the weight of the world rested on them. "I've been thinking," he said, his voice low and steady, breaking the stillness like a pebble tossed into a pond.

"About?" I managed, my tone lighter than I felt. The last thing I wanted was to crack open the emotional canister we'd been so careful to seal.

Jack shifted his weight, raking a hand through his hair. "About the hotel. About us."

My breath hitched. I felt an electric charge in the air, the kind that whispered promises and warned of impending storms. "Us?" I echoed, unsure if I wanted to pursue this line of conversation. The words hung between us like a fragile thread, ready to snap at the slightest tug.

He stepped closer, and the sun illuminated the sharp angles of his face, casting shadows that played with my heart. "I didn't just want to save the hotel. I was protecting you, or maybe just the memory of you—the girl who left this place behind years ago."

His confession swept through me like a sudden gust of wind, scattering the leaves of my carefully constructed defenses. "Me?" I murmured, my voice a mere whisper as the enormity of his words settled over us like a heavy fog.

"Yes," he said, his gaze unwavering. "You never really left, did you? You came back, and I thought, maybe..." He paused, his breath catching, and in that brief moment, I saw a flicker of vulnerability in his dark eyes. "Maybe I could convince you to stay."

The garden felt impossibly still, as if nature itself was holding its breath, waiting for my response. I had imagined this moment in a dozen different scenarios—some hopeful, some disastrous—but none had prepared me for the raw honesty in his eyes. My heart raced, pounding in my chest like a caged bird desperate for freedom. "But I have a life... a life that's waiting for me outside of this town."

Jack stepped back, the distance between us suddenly feeling like an insurmountable chasm. "And what if that life isn't what you thought it would be? What if it's just a series of weeds choking out the beauty you could have here?"

His words pierced through the haze of my thoughts. I had been running for so long, chasing after an ideal that seemed to slip further from my grasp with each passing year. "You don't know what you're asking," I said, my voice trembling. "Staying means giving up everything I've built."

He stepped closer again, that magnetic pull weaving around us like an invisible thread. "Or it means building something new, together."

The audacity of his suggestion struck me like a lightning bolt, illuminating the shadowy corners of my uncertainty. I had come back to this town, not just for the hotel but for the parts of me that had been buried under layers of obligation and expectation. "But what about you? What about the hotel?"

"The hotel is just a building," he replied, his voice steady but tinged with urgency. "It's you I can't bear to lose again."

My heart squeezed at his confession. The truth of it resonated deep within me, reverberating against the walls I had built around my heart. "Jack, I—"

He interrupted, frustration flickering across his features. "I know it's a lot to ask. But I want you to consider it. To think about staying, not just for the hotel, but for you, for us."

The air thickened with unspoken emotions, and for a moment, I couldn't tell if the tension was electric or suffocating. I dropped my gaze to the weeds at my feet, their stubbornness mirroring my own. The prospect of staying here, of allowing myself to dream of a life entwined with his, sent a shiver of exhilaration through me, but also a wave of panic. "What if I can't? What if I'm not ready?"

Jack's expression softened, his eyes gleaming with a mixture of hope and understanding. "Then let's take our time. No pressure. Just... think about it."

As the sun dipped lower in the sky, casting long shadows across the garden, I felt the weight of his words settle over me like a warm blanket. The confession hung between us, fragile yet unbreakable, a promise of what could be if only I dared to take that leap.

The sun began its slow descent, casting a warm golden hue over the garden as I processed Jack's words, a whirlwind of emotions swirling within me. I could almost hear the ancient trees whispering secrets, their leaves rustling in agreement with his plea. "You think you can just sweep in here and make me reconsider everything?" I managed to retort, trying to inject a semblance of bravado into my voice. "That's a bold strategy, Jack."

He chuckled softly, the tension breaking just enough to allow a sliver of light into our conversation. "What can I say? I've always been one for bold moves. Besides, you and I both know this place has a way of getting under your skin."

"Is that why you're here?" I shot back, half-joking. "To remind me how much I hate pulling weeds?"

His laughter was genuine, brightening the dusky garden. "No, I'm here because I thought you might need some help. Or maybe just a distraction. The weeds can wait, right?"

I quirked an eyebrow, intrigued. "You know how to garden? I thought you were more of a 'put on a suit and charm the pants off people' type."

"I can charm a weed or two," he replied, taking a step forward, the playful challenge in his eyes dancing with the fading sunlight. "How hard can it be?"

I crossed my arms, trying to appear unimpressed. "Fine. Let's see what you've got, Mr. Charmer."

He knelt beside me, determination etched on his face, and together we began to pull at the stubborn roots. The afternoon light glinted off his arms, revealing muscles that seemed to ripple with every tug. It was hard not to notice, and I quickly averted my gaze, focusing instead on the unyielding weeds. The banter flowed easily, the garden filling with laughter and the scent of freshly turned earth as we worked side by side.

"You know," I said, wiping sweat from my brow, "this might just be the best date I've ever been on."

Jack paused mid-tug, his dark eyes sparkling with mischief. "A garden date? Truly romantic."

I grinned, feeling a warmth blossom in my chest. "What can I say? I'm a sucker for dirt and hard labor."

"Next time, I'll take you out for dinner. Just don't expect me to dress up," he said with a wink, and my heart fluttered at the thought. It was so easy, this banter, a refreshing contrast to the weight of our previous conversation.

Just as I was about to reply, a sharp sound shattered our moment—a distant crash, like glass shattering. I looked up, startled. "What was that?"

Jack's expression shifted, a flicker of concern crossing his face. "I don't know, but it sounded like it came from the hotel."

We abandoned the weeds and raced towards the sound, our footsteps echoing in the stillness. The hotel loomed ahead, its once-grand façade now dulled by neglect. As we reached the entrance, the source of the noise became painfully clear. A window had shattered on the second floor, shards of glass glittering like a constellation on the ground below.

"What the hell?" I muttered, instinctively stepping closer to inspect the damage. "Did someone break in?"

Jack's jaw tightened. "It doesn't look like a break-in. More like... a mishap."

We shared a glance, both of us reluctant to approach further. "Should we call someone?" I asked, anxiety creeping into my voice.

"Let's check it out first," he said, leading the way cautiously. The old wooden stairs creaked beneath our weight, each step echoing our growing trepidation.

As we reached the second floor, the scene unfolded before us like a chaotic tableau. Furniture was overturned, and bits of glass littered the floor, reflecting the dim light streaming through the remaining windows. In the middle of the chaos stood a figure, an older man with a wild shock of white hair and a look of utter disbelief on his face.

"Dr. Prescott?" I exclaimed, recognizing him as the retired architect who had once consulted on the hotel's renovations.

He turned to us, eyes wide. "Ah, sorry, sorry! I was just—well, trying to fix things!" He gestured animatedly at a massive old chandelier, half-dismantled, dangling precariously from the ceiling.

"Fix things?" Jack echoed, trying to contain his irritation. "By pulling down the entire fixture?"

"I thought I could save it! It was a relic, you know?" Dr. Prescott stammered, a sheepish grin spreading across his face. "But then it got away from me..."

I couldn't help but laugh at the absurdity of it all. "You do realize that chandeliers don't exactly respond to 'saving,' right?"

Jack smirked, shaking his head as he stepped carefully around the glass. "This might be the worst DIY project I've ever seen."

Dr. Prescott scratched his head, looking somewhat defeated. "I just thought I could breathe some life back into this old beauty."

"Maybe next time, call a professional," Jack suggested, his tone light but firm. "Or at least someone who knows not to pull down chandeliers without safety gear."

With a resigned sigh, Dr. Prescott nodded, his shoulders sagging. "Fair enough. I guess I got a little carried away."

"Just a bit," I chimed in, unable to resist the urge to tease. "But don't worry; we've all been there."

As we helped him clean up the mess, the atmosphere shifted again, laughter mingling with the remnants of panic. With every shard of glass we picked up, the weight of my earlier conversation with Jack faded slightly, replaced by the lightness of this unexpected encounter.

Once we cleared the last of the debris, Dr. Prescott looked at us, eyes twinkling with gratitude. "I appreciate you two stepping in. The hotel's in a rough spot, and any help is welcome."

Jack exchanged a glance with me, an unspoken understanding passing between us. "We'll help. We want to see this place thrive."

Dr. Prescott smiled, his earlier embarrassment forgotten. "Then let's get to work. This hotel has stories to tell, and we're not done yet."

As I looked around at the dilapidated beauty of the hotel, a new determination ignited within me. The weight of uncertainty lingered, but so did a growing sense of purpose. Here, amidst the chaos and laughter, I felt the stirrings of a decision taking shape, one that could transform not just the hotel but my own life as well.

Dr. Prescott's fervent enthusiasm infused the air with a contagious energy, igniting a spark within me that I hadn't felt in ages. The old architect transformed before our eyes, the momentary embarrassment replaced with a zest for revitalizing the hotel. "This place holds memories," he declared, sweeping a hand dramatically toward the cracked walls and dusty banisters. "It has stories trapped in its very bones! We just need to coax them out."

"Is that what you call pulling down chandeliers?" I teased, unable to resist the playful jab as I swept up the last of the glass shards.

He chuckled, his laughter infectious. "Touché! But really, we should have a plan. Maybe a community event? A fundraiser? We can invite the locals to contribute, pitch in, share their own memories of the place."

Jack nodded, clearly caught up in the idea. "That could work. If we frame it right, people might rally to help us save this hotel." He shot me a look that felt like an invitation, and my heart raced. "You'd be a fantastic lead. You have a way of connecting with people."

"Me?" I stammered, the compliment hanging in the air like an unexpected gift. "You're talking about a hotel, not a high school reunion. I'd be trying to convince the locals to invest in the ghost of their pasts."

"Exactly," Jack replied, leaning in, a spark of mischief lighting his eyes. "And they might love the idea of a ghost story. Who doesn't want to hear about the old hotel with its charming resident spook? It's practically a marketing scheme!"

I rolled my eyes, laughing, the weight of my earlier indecision lifting slightly. "I can already see the pamphlets: 'Come for the ghosts, stay for the renovations.'"

"Perfect!" he exclaimed, a grin spreading across his face. "And who knows, maybe we could host ghost tours. Halloween's not that far away."

"Is that a ploy to get me in a spooky costume?" I shot back, raising an eyebrow. "I've seen how you dress up for Halloween parties. You're just looking for an excuse to wear that ridiculous vampire cape again."

Jack laughed, the sound rich and warm, igniting a flicker of something deeper within me. "What can I say? I wear it well."

As we fell into a comfortable rhythm, brainstorming ideas and tossing quips back and forth, I felt a shift in our dynamic. Gone was the tension of unspoken words; instead, we shared a camaraderie that made me feel alive in a way I hadn't anticipated. I caught Jack's gaze, his intensity drawing me in like a moth to a flame, but just as quickly, the moment slipped away as reality crept back in.

"What if no one shows up?" I mused, suddenly serious. "What if I'm just barking up the wrong tree?"

"Then we'll be right here to sweep up the shards," he replied, his tone resolute. "But I believe in this place. I believe in you."

His words washed over me, enveloping me in a sense of hope. Yet beneath that hope lay an undercurrent of doubt. The shadows of my past still lingered, whispering fears I thought I had left behind.

Before I could voice my concerns, the sound of footsteps echoed down the hallway, a heavy thud punctuated by a familiar voice. "You're going to want to see this!"

Turning, we spotted Lily, the local journalist and my long-time friend, bursting through the door with an air of urgency. Her auburn curls bounced wildly as she approached, her eyes wide with excitement. "You're not going to believe who I just ran into."

"Who?" I asked, my curiosity piqued.

"Simon! He's back in town!"

The name hit me like a thunderclap. Simon. The boy I had left behind. The one who had promised me the world, only to break my heart and vanish into thin air. Memories flooded my mind, the sweetness of first love tainted by the bitterness of betrayal. "Why is that relevant?" I managed to ask, forcing the words out through a tight throat.

"He's got big plans for the old mill, and he's looking for investors. I think he might be interested in the hotel too!"

A strange mix of emotions twisted within me. Excitement at the thought of revitalizing the hotel collided with the anxiety of Simon's unexpected return. "Investors?" Jack questioned, his tone shifting to something more serious. "Is he trying to buy up the whole town?"

"Seems like it. But I can't figure out why he would suddenly show up now, especially after everything," Lily said, concern etching her features.

"Maybe he's had a change of heart," I replied, but the words felt hollow. Simon's heart had been a mystery, one I hadn't solved.

Jack's jaw clenched, and I caught a glimmer of jealousy in his eyes. "Doesn't matter what he wants," he said, his voice low and steady. "We're the ones making the changes around here now."

"True," I murmured, though unease fluttered in my stomach. "But he has resources. And I..." My voice trailed off, uncertainty creeping back in.

"Don't go there," Jack interrupted, his eyes intense. "You can't let him dictate your choices. This is about you, not him."

"Easier said than done," I shot back, frustration bubbling to the surface. "He's not just anyone. He's part of my history."

"Then don't let that history haunt you."

Before I could respond, Lily interjected, her enthusiasm infectious once more. "Why don't we invite Simon to the fundraiser? Let him see how serious we are about reviving this place."

"Are you out of your mind?" I exclaimed. "You want to give him a front-row seat to our disaster? What if he tries to take over?"

"But what if he actually wants to help?" Lily countered, her tone persuasive. "He has connections. This could be what the hotel needs."

Jack frowned, clearly not convinced. "That's a risky move."

"Every move is risky," I replied, feeling a familiar spark of defiance. "If I'm going to do this, I want to do it on my terms."

The tension thickened as we exchanged glances, and in that moment, the future felt precarious, hanging by a thread. Just as I opened my mouth to argue further, a loud crash erupted from the ground floor, sending us all spiraling into alertness.

"What now?" I exclaimed, panic rising in my chest.

Before anyone could answer, the front door burst open, and a frantic figure appeared, silhouetted against the fading light. "You have to get out! Now!"

My heart raced as dread washed over me. The urgency in his voice cut through the air like a knife, and I exchanged horrified glances with Jack and Lily. The stakes had just escalated, and with it, the uncertainty of our choices—and our futures.

"What is happening?" I shouted, but the figure remained vague, only insisting that we follow. My instincts screamed for action, for answers, but as I stood there, frozen between the past and the chaos unfurling before me, I couldn't shake the feeling that everything was about to change—forever.

Chapter 19: All the Reasons to Stay

The salty breeze tangles my hair as I stroll along the beach, each step leaving an imprint in the sand that slowly fades as the waves reclaim their territory. The sun hangs low in the sky, a fiery orb spilling molten gold across the water, casting glimmers that dance like sprites. Each wave whispers secrets, stories of days gone by, lapping at my ankles as if coaxing me into its depths. With every breath, I taste the freedom in the air, mixed with the faint sweetness of the wildflowers blooming near the dunes. My heart races at the possibilities unfurling before me, like the sails of a ship catching the wind.

Jack's confession echoes in my mind, a thrilling, terrifying truth that binds me to this place. It was casual enough when he first let it slip, as if it were a stone tossed into a still pond. The ripples of his words spread out, touching everything I once held dear, everything I thought I knew about love, about home. He could have chosen anyone, yet he chose me, and it feels like the universe has shifted on its axis. I stop to watch the children building sandcastles, their laughter ringing clear like the chimes of distant church bells, each giggle a reminder of innocence, of joy. I can almost see my own children playing here one day, their tiny hands digging into the sand, their faces lit with delight. A warmth unfurls in my chest, the kind that feels like home.

At the edge of the beach, the old pier creaks underfoot, its weathered planks telling tales of fishermen and lovers who have wandered this way. I lean against a post, the wood rough against my palm, and watch the sun dip lower, a curtain call of vibrant oranges and pinks bleeding into the deepening blue of the ocean. It's beautiful, but the beauty brings with it a weight, a reminder that time is fleeting. I'm struck by the thought that I could very well be one of those lovers, but the idea sends a chill up my spine. What if I make the wrong choice? What if this idyllic life isn't what it seems?

The truth is, life in the city had become a blur of gray. I could feel the weight of my aspirations pulling me under, drowning me in a sea of obligation and expectation. Here, the colors are vivid, the air crisp with potential, yet uncertainty lurks in the corners like shadows at dusk. Just then, my thoughts are interrupted by the sound of a familiar voice, warm and rich as a freshly baked loaf of bread.

"Lost in thought again?" Jack's tone is teasing, a lilt in his voice that draws me out of my reverie. He stands a few feet away, hands tucked into the pockets of his faded jeans, a casual confidence radiating from him like the warmth of the sun. He looks so effortlessly handsome, his hair tousled by the wind, eyes sparkling with mischief. I can't help but smile back, the corners of my mouth lifting in an involuntary reaction.

"Just contemplating life's big questions," I reply, my voice light as I try to mask the storm brewing inside me. "Like how many sandcastles one can build before they all crumble into the sea."

Jack steps closer, leaning against the post beside me. His presence is grounding, a steady anchor in this whirlwind of emotions. "Aren't they all beautiful while they last?" he muses, his gaze fixed on the horizon. "Maybe it's not about how long they stand, but the joy of creating them."

The depth of his words wraps around me, tightening like a hug, and for a moment, I forget my worries. "You're starting to sound like a philosopher," I tease, nudging him lightly with my shoulder. "What's next, a lecture on the meaning of life while we sip coffee?"

"Only if you promise to listen," he grins, and the playful glint in his eyes stirs something deep within me. There's a comfort in our banter, a rhythm that feels effortless, as if we've danced this dance before, though perhaps not in this lifetime.

We watch the sun surrender to the night, painting the sky with strokes of lavender and indigo, and I find myself leaning into the moment, into him. "Do you ever think about leaving?" I ask, my voice softer now, tinged with a vulnerability I rarely show.

Jack pauses, his expression shifting as he considers my question. "Sometimes," he admits, his gaze drifting to the sea. "But there's something about this place that keeps me grounded. It's like... it's home. And I didn't even realize it until recently."

I look at him, really look at him, and see more than just the handsome facade. There's a depth to him, a richness that goes beyond the surface. He's a man who has weathered storms, who knows the weight of a secret, and yet here he is, opening up to me as the night deepens around us. "What about you?" he asks, turning the question back on me, his voice low, intimate. "What's kept you away for so long?"

It's a fair question, one I have to wrestle with. I want to tell him about the bright lights of the city, the ambition that once fueled me, but it feels so distant now. The city feels like a ghost town in my heart, empty and hollow. "I guess I was always chasing something," I say slowly, my voice tinged with reflection. "But it turns out, I was running away from what really mattered."

His eyes search mine, and in that moment, I know I've unveiled a part of myself that I hadn't meant to share. But the air between us crackles with understanding, a thread of connection weaving us together against the backdrop of the fading day. As we stand there, the waves whispering their secrets at our feet, the realization washes over me like the tide: maybe I don't have to run anymore.

The following morning, I wake to the scent of freshly baked bread wafting through the open window, mingling with the briny tang of the ocean air. Sunlight spills into my small room, illuminating the soft, pastel colors of my makeshift sanctuary. The sheets are rumpled, a reminder of restless dreams filled with laughter and waves. I stretch, feeling the warmth of the sun against my skin, and for the first time in what feels like an eternity, I'm not rushing to meet an obligation. There's no frantic race to catch a train or a deadline looming like a storm cloud. Instead, I take a moment to relish the stillness, to breathe deeply and absorb the promise of the day ahead.

After a quick shower, I pull on a light sweater, the fabric soft against my skin, and wander down the narrow staircase of the quaint cottage I've rented. The wooden steps creak beneath my feet, a sound that feels reassuringly familiar, like a friend's voice calling me home. The kitchen is bright, filled with the golden light of morning, and I make my way to the small table adorned with a vase of wildflowers. They lean slightly, their petals vibrant against the weathered wood. I pour myself a cup of coffee, savoring the rich aroma that fills the air, and grab a slice of the still-warm bread, slathering it with homemade jam—a small gift from Mrs. Hargrove, the elderly woman who runs the bakery.

With breakfast in hand, I step outside, the world bursting with color and life. Children's laughter dances on the breeze as I stroll through the winding streets, my heart buoyed by the sense of belonging that pulses in the air. I pass the post office, where Mr. Thompson is sweeping the steps with a contented smile, his silver hair glistening in the sunlight. He tips his hat at me, and I return the gesture, feeling a surge of warmth at the recognition. Just beyond, I spot Lily, the girl from the bakery, her arms overflowing with pastries as she chats animatedly with a friend. Her laughter rings out like bells, bright and joyous, pulling me into the moment.

"Hey, you!" Lily calls out, bounding over to me. "You should come by later. We're trying out a new recipe for chocolate croissants. They're a game changer!"

"Chocolate croissants?" I echo, pretending to consider it seriously. "I'll need a second to weigh the pros and cons of adding such a temptation to my life."

Lily rolls her eyes, her grin infectious. "Oh, come on! It's practically a public service to share baked goods. You'll be doing the world a favor."

We laugh together, and I feel a flicker of excitement. This is what community feels like—warmth and connection, easy banter exchanged like currency. I promise to stop by later, and as I continue my walk, I can't shake the feeling that this life, with its simple pleasures and honest connections, could be mine.

Yet, the earlier weight of Jack's confession returns, hovering just out of reach like a distant thunderhead. What if I stayed? What if this idyllic life came with its own set of complications? The thought makes my stomach twist in a curious mix of anticipation and anxiety. A small voice inside whispers warnings, reminding me of the ties I've left behind in the city, the life I built with sweat and determination. But another, bolder voice counters that those were bricks piled high in a foundation that felt increasingly unstable.

As I wander toward the beach, I spot Jack lounging on the sand, his silhouette outlined against the backdrop of endless blue. The way the sunlight glints off his dark hair makes my heart skip a beat. He looks up, catching my gaze, and the corners of his mouth lift in a smile that ignites a spark within me. I'm drawn to him like a moth to a flame, eager to close the distance that separates us.

"Hey, beautiful," he calls out, his voice smooth and warm, wrapping around me like the sun. "You look like you've just stepped out of a painting."

I laugh, a genuine sound that surprises even me. "And you look like you just rolled out of bed. Are you planning to win the 'Most Casual Beachgoer' award today?"

"Only if you promise to present it to me," he grins, sitting up straight, the casual demeanor giving way to a more serious air. "I was just thinking about you."

"Oh, were you?" I tease, settling beside him on the warm sand, the grains slipping through my fingers. "I hope it was nothing too scandalous."

"Not scandalous, but definitely profound," he replies, his expression turning thoughtful. "I was wondering what makes a place feel like home. You've been here long enough; what's your take?"

I take a moment, considering his question. "I think home is where you find comfort," I begin, "but it's also where you feel seen. It's the people, the little quirks of a town, like Mrs. Hargrove's irresistible pastries or the way the sunset lights up the pier."

Jack nods, his gaze drifting over the water. "I agree. But there's also something about memories tied to places, right? The stories we create in the spaces we occupy."

His insight stirs something within me, and I'm struck by the realization that Jack isn't just a part of this town; he is its essence, a living story that interweaves with the fabric of my newfound world. "What memories do you have here?" I ask, genuinely curious.

A shadow crosses his face, a flicker of vulnerability that makes my heart ache. "I've spent most of my life here, so there are plenty. But the ones that stand out are the quiet evenings spent fishing with my dad, or the first time I surfed that crazy wave over there." He gestures toward the rolling swell of water. "The thrill and fear mixed together, you know? Those moments taught me about courage."

I watch him as he speaks, captivated not just by his words but by the emotion behind them. There's a history etched into the lines of his face, a complexity that invites me to explore deeper. "So what keeps you from leaving?" I probe gently, not wanting to pry but unable to suppress the curiosity.

He shrugs, a gesture that feels heavy with unspoken truths. "I thought about it, especially when things got tough after... well, after losing my dad. But I guess I realized I'd rather carry those memories forward, build new ones here rather than run away."

His admission sends a thrill through me, an unexpected intimacy weaving between us like the gentle breeze. The conversation shifts, weaving from playful banter to deep reflections, and I feel the walls I've carefully constructed begin to crumble, brick by brick.

"Maybe that's what we're both searching for," I say softly, leaning slightly closer. "A place to belong. A reason to stay."

Jack meets my gaze, and for a moment, the world around us fades into the background. It's just him and me, two souls navigating the complexities of life, our hearts laid bare against the backdrop of the endless sea. The connection feels electric, a current running beneath the surface, pulling us together. The air crackles with anticipation, and I realize that in this very moment, I'm ready to embrace whatever comes next.

As the sun begins to set, painting the sky in a palette of fiery reds and soft pinks, I can't shake the feeling that something monumental is about to unfold. Jack and I sit side by side on the beach, the warmth of his body close enough that I can feel the steady rhythm of his breath. The conversation has ebbed, our playful exchanges replaced by a comfortable silence that wraps around us like a favorite blanket. I can't help but steal glances at him, my heart racing at the thought of what could be.

"What are you thinking?" Jack asks, breaking the stillness, his tone light but his eyes probing. There's a depth to his gaze that makes me feel exposed, as if he can see through the facade I've carefully constructed.

"I was just wondering how you can make being a beach bum look so appealing," I tease, nudging him playfully with my shoulder. "Seriously, do you have a secret handshake with the sun or something?"

He laughs, a sound that bubbles up effortlessly, and it warms me more than the setting sun. "Maybe I do. It's all about making sure you're on its good side. I have a few tips if you're interested."

"Tips, huh? I could use some. What do you recommend? A sun salute or a dance-off?"

"Definitely the dance-off. We can choreograph a whole routine. I'll even wear a coconut bra," he replies, his face serious but the corners of his mouth twitching with suppressed laughter.

"Please tell me you're kidding," I say, trying to suppress my giggles. But my heart is pounding in my chest, caught between the joy of his company and the reality of the life I left behind. "I'm not sure I could handle the sight of that."

Just as the light begins to fade, turning the horizon into a canvas of deep blues, I feel a shift in the atmosphere, an electricity crackling just beneath the surface. Jack turns to me, his expression morphing into something more serious. "You know, you can stay here as long as you want. You don't have to rush back."

His words hang in the air, heavy with implication. I turn to face him fully, searching his eyes for something—an affirmation, a commitment. "But what does that mean, Jack? Are you offering me a room in your house or a space in your life?"

His gaze doesn't waver, but the weight of his next words feels almost tangible. "I'm offering you a chance to build something. Together."

The world around us blurs for a moment, the sound of waves crashing against the shore fading into the background. My heart races, caught in a dizzying dance between fear and longing. I want to say yes, to leap into this life that promises warmth and laughter, but doubts claw at me, relentless and biting.

"What if it doesn't work?" I manage to ask, my voice barely above a whisper. "What if I mess everything up?"

"Then we'll figure it out," he replies, his tone steady, unwavering. "That's the beauty of it. Life is messy, and sometimes the best things come from the chaos." He leans closer, the warmth of his breath sending shivers down my spine. "I'm not asking for perfection; I'm asking for you."

A warmth blooms in my chest, blossoming into something akin to hope. I can feel the pull of this new life, a siren song beckoning me to stay. But just as I begin to open myself up to the possibility, a distant rumble of thunder interrupts the moment, ominous and unwelcome. The sky, once a gentle canvas, now threatens to unleash a storm.

"Looks like we might get some rain," Jack says, his brow furrowing slightly as he glances at the horizon.

"Perfect timing," I reply, forcing a smile despite the unease that curls in my stomach. "Maybe I'll take that coconut bra after all; it might come in handy."

He chuckles, but there's a tension that hangs between us, a flickering light dimming under the weight of uncertainty. As the first droplets begin to fall, I stand, pulling him up with me. "Let's go! I can't get soaked on my first day of freedom."

We dash toward the nearby café, laughing like children caught in the rain. The sudden downpour envelops us, the sound of rain hitting the sand becoming a rhythmic symphony, drowning out my worries. We reach the café, a cozy nook filled with the rich scent of coffee and the warm glow of fairy lights.

As we step inside, breathless and laughing, the atmosphere shifts again. The familiar faces of locals greet us, their smiles welcoming as they sip their drinks, oblivious to the tension that just moments ago crackled between Jack and me. I catch Mrs. Hargrove's eye from the corner, and she raises her cup in salute, a twinkle of mischief in her gaze.

"Just in time, you two! The storm's a perfect excuse for a cozy evening," she calls, a knowing smile spreading across her face.

Jack pulls me closer, his hand finding mine as we navigate through the small crowd, the heat of his touch sending delightful shivers up my arm. I can feel the pull of community around us, the warmth of belonging mingling with the excitement that flares each time our hands brush.

As we settle into a corner, the café fills with laughter and conversation, the atmosphere bustling with life. I can't help but smile, the magic of the evening wrapping around me like a soft blanket. Jack leans in, his voice low, just for me. "What do you think? Does this feel like home yet?"

"I think it's getting there," I reply, my heart dancing in rhythm with the storm outside.

But just as I lean into the warmth of the moment, a sudden crash of thunder rattles the windows, followed by an unexpected shout from the entrance. My breath catches as I turn, heart racing at the sight of a figure standing in the doorway, drenched and breathless. The tension shifts, and my stomach drops as I recognize the unmistakable face staring back at me, a ghost from my past I thought I had left behind.

"Surprise!" he yells, shaking off rain like a wet dog, oblivious to the stunned silence that follows. My heart races, the familiar ache of uncertainty swelling as the reality of my choices looms before me. Here, in this cozy café filled with laughter, everything I thought I wanted is suddenly overshadowed by the arrival of someone who could unravel it all.

Chapter 20: A Broken Promise

The air was thick with the smell of burnt coffee and faded dreams, the aroma swirling around me like the tendrils of memory that clung to the walls of the hotel. Each crack and creak of the old wooden floors sang a lament I had come to know too well. I stood there in the lobby, the afternoon light streaming through the large bay windows, illuminating dust motes dancing in the air like restless spirits. This was our refuge, a place where laughter once echoed and love blossomed amid the cozy nooks and crannies. Yet, today, it felt like a prison, the shadows whispering secrets I was no longer sure I wanted to hear.

Nana's secret lay hidden beneath a pile of crumpled receipts and yellowing letters, a promise buried deeper than the old floorboards that creaked under my weight. I hadn't meant to rummage through her things, but curiosity had gotten the better of me, as it so often does in this family. It was a habit I had inherited, that insatiable need to uncover the truths lurking beneath the surface. When I pulled out the crumpled papers, their edges frayed like the dreams they represented, my heart sank. The elegant scrawl of Nana's handwriting filled the pages, and the words took form in a slow, agonizing reveal. A deal with the developer. An agreement to sell the hotel. The realization hit me like a sudden gust of wind, chilling and unwelcome.

How could she? How could the woman who had poured her heart and soul into this place keep such a monumental secret from me? The weight of betrayal pressed heavily against my chest. It wasn't just the prospect of losing the hotel; it was the notion that the very foundation of our lives here was built on a foundation of sand, shifting and unstable. My fingers trembled as I folded the papers back, a tight knot forming in my stomach. This hotel wasn't just bricks and mortar; it was our history, our laughter, our life. And yet, to Nana, it might have been merely a burden, a legacy she didn't know how to carry any longer.

Jack had been a constant in my life, steady and warm like a summer's day. We had built so much together—dreams, plans, a love that felt as boundless as the sea that stretched beyond the horizon. But this news had drawn a line in the sand, a chasm forming between us. I found him in the small lounge area, his brow furrowed as he stared out the window, the sunlight playing off his hair in a way that had always struck me as impossibly beautiful. But today, there was no warmth in his expression. His eyes were stormy, a reflection of the chaos brewing inside me.

"Did you know?" His voice was barely above a whisper, thick with emotion. He didn't have to clarify what he meant. The weight of the revelation hung heavy between us like an unwelcome guest.

I shook my head, the words catching in my throat. "No. I... I just found out."

He turned to face me, his jaw tight. "So, it was always the plan. She was just waiting for the right moment."

"It's not like that!" I protested, the sting of his accusation igniting a fire within me. "Nana loved this place. It was her home."

"Or maybe it became a cage," he shot back, and his frustration cut deeper than I expected. "How long have we been pretending everything was fine, when clearly it wasn't?"

The truth of his words resonated painfully. I wanted to lash out, to defend Nana as if she were an extension of myself, but the weight of the hidden deal loomed large, and I was left speechless. I could feel my heart thudding in my chest, each beat a reminder of how quickly everything could unravel.

"We need to talk to her," Jack finally said, his voice a mixture of anger and sorrow. "We can't just let this go. Not after everything."

I nodded, the reality of our situation settling like a thick fog around us. "You're right. She needs to explain." But a part of me trembled at the thought of confronting Nana. What if her reasoning was sound? What if she had a good reason for keeping such a monumental secret?

As we climbed the winding staircase, the air grew colder, the wallpaper peeling in places like the memories I was trying to hold onto. Each step felt heavier than the last, the anticipation of the confrontation clawing at my insides.

When we reached Nana's door, the familiar scent of lavender and old books wafted through the crack, a comforting balm that felt at odds with the tension brewing between us. I knocked lightly, a small gesture that felt monumental in the face of the storm we were about to unleash.

"Nana?" My voice trembled slightly, and I could feel Jack's presence beside me, his warmth a stabilizing force. "Can we come in?"

"Just a moment!" Her voice, usually so vibrant, sounded distant, as if she were underwater. It took a heartbeat for the door to creak open, revealing her delicate frame, wrapped in a knitted shawl that seemed to blend with the fading light of the room. Her eyes were wide, an unreadable expression shadowing her features.

"What's the matter, dear?" she asked, the concern in her voice almost breaking my heart.

But I didn't have time for pleasantries. "We found something, Nana," I said, my voice steadier than I felt. "About the hotel."

Her face paled, the color draining from her cheeks. "Oh, honey, I—"

"It's about the deal you made," Jack interjected, his tone unforgiving yet tinged with sadness. "You should have told us."

The silence that followed felt like an eternity, stretching out until it was almost unbearable. I searched her eyes for answers, but all I found was a deep well of regret, swirling with unspoken fears and burdens too heavy to bear.

Finally, she sighed, a sound so defeated it cut through the tension like a knife. "I never meant for you to find out this way."

Her voice trembled, and I felt my resolve waver. "Then tell us, Nana. Why didn't you trust us?"

The answer hung in the air, charged with possibility and fear, and I realized that the shattered pieces of our lives were now in her hands. Whatever she said next would shape the future of everything I held dear, and I braced myself for the truth.

The room was heavy with an awkward silence, each second stretching thin as we stood there, the three of us suspended in a moment that felt impossibly fraught. Nana's eyes darted between Jack and me, searching for something—an escape route, perhaps, or a flicker of understanding that might absolve her of the burden she had carried alone for so long. The lavender-scented air, usually comforting, felt stifling, wrapping around me like an unwanted shroud.

"Why now, Nana?" I finally managed, my voice wavering slightly. "Why didn't you tell us? We could have figured this out together."

Her face twisted with emotions I couldn't fully decipher—fear, regret, and something deeper, a weariness that suggested she had fought a long and solitary battle. "Because I thought I was protecting you both," she said, her voice steady but tinged with sorrow. "I didn't want to burden you with my struggles. I wanted you to love this place as I do, without knowing the shadows that lurked in the corners."

"Protecting us or yourself?" Jack challenged, his frustration bubbling just beneath the surface. He was like a storm on the verge of breaking, and I could see the conflict waging within him. "You don't get to make decisions about our lives without us. This is our home too!"

I winced at his tone. It wasn't like Jack to raise his voice, but I could hardly blame him. We were all feeling the weight of this revelation, and emotions had a way of spilling over when the truth came knocking. "We just want to understand," I added, attempting to soften the tension that had tightened the air between us.

Nana looked at me, her gaze intense and unwavering. "I feared that if I told you, it would change everything. I didn't want you to look at me with pity or—worse—anger." Her voice cracked, the vulnerability laying bare the strength she had always portrayed. "I didn't want you to think I was giving up on the dream."

"The dream?" Jack echoed, incredulous. "You call this a dream? It's more like a ghost story waiting to happen."

I shot him a warning glance, the tension between them palpable. "We're all scared, Nana. But we need to face this together. Hiding it won't make it go away."

A deep sigh escaped her, and she sank into the armchair by the window, the fabric worn and familiar. "I didn't want to admit that I'm tired, that I've been holding this hotel together with little more than memories and old hopes. The repairs, the finances... it all became too much. I thought if I made the deal quietly, I could avoid facing the inevitable."

The confession hung in the air, dense and heavy, the implications settling like ash after a fire. It was hard to reconcile the woman I knew—the vibrant, spirited matriarch—with the image of someone trapped under the weight of her own choices. "But Nana, this hotel is your legacy. It's everything you've built. Don't you want to fight for it?" I pleaded, desperate to rekindle that spark of passion I knew lay beneath her fatigue.

She looked at me then, her eyes glistening. "What if I've fought enough? What if I'm tired of fighting?"

"Then let us help," I urged, stepping closer. "We can figure this out together. I won't let you carry this alone."

Jack's expression softened slightly, the storm inside him calming. "We'll find a way to keep this place. We can look at the numbers, see what it would take to make it work."

Nana shook her head slowly. "I don't want you two to be shackled to a sinking ship. This isn't just about numbers; it's about dreams that have faded over the years."

"Maybe those dreams can be rekindled," I said, the thought suddenly sparking in my mind. "What if we turned it around? What if we brought new life into this place?"

Jack's brow lifted, and I could see the wheels turning in his head. "You mean like hosting events? Bringing in more tourists? We could turn the upstairs into guest rooms or even a boutique."

Nana stared at us, her expression shifting from skepticism to something that resembled hope. "You really think that would work?"

"Why not?" I replied, my heart racing at the thought. "We can make this hotel not just a place to stay, but an experience. A destination. People are always looking for unique places."

"And we could host community events, collaborate with local artists, create a sense of belonging," Jack added, excitement creeping into his voice. "Imagine this lobby filled with laughter, music, and life again."

Nana's eyes sparkled for the first time since we'd begun this conversation. "That... that could be something special."

"I'll help with the marketing," I offered, feeling a rush of adrenaline at the prospect. "We can create a website, use social media to tell our story. People love authenticity. They want to connect."

Jack grinned, and for a moment, the weight of our earlier confrontation felt lighter. "We can host pop-up markets, weekend retreats, maybe even cooking classes featuring your recipes, Nana. You have such a talent."

Her cheeks flushed with color, and I could see the spark of her old self beginning to flicker back to life. "I've always wanted to share my love for cooking."

"Then let's do it!" I exclaimed, feeling the fire of possibility igniting within me. "Let's breathe new life into this place, one event at a time."

For a moment, the three of us stood there, a trio of hope and possibility. We could forge a new path together, reimagine our future, and build a legacy that wasn't just about survival but about thriving.

But even as the excitement coursed through me, a nagging worry loomed at the edges of my mind. Would it be enough? Could we truly breathe life back into this hotel? I pushed the thoughts aside, focusing on the warmth of Jack's hand brushing against mine, the comfort of Nana's hopeful smile.

"Let's start tomorrow," I said, my voice a mix of determination and thrill. "We'll brainstorm ideas, make a list of what needs to change, and get to work."

Nana nodded, her resolve returning, a light reigniting in her eyes. "Alright then, let's do this."

Just as hope began to unfurl its delicate wings, the sound of heavy footsteps echoed from the hallway, breaking our moment. The door swung open, revealing the developer himself, a tall figure framed against the light, his presence a dark cloud looming over our newfound optimism.

"I'm here to discuss the property," he said, his voice smooth as silk but carrying an edge that sent chills down my spine. "I believe it's time we had a serious talk."

A shiver coursed through me, the taste of hope bittered by the intrusion of reality. I glanced at Jack and Nana, the determination in their eyes battling against the apprehension clawing at my insides.

The game had changed, and I realized that the path ahead might be more treacherous than I had anticipated.

The developer stepped into the room with an air of authority that felt like a winter wind sweeping through a warm summer's day, a chill that made me instinctively step back. His presence darkened the vibrant hopes we had just begun to weave, snatching away the fragile threads of optimism we had dared to grasp. He was dressed in a tailored suit, a crisp white shirt contrasting starkly with the deep green walls of our once-comforting sanctuary. I felt suddenly exposed, as if I were standing in front of a judge instead of someone merely seeking a conversation.

"Good afternoon," he said, flashing a smile that didn't reach his eyes. "I trust you're all well?" The glint in his gaze suggested he was enjoying the power he wielded, and my stomach churned in response.

Jack's posture stiffened beside me, his earlier enthusiasm evaporating like mist in the morning sun. "What do you want?" he asked, a steel edge to his voice that didn't betray his unease but reinforced it.

The developer leaned against the doorframe, hands casually tucked into his pockets, exuding a sense of entitlement. "I believe we need to have a serious discussion about the future of this property." His tone dripped with condescension, as if he were addressing children rather than the rightful stewards of this hotel.

Nana straightened, her earlier resolve wavering but still present. "We've already made it clear that we're not interested in selling. This hotel is not just property to us; it's home."

"Oh, but that's where you're mistaken." He stepped further into the room, filling the space with an unsettling energy. "It might be home to you, but to me, it's a lucrative investment opportunity. And it's one I intend to capitalize on, whether you like it or not."

My heart raced, the air thickening with the tension between his calculated ambition and our desperate determination. I could see the flicker of doubt in Nana's eyes, the weight of her earlier admission creeping back like a shadow.

"We've got plans," I blurted out, surprising even myself with the outburst. "You think you can just waltz in here and take what's ours? We're going to revitalize this place and make it thrive."

He chuckled, the sound low and disconcerting, a predator amused by the defiance of its prey. "Revitalize? I admire your enthusiasm. But let's be realistic. You're up against a mountain of debt, maintenance issues, and the threat of a collapsing market. It's only a matter of time before this place becomes a burden too heavy to carry."

Jack stepped forward, his jaw clenched, a fierce protectiveness radiating from him. "And you think you can just swoop in and make it all better? You'll just turn it into some cookie-cutter tourist trap, won't you?"

The developer's smile widened, revealing too many teeth. "I'll make it a destination. A place where people want to spend their hard-earned money. What do you think it's worth in its current state? A fraction of what I can offer you. You know it's true."

Nana's hands trembled slightly, and I could feel the tremors of her doubt shaking the very foundations of our resolve. "You may think you have the upper hand," she began, her voice steadier than I felt, "but you underestimate what this place means to us. It's not just a financial venture; it's a legacy."

"Legacy," he scoffed, his gaze dismissive. "What good is a legacy if it crumbles to dust? You're living in the past, clinging to something that's already fading. But I can offer you a fresh start—no more worries, no more upkeep. Just cash in hand."

It felt like a slap, his words echoing painfully in the silence that enveloped us. I exchanged a glance with Jack, both of us grappling with the reality we were facing. I didn't want to lose this place, our home, our sanctuary filled with the echoes of laughter and love. But what if we were too far gone? What if his words were steeped in an unsettling truth?

"What's your offer?" I asked, my voice a mere whisper, trembling under the weight of my own inquiry.

The developer straightened, the glint of ambition in his eyes sharpening like the edge of a knife. "Let's say I'm willing to buy this beautiful establishment for a handsome sum. Enough to erase your debts and give you both a nice little nest egg to start fresh elsewhere. You could go anywhere, do anything. Think of it as an opportunity."

Jack opened his mouth to respond, but I cut him off. "And then what? You tear it down and put up a parking lot or another chain restaurant? Is that really what you want? To erase everything this place represents?"

"Business is business," he replied, shrugging as if the loss of our memories meant nothing. "And frankly, I'd be doing you a favor."

I stepped closer, emboldened by a fire that had ignited within me. "You think we're going to roll over just because you dangle money in front of us? We're not leaving this place without a fight."

His laughter echoed off the walls, a sound devoid of warmth. "Ah, the fire of youth. It's commendable but misguided. You have no idea what you're up against."

"What are you talking about?" Jack snapped, his patience thinning.

"Just consider this," the developer continued, his tone slick with malice. "I have the means to make things very difficult for you if you decide to be stubborn. Lawsuits, permits, the media—oh yes, I have ways to ensure this hotel's past comes crashing down around you."

My stomach sank at his implications, a wave of dread washing over me. "You wouldn't dare."

"Wouldn't I?" He leaned closer, his voice a low whisper that sent chills down my spine. "I'm not just a businessman; I'm a man with power. And power can be... persuasive."

The threat lingered in the air, a dark cloud ready to burst. I felt the walls closing in, the safety of our dreams at the mercy of a man who viewed them as mere dollars and cents. Jack and I exchanged another glance, both of us searching for a flicker of reassurance, some glimmer of a plan that could shield us from the onslaught of reality.

"Enough," Nana interjected, her voice cutting through the tension like a blade. "You may have power, but you don't have our love for this place, our determination. We will not be intimidated by threats."

"Intimidation?" He chuckled again, but this time there was something colder behind it. "I'm merely offering you a lifeline. But if you prefer to drown in your own pride, that's entirely your choice."

The audacity of his words filled the room with a thick, oppressive air, and I could feel my heart racing in response to the escalating tension. "We'll think about your offer," I managed, even as dread coiled around my chest. "But you're not taking this from us without a fight."

The developer smiled, the kind of smile that sent shivers down my spine. "I look forward to seeing how this plays out. Just remember, the clock is ticking. I won't wait forever."

With that, he turned and strode out of the room, the echo of his footsteps trailing behind him like a shadow, leaving us in a suffocating silence. The moment he was gone, the walls felt as if they were closing in, a sudden weight pressing against my chest, and I could see the uncertainty etched on Jack's face.

"Nana, what do we do now?" I asked, my voice trembling as the reality of our situation crashed over me like a tidal wave.

Nana's expression was a mix of fear and resolve, her hands clasped tightly together as if holding onto a lifeline. "We fight. We dig our heels in and remind him what this place truly means to us. But first, we need a plan."

"Right," I said, the adrenaline coursing through me. "We can't let him win. We'll bring the community together, get their support. We'll show him that this hotel is more than just a building; it's a part of all of us."

Jack nodded, determination sparking in his eyes once more. "But we'll need a strategy. We can't just dive in blindly."

"Agreed," Nana said, her resolve strengthening. "We'll need to gather information, understand our options. Maybe even reach out to others who've fought against similar threats."

Just as we began brainstorming, the sound of a phone ringing shattered the tension in the air, and I reached for my phone, a sense of foreboding washing over me as I glanced at the screen. The number was unfamiliar, but something deep within me urged caution.

"Do you want me to answer?" Jack asked, eyeing me with concern.

"Just a moment," I replied, my voice a whisper as I hesitated, the weight of my decision pressing heavily on my chest.

But curiosity won out, and I swiped to answer. "Hello?"

The voice on the other end was smooth, almost silky, and sent chills racing down my spine. "I believe you have something of mine, and it's time we had a conversation."

My heart raced as I exchanged a glance with Nana and Jack, the atmosphere shifting once more, danger lurking just beneath the surface. "What do you mean?" I managed to say, the words barely escaping my lips

Chapter 21: The Breaking Point

The storm raged outside, winds swirling like a restless spirit around the old house, its creaking timbers echoing the tension inside. I stood in the cramped confines of my room, the walls painted a soft lavender that now felt oppressive, a reminder of a life once painted in brighter hues. My hands trembled as I tossed clothes haphazardly into my suitcase, the fabric brushing against each other like whispers of the memories I was about to abandon. With each item I packed, the weight in my chest grew heavier, an anchor dragging me back to the place I wanted so desperately to escape.

Jack's voice pierced through the storm's roar, cutting sharper than any lightning strike. "You think running away will fix anything?" His anger radiated from him like heat from a fire, and even though I wanted to be brave, I felt like a moth flapping helplessly against the glass, desperate for freedom but trapped in this reality. I could see the disappointment in his eyes, a flicker of something deeper that twisted in my gut. He was standing in the doorway, arms crossed tightly against his chest, the storm outside mirrored in the storm brewing within him.

I turned away, unable to meet his gaze. "It's not running away. It's about standing up for myself. This place—" I gestured wildly, the suitcase slipping from my fingers momentarily before I steadied it. "It's built on lies, Jack. Lies that have kept us shackled for too long."

"Is that what you really believe? That you're the only one who's suffered here?" His voice cracked with frustration. "I'm not just some villain in your story, Clara. I have my own pain. We both do." The words hung in the air, a palpable tension that seemed to thrum like a guitar string ready to snap.

I knew he was right. But in that moment, all I could see were the years of hurt stacked against us like a mountain too steep to climb. Nana's secrets, the weight of expectations, and the deep-seated family tensions that had seeped into the very fabric of our lives—it all felt insurmountable. "I didn't ask to be part of this tangled web, Jack," I shot back, my voice trembling as I finally turned to face him. "But I won't keep playing the part of the dutiful granddaughter or the understanding girlfriend. Not anymore."

As I zipped the suitcase, the sound was jarring, punctuating the heavy silence that settled between us. I wanted to scream, to throw something, to make him understand that I had spent too long trying to be everything to everyone else. "Maybe if you would just listen—"

"Listen to what? That you're leaving? That you think I'm the enemy?" His frustration morphed into something darker, a shadow creeping over his features. "You're not the only one with choices here, Clara. What do you think this means for me? For us?"

The weight of his words hit me harder than any storm gust could. The realization that this wasn't just my decision, that my leaving would change everything, gnawed at my insides. I wanted to explain, to justify my actions, but the truth was, I didn't even fully understand them myself. "I need to find my own path, Jack. And I can't do that here," I managed, my voice barely above a whisper.

He stepped closer, his frustration melting into something softer, more vulnerable. "But what about us? Do you really think you can just walk away and leave everything behind? Our plans, our dreams? The moments we've shared?" His words wove through the room like a melody, each note a reminder of the life we had built together, now teetering on the edge of oblivion.

"Those moments feel like a lifetime ago," I replied, the tears I had been holding back finally spilling over. "I don't know who I am anymore, Jack. All I see are the shadows of what could have been. I don't want to drown in this—" I gestured again, this time encompassing not just the house, but the entire town that had begun to suffocate me. "I can't keep pretending that everything is fine when it's not."

He looked at me, a mix of pain and understanding etched across his face. "Clara, you're not alone in this. We can figure it out together. We can face whatever shadows are looming over us, but you have to trust me." His voice softened, and I felt a flicker of hope ignite within me, a warmth pushing against the cold dread settling in my stomach.

I wanted to believe him. I wanted to reach out and pull him into an embrace that would shield us from everything that threatened to tear us apart. But the memory of the lies, of Nana's secrets hidden beneath the floorboards and the whispers that echoed in the corners of this house, flooded my mind. "You don't understand," I whispered, the weight of my decision heavy in the air. "I need to break free. For me."

Silence wrapped around us like a fog, thick and suffocating. The wind howled outside, shaking the windows again, but inside, the storm felt more turbulent. I took a deep breath, steeling myself for what I knew I had to do. My heart pounded, each beat a reminder of the life I had lived and the one I was about to step into. I moved toward the door, the suitcase trailing behind me like a faithful companion.

"Clara, wait!" His voice echoed through the air, filled with desperation. I paused, half-turned, caught between the past I was desperate to leave and the uncertain future that awaited me. "Don't just go. Not like this. Please."

It was the "please" that pierced my resolve. It wrapped around me, heavy and thick, making it impossible to ignore. I closed my eyes, fighting the urge to turn back, to succumb to the warmth of his plea. But I knew—deep down, I knew—there was no going back. The path ahead was shrouded in shadows, but perhaps it was also lined with the possibility of finding myself again, free from the weight of everyone else's expectations.

With one last glance at the life I was leaving behind, I pushed the door open, stepping out into the storm, where the rain lashed against my skin, cold yet invigorating. I could feel the road ahead twisting and turning, a blank canvas awaiting the brush of my choices. And though I felt as if I were shedding a piece of my soul, I also felt the spark of something new, something thrilling, as I stepped away from the past and into the chaos of the unknown.

The rain pounded against the windshield like a relentless percussion, each drop a reminder of the tears I'd held back just moments before. As I navigated the winding roads out of town, the familiarity of my surroundings blurred into a gray haze, merging with the storm as if the landscape itself was mourning my departure. I caught glimpses of the diner where Jack and I used to laugh over milkshakes, the park bench where we shared secrets under the stars, and the library that housed countless afternoons spent in each other's company. Each sight pulled at my heartstrings, a cruel juxtaposition against my desperate resolve.

A cacophony of emotions surged within me—fear, anger, sorrow—each one battling for dominance. My knuckles whitened around the steering wheel, the intensity of my grip a futile attempt to maintain control over a life that felt utterly chaotic. I wanted to scream, to unleash the turmoil, but the only sound filling the car was the growl of the engine and the pitter-patter of rain. It was as if the world outside was determined to drown out my thoughts, to remind me that I was leaving a storm behind, but one that had forged me into who I was, however fractured.

Just as I was beginning to find a rhythm in my thoughts, my phone buzzed on the passenger seat, shattering the stillness. I glanced at the screen, half-hoping it was Jack. A flicker of anticipation danced in my chest before I saw the name: Nana. The sharp pang of guilt tightened its grip around my heart. Even in the midst of my rebellion, I couldn't help but feel like I was abandoning her too.

I picked up the phone hesitantly, letting it ring until the voicemail picked up. "Clara, dear, I know things are tumultuous right now. Please come home. We need to talk." Her voice trembled slightly, a soft quiver that gnawed at my insides. It was always difficult for Nana to ask for help; pride and fear had wrapped around her like ivy, making it hard to see the woman beneath. Yet, in this moment, the weight of her vulnerability pressed down on me, a reminder that perhaps I wasn't the only one tangled in this web of secrets and lies.

"Home," I murmured to myself, the word tasting bittersweet on my tongue. It was a concept that had become increasingly complicated. I had thought of it as a sanctuary, a place where love flourished despite the imperfections. But now, it felt more like a prison, constructed of expectations I could no longer bear. "Not anymore," I whispered, the resolve settling back into my chest as I pressed the accelerator.

The road stretched ahead like a lifeline, pulling me toward the unknown. Just as I was settling into the rhythm of solitude, my phone buzzed again. This time, it was a text from Jack. A single line, but it hit me like a punch to the gut: "I can't just let you go without a fight." My breath caught in my throat, the defiance in his words igniting something fierce within me. I knew he was right, but that didn't make it easier.

"Don't do this, Jack," I muttered under my breath, gripping the wheel tighter as if it could anchor me against the tumult of emotions crashing around me. I was caught between two worlds, one that wanted to keep me shackled and another that beckoned me toward freedom.

As I drove, the scenery morphed from the familiarity of town into the wild embrace of trees and open fields, nature's raw beauty a stark contrast to the turmoil in my heart. I glanced up, catching sight of a bright flash of lightning in the distance, illuminating the sky for a fleeting moment. It felt like a sign, a reminder that even in chaos, there was beauty. With a resolute exhale, I picked up my phone and typed a response. "I need time. I need to figure out who I am without the shadows." I hesitated before hitting send, the weight of my choice sitting heavily on my chest.

My phone buzzed almost immediately, the screen lighting up with his reply: "I'll be waiting. You're not alone in this." His words stirred something deep within me, a flicker of hope battling against the shadows of doubt. Maybe he was right; maybe I didn't have to do this alone. But the question lingered—was I truly ready to confront the depths of my own heart, to wade through the murky waters of my past and emerge whole on the other side?

The road twisted and turned, leading me deeper into the unknown, where the trees stood tall like sentinels, guardians of secrets I had yet to uncover. As I drove further, I spotted a roadside café nestled among the trees, its bright yellow sign offering a promise of warmth and respite. A flash of whimsy surged through me, an urge to stop and gather my thoughts over a cup of coffee rather than barreling blindly into the storm of uncertainty ahead.

With a decisive turn of the wheel, I pulled into the gravel lot. The café looked inviting, its windows aglow with soft light, the scent of fresh pastries wafting through the air like an embrace. As I stepped inside, a bell chimed softly above the door, announcing my arrival to the few patrons scattered about. The walls were adorned with local art, each piece telling a story of love, loss, and everything in between. I felt an overwhelming sense of connection, as if the café itself were whispering that it understood my turmoil.

I approached the counter, where a barista with vibrant green hair greeted me with a smile that felt like a warm hug. "What can I get you?" she asked, her eyes sparkling with mischief.

"Something strong. I need to make sense of my life," I replied, half-joking but wholly sincere.

She chuckled, a sound bright enough to pierce through my heaviness. "I think we can manage that. How about a double shot of espresso? It'll kick you into gear."

I nodded, grateful for her unintentional encouragement. As she prepared my drink, I took a moment to absorb my surroundings—the chatter of the patrons, the clinking of cups, the aroma of baked goods mingling with the rich scent of coffee. It was a cocoon of comfort, a stark contrast to the storm raging outside and the tempest brewing within me.

The barista slid my drink across the counter, and I took a moment to relish the sight of the dark, glossy liquid, steam rising like a gentle reminder that there was warmth to be found, even in the coldest of storms. "Enjoy," she said, flashing me a smile before turning her attention to another customer.

I found a small table by the window, the rain creating a rhythmic pattern against the glass. As I took a sip of the espresso, the rich flavor ignited my senses, and for a brief moment, I felt a flicker of clarity amidst the chaos. I pulled out my phone again, contemplating the text thread with Jack. I had a decision to make—whether to continue to distance myself or to reach out, to let him know that while I was searching for myself, I didn't want to lose him entirely.

The rain continued its relentless dance outside, each drop a reminder that storms could be both beautiful and destructive. I set the cup down, staring out at the world blurred by raindrops, my heart racing with the weight of my thoughts. The journey ahead was uncertain, but maybe—just maybe—there was a chance for something new, something vibrant, just waiting to be discovered in the chaos of it all.

The warmth of the café enveloped me, a stark contrast to the chill of the rain-soaked world outside. Sipping my espresso, I allowed the rich, bitter flavor to pull me deeper into thought. This little sanctuary, with its mismatched chairs and quirky decorations, felt like a refuge from my chaotic life. The barista bustled around, her laughter mingling with the aroma of freshly baked pastries, and for a moment, I let the weight of my worries slip away. But beneath that calm surface, a storm still brewed, the uncertainty swirling around me like the dark clouds that hung low in the sky.

As I settled into my thoughts, I couldn't shake the feeling that I was teetering on the edge of a precipice. My phone vibrated on the table, pulling me back to reality. I glanced down to see another message from Jack. "I know you need space, but don't shut me out completely. I'm here." Each word felt like a lifeline thrown into turbulent waters, a reminder of the connection we shared. I bit my lip, debating whether to respond. Part of me yearned to reach out, to assure him that he wasn't alone in this, while another part clung to the idea of independence, the need to carve out my own identity away from the shadows of my past.

Before I could make a decision, the café door swung open with a sharp creak, letting in a gust of cold air that sent a shiver down my spine. My heart raced as a figure stepped inside, water cascading off their coat. Jack stood there, soaked and determined, his dark hair plastered against his forehead. The sight of him ignited a flurry of conflicting emotions—a fierce urge to run into his arms collided with the reality of the distance I was trying to create.

"Clara," he said, his voice low but steady, cutting through the din of the café. He scanned the room until his eyes found mine, a mix of relief and worry flickering across his features. "I thought I might find you here."

"Surprised?" I shot back, trying to sound casual, but my heart betrayed me, racing in a way that felt both thrilling and terrifying.

He stepped closer, the warmth radiating from him somehow wrapping around my heart. "No, not really. You always did love this place."

"Must be the espresso," I quipped, attempting to lighten the tension, but it felt heavy in the air between us, thick with unsaid words and unresolved feelings.

"I came to talk," he said, and there was an edge in his voice, a desperate need for connection that tugged at me. "I know you think leaving is the answer, but have you really thought this through?"

I crossed my arms, stubbornness flaring. "I need to think. Alone. You have to understand that."

"I do understand," he replied, his voice softening. "But what I don't understand is why you think running away will change anything. You can't escape what's inside you."

My chest tightened at his words. He had a point, but the idea of confronting my inner turmoil felt daunting. "Maybe it's not about escaping. Maybe it's about finding myself in a place where I can breathe."

Jack sighed, his frustration morphing into something deeper. "And what happens if you find out you don't like what you see? What then?"

I opened my mouth to respond but faltered, the truth hanging in the air like a storm cloud. The uncertainty was suffocating. "I... I don't know," I admitted, the vulnerability spilling out before I could stop it.

He took a step closer, his presence enveloping me. "What if you find that you still love the things you're trying to leave behind? What if you still love me?"

My breath caught, a rush of warmth and fear coursing through me. I wanted to scream at him for even suggesting it, but in my heart, I felt the echo of his words resonate with something I couldn't deny. "This isn't about love," I said, my voice trembling. "It's about survival, Jack. I have to survive this."

"And what if survival means losing me?" he asked, his gaze piercing through me, searching for the truth. "You think that's what you want?"

Silence enveloped us, thick with unspoken fears and regrets. I could feel my heart thudding in my chest, a relentless reminder of the turmoil swirling inside me. I took a deep breath, gathering my thoughts, but before I could respond, the bell above the door chimed again, drawing our attention.

A woman stepped inside, her face pale and drawn, a striking contrast against the vibrant café. She looked frantic, her eyes darting around until they landed on me. "Clara! Thank God you're here!"

I shot a confused glance at Jack before turning my full attention to the woman. "Do I know you?" I asked, my heart racing again, this time from sheer bewilderment.

"It's Amelia, from the library! You have to come quickly—there's been an accident!"

The room spun around me, the warmth of the café evaporating in an instant, replaced by a chilling sense of urgency. Jack's expression morphed from confusion to alarm as he stepped protectively closer, concern etched on his face. "What happened?"

"There was a fire!" Amelia exclaimed, her voice trembling. "It started in the archives. They think it might be connected to the renovations. They need everyone to evacuate—now!"

Panic surged through me. "The library! My—my grandmother's journals!" I exclaimed, fear gripping my chest. Those journals held the truths I had sought, the connections to my family's past that I could no longer ignore. "Nana's stories!"

"I don't know if we can save them!" Amelia cried, tears glistening in her eyes. "They're trying to get everyone out, but it's spreading too fast."

I felt the ground shift beneath me, the weight of everything I was trying to escape crashing back in an instant. "We have to go!"

I shouted, adrenaline coursing through my veins, and as I turned toward the door, I felt Jack's hand grasp my arm, anchoring me momentarily.

"Wait," he urged, his expression a mix of determination and fear. "We can't just leave without a plan. You could get hurt."

"I can't just stand here, Jack!" I yelled, the panic clawing at my insides. "My past is literally on fire! We have to go, now!"

Without waiting for his response, I tore out of the café and into the storm, the rain mixing with my tears as I sprinted toward the library. The world around me blurred, the only thought in my mind was to save what I could of my family's legacy, the pieces of history that could hold the key to understanding who I was. As I raced through the downpour, the sounds of sirens wailed in the distance, an ominous chorus heralding the chaos that awaited us.

But as I approached the library, the sight that greeted me stole my breath. Flames licked at the building, painting the night sky a haunting orange, and I realized with a jolt that the past I had sought to escape was now enveloped in smoke and fire. The truth I had been running from, the answers I desperately needed, were slipping away before my eyes. And in that moment, as I stood at the edge of destruction, I felt the ground beneath me give way, plunging me into uncertainty once again.

Chapter 22: A New Beginning

The clamor of New York wrapped around me like an old, familiar blanket, albeit one that felt a touch too scratchy. The honks of taxis merging with the murmurs of street vendors created a cacophony that should have brought comfort, yet instead left me disoriented, as if I were a misplaced piece in a jigsaw puzzle. I navigated the bustling streets with the determination of someone who had conquered them before, yet the rhythm felt foreign, almost like a dance I had forgotten. The bright lights and towering skyscrapers loomed over me, relentless reminders of the life I had temporarily stepped away from.

Every corner I turned unleashed a tide of memories. The coffee shop on Fifth that brewed the richest espresso I'd ever tasted, the park bench where I'd spent countless afternoons, lost in novels that whisked me away from the city. Yet now, the aroma of roasted coffee beans did little to quell the pangs of nostalgia. My senses were on high alert, attuned to the heartbeats of the city, but my own heart drummed an erratic, dissonant beat. I should have felt at home, yet my footsteps echoed with a sense of longing that seemed to deepen with every passing hour.

I settled into my cubicle at the marketing agency, the air thick with the scent of burnt coffee and the gentle hum of conversations blending with the clicking of keyboards. My colleagues were enveloped in their work, vibrant and dynamic, yet I felt like a ghost in the midst of their bustling lives. Each email I sent felt like a hollow reminder of what I used to be, a point on a graph without a real trajectory. The days blurred into a haze of deadlines and strategy meetings, my mind constantly wandering back to the coast, to the sun-kissed mornings spent with Jack, his laughter ringing like a melody I couldn't quite shake off.

"Hey, Earth to Sarah!" Jess, my desk neighbor, leaned over, her voice breaking through my fog. Her bright blue hair caught the light in a way that always made me smile, a sharp contrast to my mundane brown locks. "You in there or just daydreaming about some ocean paradise again?"

"Maybe both," I replied, a wry grin spreading across my face. "I could use a little beach therapy right about now."

Jess chuckled, her laughter bright and infectious. "You know, there's a bar downtown that has this amazing rooftop view. It might not be the coast, but it'll remind you of the skyline at least."

I appreciated her effort to draw me out of my funk. "Sounds tempting," I replied, though my heart wasn't quite in it. The truth was, I was still tethered to my memories of those crisp, salty breezes and quiet mornings with Jack, where the world felt like it belonged to us alone.

The week drifted by, a blend of work obligations and a growing restlessness that settled in the pit of my stomach. Every evening, as I stepped out into the sea of humanity that was New York City, I felt that familiar tug—an unyielding pull back to the life I had left behind. I longed for the simplicity of those days, where my biggest decision was whether to order a second slice of pie or save room for the chocolate cake at the local diner.

It wasn't until the weekend that I stumbled upon Nana's letter, the words scrawled in her shaky but unmistakable handwriting, tucked away in the folds of my suitcase. I had been unpacking, hoping to reclaim some semblance of order in my chaotic life, when her familiar looped letters leapt out at me like a beacon of light. I settled onto the edge of my bed, the letter trembling in my hands as I opened it, the scent of her favorite lavender sachet still lingering within the pages.

"My dearest Sarah," it began, the warmth of her love radiating through the ink. "If you're reading this, I hope you've found your way back to yourself. Life isn't about the obligations we feel. It's about the paths we choose, the adventures we embark on. Remember, my love, you have the strength to carve your own way, wherever that may lead you."

Tears prickled at the corners of my eyes as her words washed over me, each line unfurling layers of hope and encouragement I had buried beneath my own uncertainties. Nana had always been my guiding star, the one who taught me the beauty of independence and the importance of following one's heart. Her letter was a reminder that I didn't need to be tied to the past or the expectations of others; I could, in fact, choose my own direction.

With that realization, the restlessness that had consumed me began to transform into something more profound—an awakening. It wasn't merely about going back to the coast or staying in the city; it was about embracing the life that lay before me, full of possibilities and potential. I could craft my own adventure, a blend of both worlds.

I sat back, envisioning the sun setting over the water, casting a golden hue over the horizon, and Jack's laughter echoing in the distance. A rush of determination surged through me. Maybe I didn't have to choose. Maybe I could merge the vibrancy of the city with the tranquility of the coast, finding a way to keep both pieces of my heart intact.

With renewed clarity, I reached for my phone, the familiar sensation of excitement coursing through my veins. As I dialed Jack's number, my heart raced with the possibilities that awaited. The ringing felt like a countdown, each beep pulling me closer to a decision that could redefine everything.

As Jack's voice filled the line, a warmth spread through me, like the first rays of sunlight peeking through a dreary morning fog. "Sarah?" he asked, his tone a mixture of surprise and a hint of that familiar teasing lilt that always made my heart race. "I didn't expect to hear from you. What's up? Did you accidentally dial someone else while lost in a daydream?"

"Maybe I did," I replied, a smile creeping onto my lips. "But the daydream's not as interesting without you in it. I'm kind of at a crossroads here, and I could use your perspective. How do you feel about the idea of... flexibility?"

"Flexibility?" he echoed, laughter bubbling in his voice. "Are we talking yoga, or are you considering a career change to acrobatics? Because I'm not sure you could manage the splits."

"Ha ha. Very funny," I shot back, my heart lifting at our banter. "No, I'm thinking more along the lines of life choices. What if we could—"

"—not have to choose between two places?" he interrupted, his voice suddenly serious, the laughter dissipating. "Is that what you're getting at? Because, Sarah, I've been mulling over a similar thought."

The breath caught in my throat. "You have?" I felt the world tilt slightly, as if the foundations of my reality had shifted. "You mean... you'd be okay with me coming back to the coast? Like, in any capacity?"

"Why wouldn't I be?" he asked, his tone softening. "You belong here just as much as you do there. You always have. But what's got you thinking this way? Is it really just the letter?"

"It's more than that," I admitted, the words spilling out before I could catch them. "It's about feeling like I'm living a half-life here, like I'm stuck in a loop that doesn't quite fit. And your voice, your laughter, reminds me that there's still something real waiting for me."

"Sarah," he began, his voice low and steady, "you don't have to make any decisions right this second. Just think it through. What if you came back to the coast, spent some time here, and figured out how to balance both worlds?"

His suggestion hung in the air, both enticing and terrifying. I could almost hear the waves lapping at the shore, a siren's call pulling me back to the life I had left. But with each pulse of desire, the weight of the city pressed down on me, reminding me of the life I had built, the friends I had forged in the melting pot of chaos. "But Jack, what about the city? What if I'm just running away?"

"Isn't that the beauty of it?" he countered. "Running isn't always about escaping; sometimes, it's about chasing after what truly matters. And you can't know what you want unless you explore both sides."

As I mulled over his words, the city around me faded. I envisioned a life split between two worlds: the tranquil beauty of the coast, where the sunsets painted the sky in vivid hues, and the electric energy of the city that thrummed beneath my feet. Could I truly find a way to weave them together, to create a tapestry that was uniquely mine?

"Let's meet," I said suddenly, my heart racing at the thought. "Tomorrow. At our spot by the water. I want to see the coast again, to feel the sand beneath my feet and figure this all out."

"I'd like that," he replied, a hint of excitement threading through his words. "I'll even bring a picnic. You know, to help you ponder your life choices in style."

"Only if you promise not to burn the sandwiches this time," I teased, my heart lifting at the thought of sharing that familiar space with him again.

"I make no promises," he shot back, laughter dancing between us, the bond we shared undeniable despite the distance. "But I'll see you tomorrow, Sarah. Bring your best beach blanket."

As we hung up, I felt lighter, like the shadows that had been clinging to me began to dissipate. I had a plan—a tentative, hopeful plan. The city buzzed around me, yet the thought of the coast electrified my veins. I spent the rest of the day lost in a haze of anticipation, thoughts swirling like autumn leaves caught in a gust of wind.

The next morning dawned bright and clear, the air fragrant with promise. I slipped into a pair of well-loved sandals, threw on a loose sundress that danced with each step, and grabbed a canvas tote for the picnic. As I stepped out into the bustling street, the cacophony felt different—more vibrant, alive with potential rather than just noise.

The subway ride felt like a trip through memory lane, each stop sparking images of the past. I felt a magnetic pull toward the coast, a pull that promised not just nostalgia, but also the chance to reclaim parts of myself that had been lost in the shuffle of urban life.

When I finally arrived at the beach, the salty breeze wrapped around me like a welcome hug, and the rhythmic sound of the waves crashing against the shore seemed to whisper secrets only I could hear. I spotted Jack already sprawled on the sand, his sun-kissed skin glistening in the sunlight. He waved, and the sight of him sent a surge of warmth through me.

"Look who decided to grace us with her presence!" he called out, a teasing grin illuminating his face. "I was beginning to think you'd gotten lost in the subway tunnels or something."

I laughed, shaking my head as I approached him, feeling the warm sand between my toes. "I would never miss a chance to see the ocean—and you."

"Smart choice," he said, patting the blanket beside him. "I brought a surprise." He reached into the tote next to him and revealed a thermos. "Homemade lemonade, no burning involved."

I raised an eyebrow, a smile playing on my lips. "This, I have to see to believe."

He poured the vibrant liquid into two mismatched cups, and as I took my first sip, the refreshing tartness exploded on my tongue, instantly transporting me back to lazy summer days spent at this very beach. "This is amazing!" I exclaimed, grinning at him.

"Of course it is. I make a mean lemonade," he said with mock seriousness. "But don't get used to it. I can't be your personal chef forever."

"Just until I figure out this whole life thing," I countered, the weight of my uncertainties easing slightly under the sun's golden glow. "You might have a future in the culinary arts if you keep this up."

As we settled into easy conversation, sharing stories and laughter, the sea breeze tousled our hair and our worries felt distant. I let myself relax, the tension of city life slipping away like a forgotten dream. Jack's presence was grounding, yet also exhilarating—a reminder that life was meant to be embraced, not merely survived.

"I was thinking," I said after a moment, glancing out at the waves. "About what you said yesterday. About flexibility."

"Uh-oh," he replied, a playful frown crossing his face. "When you start thinking, trouble usually follows."

"Shut it," I laughed. "I'm serious. I think you're right. Maybe I don't have to choose between the city and the coast. I can create something new, something that blends both worlds."

"Now you're talking," he said, leaning forward, his excitement palpable. "You've got this, Sarah. I knew you would come to see it."

We spent the afternoon immersed in discussion, dreams spilling forth as the waves lapped at the shore. Every idea felt like a spark igniting a fire within me. The possibilities unfolded like the very ocean before us, vast and endless, each wave a reminder that life could be fluid, ever-changing.

But just as the sun began to dip towards the horizon, painting the sky in shades of pink and orange, a figure appeared on the beach—one I hadn't anticipated. A woman stood in the distance, her silhouette framed by the setting sun. My heart plummeted as recognition surged. It was Claire, my former boss, striding toward us with purpose, her expression unreadable.

Jack and I exchanged glances as Claire approached, an uninvited storm cloud on our sun-soaked afternoon. Her sharp heels clicked against the boardwalk, each step echoing a sense of authority that was hard to ignore. I felt the playful energy between us fade, a chill slicing through the warmth of the sun.

"Sarah," Claire called out, her voice dripping with a mix of surprise and something I couldn't quite place—was it disappointment? "There you are. I've been looking for you."

"Lucky me," I managed, a nervous laugh bubbling up as I shifted slightly away from Jack. My heart raced, caught between wanting to shrink away and needing to stand my ground. "What brings you to the coast?"

"Oh, you know," she said, her tone airy, almost dismissive. "Business. But clearly you've taken a sabbatical to find yourself by the beach." Her gaze flicked to Jack, assessing him like a rare specimen. "And who's this?"

"This is Jack," I said, a defensive edge creeping into my voice. "My friend."

"Friend," she echoed, raising an eyebrow with a slight smirk that felt more like a challenge than a curiosity. "Charming. I hope he's not distracting you from your responsibilities."

"Hardly," I replied, my voice firmer than I intended. "We were just discussing the importance of flexibility in life choices, actually."

Claire's expression hardened momentarily, and I couldn't help but notice the way her perfectly manicured nails dug into the strap of her designer bag. "Flexibility? That's a lovely concept. But I would think after everything you've invested in New York, you'd be more focused on your career."

I bristled. "And what's that supposed to mean?"

"Oh, you know," she said, waving a hand dismissively as if brushing away a pesky fly. "You're at a turning point. The agency's been buzzing about you since you left. People are wondering if you're going to return. They miss your creativity."

The mention of my old life sent a jolt of anxiety through me, reminiscent of stepping off a ledge without knowing how far I'd fall. "I needed a break, Claire. To figure out what I really want."

"And have you?" she pressed, her tone sharpening. "Because it's not too late to come back. I could use someone with your skills. Your talent deserves to be showcased, not hidden away in a quaint beach town."

"Hidden?" I laughed, a little too harshly, the sound tinged with disbelief. "I'm not hiding, Claire. I'm exploring."

"Exploring," she echoed, her voice dripping with skepticism. "How romantic. But what does that exploration amount to? Just another way to avoid commitment?"

"Is that really what you think of me?" The sting of her words was like a slap, and I could feel my cheeks heat with a mixture of embarrassment and anger.

Jack shifted slightly, his gaze moving between Claire and me. I could tell he was weighing whether to intervene or let me handle this myself. "Sarah's just taking some time to find her footing," he finally said, his voice calm but firm. "It's a big decision, and she deserves space to figure it out."

Claire's eyes narrowed, clearly unimpressed. "Space is great, but time is a luxury we don't always have. I wouldn't want to see you waste your potential, Sarah. You have too much to offer."

"Thanks for the pep talk, Claire," I retorted, the frustration bubbling over. "But I think I'll decide what I want without your guidance."

"Good luck with that," she replied, a disingenuous smile plastered on her face as she turned on her heel, but not before throwing one last dagger my way. "Just remember, opportunities don't wait forever."

As she walked away, the warmth of the sun felt dimmed, the weight of her words lingering in the air. I turned to Jack, my heart still racing. "That was—"

"Intense?" he finished for me, arching an eyebrow.

"Putting it mildly," I sighed, running a hand through my hair. "I thought I was over her influence, but clearly, I have a long way to go."

Jack shook his head, a look of concern etched on his features. "You know she's wrong, right? You're not wasting your potential. You're figuring out who you are outside of her expectations."

"I know, but it's hard not to feel the pressure. Every time I take a step back, she's there, reminding me of what I left behind. And I want to be strong about this, but…"

"But you still care what she thinks," Jack finished, empathy in his gaze. "And that's okay. It's a tough balance. But you've made it this far, and you're doing great."

The encouragement in his voice wrapped around me like a warm blanket, but Claire's words echoed in my mind, refusing to let go. "Do you really think I'm doing okay?"

"Absolutely." He leaned in closer, lowering his voice. "You're here, living your truth. That counts for something."

A slight smile crept onto my face, the tension easing just a bit. "You really think I can make this work? Balancing the coast and the city?"

"Why not?" he asked, an easy grin spreading across his face. "You're a creative genius. If anyone can navigate two worlds, it's you."

I took a deep breath, letting the ocean air fill my lungs, feeling slightly buoyed by his confidence in me. "Thanks, Jack. I really needed to hear that."

As we resumed our conversation, the sun dipped lower in the sky, painting the horizon with shades of orange and pink. Just when I thought I could shake off Claire's ominous presence, I caught sight of her silhouette in the distance again. She was talking to someone—no, more like arguing. The man with her looked strangely familiar, and my heart skipped a beat as recognition flooded through me.

"Is that...?" I whispered, squinting against the sunlight.

Jack followed my gaze, and his brow furrowed in confusion. "Who? Do you know him?"

"Yeah," I said, dread curling in my stomach. "That's Greg, my former coworker. He's been trying to climb the corporate ladder at the agency. I wonder what they're discussing."

The scene unfolded like a slow-motion train wreck, Claire gesturing emphatically while Greg leaned in, his face tight with intensity. Whatever they were discussing didn't look friendly. I felt the need to know what was going on, the urgency thrumming in my veins.

"Maybe we should go over there," I suggested, standing up. "I don't like the vibe."

"Are you sure? It looks like they're in the middle of something important."

"I have to know," I insisted, my heart pounding as I moved toward them, propelled by a mix of instinct and anxiety.

As we approached, the tension in the air crackled like static electricity. Claire's voice was raised, her frustration palpable. "You can't just do this without consulting me first! We had an agreement!"

Greg responded, his voice low but urgent. "You're playing with fire, Claire. This could backfire on all of us. You don't want to be the reason for Sarah's downfall."

My heart sank. What were they plotting? I stepped closer, trying to catch every word, but just as I was about to call out, Jack grabbed my arm, concern flickering in his eyes.

"Are you sure this is a good idea?" he whispered.

Before I could respond, Claire turned sharply, her gaze locking onto mine. The surprise quickly morphed into something cold and calculating. "Well, well, if it isn't the girl who ran away."

I froze, caught in the crossfire of their unexpected confrontation. Jack stiffened beside me, and the weight of Claire's words hung in the air like a dark cloud. I could feel the momentum shifting, the stakes rising, and for the first time, I wasn't sure if I was ready for the battle that lay ahead.

Chapter 23: Coming Home

The moment I stepped into the hotel lobby, the familiar scent of aged wood and the lingering aroma of freshly brewed coffee enveloped me like an old friend. The elegant chandeliers above shimmered with a soft glow, casting delicate shadows on the marble floor. Each step I took resonated with echoes of laughter and whispered secrets, memories swirling around me like autumn leaves caught in a gentle breeze. I had imagined this moment countless times while I was away, but nothing could prepare me for the stark reality that lay ahead.

The reception desk, once a bustling hub of friendly faces and warmth, now felt like a fortress. I caught sight of Claire, the receptionist, her eyes narrowing slightly as she recognized me. There was a tension in the air, thick and palpable, as if the hotel itself had held its breath since I left. Her expression, a mixture of surprise and wariness, reflected the change in the town I had once called home. The absence of my presence had carved a hollow space, one that had begun to fill with suspicion and unresolved hurt.

"Welcome back," she said, her voice polite but clipped, lacking the exuberance I remembered. I nodded, attempting to mask my own apprehension with a casual smile. It was a smile that felt too tight, too rehearsed. I had to push through this wall of ice, reminding myself that I was no longer the woman who had fled. I was back, and I needed to reclaim what was mine.

As I made my way down the familiar corridors, the worn carpets whispered stories beneath my feet, each thread woven with laughter, tears, and late-night conversations. I could hear the faint sounds of clinking glasses and muffled chatter drifting from the bar, where I had shared countless moments with Jack. The thought of him sent a jolt of energy coursing through me, igniting a flicker of hope amidst the uncertainty. Yet, it was also a reminder of the distance that had grown between us.

The bar was dimly lit, shadows dancing across the walls as I stepped inside. Jack stood behind the counter, his back to me, busy pouring a drink. I hesitated for a moment, letting the warmth of the room wash over me. I wanted to be swept away by nostalgia, but the reality was that I had left him and this place behind, and the memories now felt like ghosts haunting me. When he turned, our eyes locked for a brief moment that felt electric, and I could see the surprise flicker across his face before it was replaced by a carefully crafted mask of indifference.

"Didn't expect to see you back so soon," he said, his tone casual, but the tightness around his mouth betrayed him. I was taken aback by the coldness in his voice. This was not the man who had whispered sweet nothings to me beneath the stars, the one who had promised we would weather any storm together. This was a stranger cloaked in familiar skin.

"I needed to come back," I replied, trying to inject warmth into my voice. "There are things we need to talk about." The words hung between us, thick with unspoken feelings and unresolved conflict.

"Like what? You made your choice when you left," he replied, pouring another drink, his hands steady but his eyes betraying a flicker of something deeper. Anger? Hurt? Maybe both.

"I didn't leave because I wanted to," I pressed, desperation creeping into my tone. "I thought it was the only way to protect us, to protect the hotel. But being away... it only made me realize how much I love this place, and you."

"Love? That's rich coming from the woman who packed up and ran without a word," he snapped, the glass in his hand trembling slightly as he set it down with a clatter. "What did you think would happen? That we'd just pick up where we left off?"

I felt a pang in my chest at his words, a rush of anger mixed with hurt. "I was scared, Jack! I thought I was doing the right thing, and I was wrong! I see that now. Can't you see it too?"

He took a deep breath, his shoulders tensing as he moved closer. "You think it's that simple? You think you can just waltz back in and everything will be fine? The town has changed. I've changed. And you... you have no idea what it's been like since you left."

"I know I messed up. But I'm here to fix it," I said, my voice rising with determination. "I want to fight for the hotel, for us, for everything we built together. I know it won't be easy, but I'm willing to try. Are you?"

Silence enveloped us, heavy and suffocating. I could see the battle waging behind his eyes, the struggle between desire and hurt. It was a tension I had felt countless times before, but now it felt like a rift had opened between us, deeper and more jagged than ever. I wanted to reach out, to bridge that gap, but the walls he had erected seemed insurmountable.

"I don't know if I can trust you again," he finally admitted, his voice low, laden with emotion. "You made your choice, and choices have consequences."

"Then let me show you I'm worth that trust. Let me prove to you that I'm not the same person who left," I urged, my heart pounding in my chest. "We can't let the hotel—or us—fade away because of one mistake."

The fire in my chest burned brighter, a spark igniting something deep within me. I had come back for more than just the hotel; I had come back for him. As his gaze softened, I dared to hope that maybe, just maybe, we could find a way back to each other.

The air between us crackled with an intensity I hadn't felt in ages, as if the universe had conspired to thrust us into this moment, fraught with tension and possibility. Jack leaned against the polished bar, his arms crossed, exuding an aura of defiance that only fueled my determination. The low light of the room caught the sharp angles of his jaw, highlighting the weariness etched into his features. This was a man who had carried the weight of my absence, and the sight of him made my heart ache with regret and longing.

"I know I hurt you," I said, taking a cautious step closer. "But I've come to understand that running away was never going to solve anything. I thought leaving would protect you, protect the hotel. Instead, it just created a void."

Jack's eyes narrowed, and he opened his mouth to respond, but I pressed on, desperate to break through the wall he had constructed. "The hotel is not just a building to me. It's the embodiment of every dream we shared, every late-night conversation, every moment that made us feel alive. I want to fight for that dream, for us."

He shook his head slowly, as if trying to rid himself of the weight of my words. "It's not that simple. You left, and you left me to pick up the pieces. You can't just stroll back in like a hero returning from battle. You don't get to rewrite history."

The hurt in his voice hit me like a physical blow, and I found myself wrestling with the urge to retreat. But this time, I would not back down. "Maybe I don't get to rewrite history," I countered, my voice gaining strength. "But I can write a new chapter. We can write a new chapter together. Isn't that worth fighting for?"

Jack's expression softened, if only for a moment, revealing the vulnerability hidden beneath his bravado. The tension in the room shifted, a fragile thread pulling taut as we stood on the precipice of something—fear, hope, regret—all swirling in a dizzying dance.

"Do you even know what you're asking for?" he said, his voice barely above a whisper. "Trust isn't easily given, especially after what you did."

"Then let me earn it," I said, my heart racing. "Give me a chance to show you I'm not the same person who ran away. I'm here now, and I want to help—help you, help the hotel, help us."

A silence fell between us, heavy and profound, and I could see him waging a war within himself. His eyes darted away, taking in the faded photographs lining the walls, remnants of a time when life felt simpler, when love and laughter danced through every corner of this place.

"It's not just about you, you know," he finally said, returning his gaze to mine, the storm of emotions swirling in the depths of his eyes. "There are people in this town who relied on you, who looked to you for support. When you left, it felt like a betrayal."

"I never meant to betray anyone," I replied, my voice thick with emotion. "But I realize now that my absence did more harm than good. I'm here to make amends, to be part of this community again."

He studied me for a moment, as if gauging my sincerity. "You really think you can just waltz back in and make everything right? The hotel is struggling, and I've had to take on responsibilities that you left behind. I don't know if I can trust you not to run again."

"Then let's face it together," I implored, desperation creeping into my tone. "I want to help with the hotel's issues. We can come up with a plan, bring the town back together. There are people who want to see this place thrive, who miss the heart and soul it once had."

His expression shifted, doubt giving way to curiosity. "You're willing to jump back into this mess after everything?"

"Absolutely," I said, my resolve firm. "I'm ready to roll up my sleeves and fight for this place. For us."

With a sigh that seemed to carry the weight of the world, he ran a hand through his hair, revealing a flash of uncertainty. "You don't know what you're asking. It's a lot of work. It's going to take time, and it's going to hurt."

"Life is messy, Jack. I get that now," I replied, trying to keep my voice steady despite the turmoil inside. "But isn't that what makes it worth it? The struggles, the victories, the moments that make you feel alive?"

He studied me again, the tension lingering in the air like a tightrope between us. I could see him grappling with the ghosts of our past, the unhealed wounds that lingered like scars across his heart.

"Okay," he finally said, his voice low, but there was a hint of something—perhaps a flicker of hope. "If you're serious about this, we need a plan. The hotel needs to draw people back in, and it's going to take a lot more than just pretty words."

"I'm all in," I replied, feeling a rush of adrenaline course through me. "Let's brainstorm. We can revive the old events—those quirky little festivals that used to draw crowds. What about the summer fair? Or the wine tasting nights? We can host themed weekends to attract visitors. There's so much potential."

The corners of his mouth twitched slightly, almost in a smile, but he quickly masked it with skepticism. "You think it'll be that easy? People aren't just going to flock back because of a few events."

"No, but they might if they see a spark again," I shot back, emboldened by my own enthusiasm. "We just need to ignite that flame. And once they come back, we can show them what this place truly means."

Jack leaned back against the bar, a thoughtful look crossing his face. "You really believe we can turn this around?"

"Absolutely," I said, my voice steady. "We just have to get started."

He chuckled softly, the tension in his shoulders easing just a bit. "Well, if we're doing this, we better start soon. I'll gather the staff for a meeting tomorrow morning. You can lay out your ideas, see who's willing to jump on board."

A wave of relief washed over me, mingling with excitement. "Thank you," I said, the words spilling from my lips with genuine gratitude. "This means more than you know."

"Just remember," he cautioned, his expression turning serious again, "this is going to be hard work. You're not going to get a free pass just because you returned."

"I wouldn't dream of it," I replied, a grin breaking through the seriousness of our conversation. "I've got a lot to make up for. And I promise, you'll see—I'm not going anywhere this time."

The flicker of something—was it trust?—flashed in his eyes, and for the first time since I'd arrived, I felt a surge of hope. Together, we might just be able to weave a new story for the hotel, for the town, and perhaps even for us.

The next morning arrived with a mist that clung to the windows, weaving through the hotel's antique curtains like a cautious guest. I stood at the small desk in my room, sunlight filtering through the glass and illuminating the dust motes swirling lazily in the air. Today was crucial; today was when I would lay out my vision for the hotel and the town. I took a deep breath, my heart racing with anticipation and dread. The smell of brewed coffee wafted through the hall, a warm embrace amidst the uncertainty.

As I descended the staircase, the polished wood creaked underfoot, each step resonating with the ghosts of my past. I paused briefly at the door to the bar, where Jack and I had shared laughter and dreams. I could almost hear the echo of our conversations, a haunting melody of what once was and what could still be. Steeling myself, I pushed the door open, greeted by the sight of familiar faces: the staff gathered, some casting glances my way, others openly scrutinizing me.

Jack was at the head of the table, his presence commanding yet weary. The way he ran a hand through his hair spoke of a restless night. "Thanks for coming, everyone," he said, his tone professional, but his gaze lingered on me with a mix of caution and curiosity. "We're here to discuss how to breathe new life into the hotel."

The murmurs of uncertainty echoed around the room. I could feel their skepticism wrapping around me like a cold fog, but I couldn't let it deter me. "I appreciate you all being here," I started, trying to project confidence even as my hands trembled slightly. "I know things have been tough, but I truly believe we can turn this place around. Together."

"What's your grand plan?" one of the waitresses, Megan, asked, her tone dripping with sarcasm. "Just what are we supposed to do—throw a party and hope people magically show up?"

"Not just any party," I replied, finding my footing. "I'm talking about revitalizing our community events. Let's bring back the summer fair with a twist. We can introduce themed nights—murder mystery dinners, craft beer tastings, maybe even a farmers' market in the garden. We have to remind people what this hotel represents: a place of connection, joy, and community."

Jack's eyes sparkled for a moment, and I could sense a shift in the room as some of the staff leaned forward, their skepticism wavering. "That might actually work," he said slowly, as if he were testing the idea. "People miss those events. But what's the catch? We can't afford to invest too much upfront without assurance of a return."

"We won't need a big budget," I countered, encouraged by Jack's tentative approval. "We can reach out to local businesses for sponsorships and collaborate with artists and farmers. They'll benefit from the exposure, and we'll create an atmosphere that draws people back to the hotel. Think of it as an investment in our future."

A murmur of excitement rippled through the staff, but Megan crossed her arms defiantly. "And what if it doesn't work? We could end up with empty halls and more disappointed guests."

"Then we learn from it," I said, my voice steady. "I've learned that you can't succeed without taking risks. If we fail, we regroup and try something else. But if we don't try at all, we'll lose everything."

Jack's gaze remained locked on me, his expression unreadable. There was a flicker of something in his eyes—hope? Frustration? It was maddening, not knowing which way he leaned. "Let's give it a shot, then," he said finally, breaking the tension. "But it has to be all hands on deck. We'll all be working extra hours, and I want to see everyone committed to this."

A collective nod spread across the room, and I felt a wave of relief wash over me. "We'll meet every week to discuss progress and brainstorm new ideas. I'll work closely with each of you to ensure you feel supported."

As the meeting wrapped up, Jack stayed behind, clearing the table while the others drifted away, chatting animatedly. The atmosphere shifted from one of apprehension to cautious optimism, but I couldn't shake the feeling that Jack was still holding back. I approached him, my heart pounding. "You're really on board with this?"

"I'm willing to see where it goes," he said, not meeting my gaze as he stacked the chairs. "But if it falls apart, you need to be prepared to handle the fallout. This isn't just about you anymore; it's about the whole town."

"I understand," I replied, my stomach tightening. "And I promise I won't bail. I'm in this for the long haul, no matter what."

Just then, the front door swung open, letting in a gust of cool air. I turned to see a figure silhouetted against the light. It was a man I didn't recognize, dressed in a dark coat, his demeanor exuding an air of authority that immediately put me on edge. "Excuse me," he said, his voice deep and resonant. "Is the manager available?"

Jack turned to him, a frown creasing his brow. "That would be me. What can I do for you?"

The man stepped forward, his expression grave. "I'm with the town council. We need to discuss some urgent matters regarding your hotel. There have been complaints."

My heart sank. Complaints? The hotel had been trying to revive itself, not draw unwanted attention. "Complaints?" I echoed, confusion mixing with dread. "About what?"

The man glanced between Jack and me, his gaze piercing. "It seems the renovations you've been undertaking have raised some concerns. There are reports of structural issues that need immediate attention before we can allow any more events to take place."

Jack's face hardened, and I felt a chill creep into the room. "Structural issues? We've had the place inspected."

"Not recently enough," the man replied coolly. "If you want to proceed with any events, we'll need to conduct a full inspection—and that will come at a cost."

"Wait, you can't be serious," I interrupted, panic rising in my chest. "We're just starting to rebuild, and now we have to deal with... with structural issues?"

"Trust me, you don't want to ignore this," he said, his voice unwavering. "If there's anything unsafe, the town won't hesitate to shut you down."

Jack's jaw clenched, and I could see the gears turning in his mind, grappling with the sudden weight of this new obstacle. "How long do we have?"

The man paused, letting the tension hang thick in the air. "You have until the end of the week to sort this out. If the council sees fit, your events could be put on hold indefinitely."

As he turned to leave, I felt my breath catch in my throat. Everything we had just started to build felt like it was crumbling before our eyes. I exchanged a frantic glance with Jack, and in that moment, the gravity of our situation settled heavily between us. We were on the brink of something—something that could either uplift us or tear us apart.

"Jack," I said, feeling the adrenaline surging through me, "we have to act fast. We can't let this happen."

He nodded, determination etched into his features. "You're right. We'll find a way to resolve this."

Just as the words left his lips, a loud crash echoed from the back of the hotel, reverberating through the walls. A mixture of dread and urgency shot through me as I turned toward the sound. "What was that?"

"I don't know, but we need to check it out," Jack said, moving toward the exit with purpose. I followed closely, my heart racing as uncertainty loomed over us, the promise of change now tinged with peril.

As we approached the back door, I could feel the weight of the moment pressing down on me, the feeling that we were standing on the edge of something monumental. Whatever lay beyond that door could alter the course of our efforts forever. Jack opened the door, and I gasped as a cloud of dust erupted into the air, obscuring my view. I squinted through the haze, anxiety prickling my skin.

"Jack!" I shouted, pushing through the cloud. "What happened?"

And then I saw it—a gaping hole in the wall of the storage room, debris scattered across the floor, and a flicker of movement just beyond the wreckage. My heart dropped as a shadowy figure slipped into the shadows. "Stop!" I yelled, my voice cracking as adrenaline coursed through me.

But the figure was already gone, leaving behind a mystery that would haunt us.

Chapter 24: Forever Is Here

The final days of summer draped themselves over Cedar Creek like a soft, golden shawl, bringing a gentle warmth that lingered in the air. The scent of sun-baked earth mingled with the tang of salt from the nearby coast, creating a fragrant reminder of the ocean just beyond the horizon. The hotel stood proudly at the town's edge, a historical gem with its weathered wood and faded paint, its very walls whispering stories of laughter, heartache, and love. It was far from perfect—there were leaks in the roof, and the plumbing grumbled like an old man on a cold morning—but it felt like home. I hadn't realized how much I'd craved this sense of belonging until I found it nestled within these imperfections.

Mornings began with the sun streaming through the cracked windowpanes, casting a mosaic of light and shadow across the wooden floors. I'd brew coffee in the little kitchenette, the aroma rich and inviting, wrapping me in a cocoon of warmth as I stood by the window, watching the town wake up. The local bakery would fire up its ovens early, sending wafts of fresh bread and pastries that beckoned like a siren's call. I'd often catch myself smiling at the sight of the baker, Mrs. Elkins, bustling about with her flour-dusted apron, her laughter echoing down the street. She reminded me that small-town life had its own rhythm, a cadence that was both comforting and invigorating.

Jack appeared more often, slipping into my life like a familiar melody I didn't realize I'd missed. His presence was both a balm and a spark, igniting something deep within me that I thought had been snuffed out for good. He worked tirelessly to restore the hotel alongside me, our days filled with laughter and a shared purpose that felt thrilling. It was in these moments of labor—hauling boxes of old linens, painting walls the color of sea glass, or scrubbing down the sun-drenched patio—that I discovered the joy of collaboration, the beauty of building something tangible together.

"Did you really think you could hide that from me?" he teased one afternoon, catching me sneaking a blueberry scone from the bakery. The lightness in his voice sent butterflies fluttering in my stomach. I feigned innocence, my mouth full of pastry as I grinned like a child caught with a hand in the cookie jar.

"I have no idea what you're talking about," I mumbled, crumbs escaping my lips.

Jack leaned against the doorframe, arms crossed, a playful smirk playing at the corners of his mouth. "You know, if you wanted to share, all you had to do was ask. But now I'm going to have to take half of that for myself."

"Not a chance!" I exclaimed, holding the scone protectively against my chest, pretending it was the Holy Grail. "This is all mine."

He chuckled, a deep, rich sound that rolled over me like the tide. "You'd make a terrible pirate, you know that? You're supposed to share the treasure."

"Maybe I'm just hoarding my riches for a rainy day," I replied, adopting a mock-serious tone. "What if I get caught in a storm and need sustenance? What then?"

"Ah, but you see, it's never about the treasures we hoard; it's about the company we keep," he said, stepping closer, his gaze locking onto mine with an intensity that made my heart race.

In that moment, I felt the world around us blur into insignificance, leaving only the two of us—Jack and me—caught in a moment that was both mundane and electric. My defenses began to crumble, and I found myself craving more than just stolen glances and playful banter. I wanted to dive into the depths of what we were building, to explore the uncharted territory of our connection.

As the sun dipped below the horizon, painting the sky in hues of orange and lavender, the hotel came alive with laughter and chatter.

Locals streamed in, excited to support the reopening after months of uncertainty. The atmosphere buzzed with energy as we transformed the space into something welcoming, a haven for weary travelers and a gathering place for friends. The dining area overflowed with food, the kitchen filled with the aromas of roasted vegetables and rich sauces that danced on the edge of my senses. I relished every moment, each smile exchanged and each laugh shared, feeling as if the town was slowly wrapping its arms around me, pulling me closer into its embrace.

But it wasn't all smooth sailing. As I tried to navigate my feelings for Jack, a shadow loomed just beyond the horizon, an unexpected twist that threatened to unravel everything I had begun to stitch together. One rainy afternoon, as I sorted through a box of old guest records, I stumbled upon a letter hidden beneath the brittle pages, its ink faded but legible. My heart sank as I recognized the familiar handwriting. It belonged to my mother.

In the letter, she spoke of dreams unfulfilled, of regrets tangled in love and loss. She mentioned a man named Thomas, someone I'd never heard of before, a name that resonated with echoes of the past, of a life she had lived long before mine. My pulse quickened as I read her words, the weight of her choices pressing down on my chest. The letter felt like a ghost returning to haunt me, stirring a tempest of emotions I thought I had put to rest.

"Hey, you okay?" Jack's voice pulled me back to the present, grounding me as he stepped into the room, concern etched across his features.

"Yeah," I managed to reply, but the tremor in my voice betrayed me.

He took a step closer, his brow furrowing. "You don't look okay. What's going on?"

"I found something," I said, holding up the letter, my hands shaking. "It's from my mom."

Jack's gaze softened, and he moved to sit beside me, his warmth seeping into my side like the sunlight filtering through the window. "Do you want to talk about it?"

I hesitated, the storm brewing inside me clashing against the calm that surrounded us. There was so much to unravel, so many layers of my past that I hadn't shared with him. Yet, as I looked into his eyes, I saw the promise of understanding, the desire to be there for me even when the weight of my history threatened to pull me under.

"I...I think I need to," I whispered, the words tumbling from my lips, unbidden but necessary. And in that moment, with the storm clouds gathering outside, I realized that sharing my burdens might just lighten my heart—and perhaps bring Jack and me closer than ever.

The rain drummed a steady rhythm against the roof, a gentle reminder of the tempest brewing within me. I sat beside Jack, the letter from my mother crumpled in my hand like an unwanted guest at a party. Each word felt like a puzzle piece I was desperately trying to fit into a picture I couldn't see. As I stared out the window, droplets sliding down the glass like tears, I realized I had spent so much time running from my past that I hadn't considered how it might shape my future.

"What does it say?" Jack's voice was low, filled with an openness that urged me to let him in. The concern etched in his features mirrored the tempest I felt, swirling with confusion and apprehension.

"It's about her life before..." I hesitated, not sure how to navigate this revelation. "Before me. She talks about choices she made, a man named Thomas, and how she often felt trapped." I bit my lip, glancing sideways at him. "I didn't even know about him."

He leaned in closer, his presence wrapping around me like a warm blanket. "That's a lot to unpack. Do you want to read it together?"

I nodded, swallowing the lump in my throat. With each word I read, I could feel the weight of my mother's regrets, the echo of dreams lost in the shadows of her decisions. "She wanted to travel the world, explore life beyond this town. But then... she got pregnant and settled down. I always thought she was happy with her life here."

Jack shifted, his elbow resting on the arm of the couch, his gaze fixed on me with a focus that was both reassuring and intense. "It's tough when you find out that people you love carry burdens you never knew about. It doesn't mean they loved you any less."

I took a deep breath, the truth of his words settling into the spaces of my heart. "She mentions him as if he were a ghost haunting her. What if she resented me for being the reason she didn't chase those dreams?"

"Maybe she just wanted to protect you from that disappointment," Jack suggested gently. "But it sounds like she also wished for you to find your own path, one that doesn't feel like a chain dragging you back."

His insight cut through my muddled thoughts, and I felt a flicker of clarity emerge from the chaos. "You're right. I've been so caught up in her shadow that I forgot to step into my own light."

Jack nodded, his expression shifting from concern to something deeper, something that felt like understanding. "We all have a past, but it doesn't define who we are. It's what we do with it that matters."

There was a moment of silence, the kind that vibrated with unspoken truths, and I could feel the tension between us shifting. My heart raced at the thought of revealing my fears, of laying bare the uncertainties that clung to me like cobwebs. "I don't want to end up like her," I confessed, my voice barely above a whisper. "Living with regrets, wondering 'what if.'"

"Then don't," he said, the weight of his words settling between us like a pact. "You're in control of your story now. You can write a different ending."

I met his gaze, a swell of gratitude washing over me. "You make it sound so easy."

"Trust me, it's not," he replied, a wry smile dancing across his lips. "But I'm pretty sure it starts with blueberry scones."

I chuckled, the tension easing as we shared a moment of levity. "Are you suggesting we steal some more?"

"Why not? It's a perfect day for a heist, and I hear Mrs. Elkins has a fresh batch just cooling."

Before I could respond, he was up and out the door, a whirlwind of energy as he dashed into the rain. I watched him, a smile creeping across my face, my heart warming at the sight of him leaping over puddles like a kid again. He was a beacon of light in my chaotic world, and for the first time in weeks, I felt a glimmer of hope shining through the shadows.

We returned to the hotel, our hands full of warm pastries, laughter echoing in the now-vibrant lobby. The smell of freshly baked goods filled the air, a sweet balm for our heavy hearts. I watched as Jack interacted with the guests, his charm effortlessly drawing them in. The way he spoke with each person, making them feel seen and valued, ignited something deep inside me.

"Who knew you had such a knack for hospitality?" I teased, nudging him playfully. "Maybe I should put you on the payroll."

He winked, brushing crumbs from his hands. "Only if you promise to keep the scones coming. I'll work for baked goods alone."

"I'll consider it," I said, a twinkle in my eye. "But only if you promise to wear a chef's hat while doing it."

"Deal," he laughed, running a hand through his damp hair. "But I draw the line at an apron. That's just too far."

We continued to banter, our laughter echoing like music through the halls, and as the sun began to peek through the clouds, casting golden rays across the hotel's interior, I felt the weight of my mother's letter lift slightly. There was still much to unravel, but with Jack beside me, I felt empowered to face whatever lay ahead.

As the afternoon slipped into evening, the hotel filled with the warm glow of candlelight. I had organized an impromptu gathering for the locals to celebrate the recent renovations and welcome the returning tourists. Jack and I moved among the guests, our spirits buoyed by the warmth of camaraderie, the air thick with laughter and stories shared over glasses of wine and plates of charcuterie.

"Isn't this lovely?" I mused, leaning into Jack as we surveyed the crowd. "Everyone seems so happy."

"Yeah, it feels like the town's coming back to life," he replied, a hint of pride lacing his voice. "You've done an incredible job, you know. It wouldn't be the same without you."

I shrugged, but his compliment warmed my heart. "I couldn't have done it without you. You've been my secret weapon."

"More like your accomplice," he quipped, a playful glint in his eye.

Just then, Mrs. Elkins approached, her cheeks flushed with excitement. "This is fantastic! I haven't seen so many smiling faces in ages. You two really outdid yourselves."

"Just wait until you try the desserts," I said, motioning toward the dessert table, overflowing with cakes and pastries. "We might have a few more surprises in store."

She clapped her hands, eyes sparkling with delight. "Oh, I do love surprises! Just as long as they don't involve any more rain. We've had enough of that for a while."

Jack and I exchanged glances, the unspoken understanding between us deepening. In this moment, surrounded by laughter and warmth, I felt a sense of clarity wash over me. The shadows of the past might linger, but I was ready to embrace the light, ready to write my own story—one filled with hope, laughter, and perhaps a few unexpected twists along the way.

As the night unfolded, I reveled in the joy around me, the rhythm of connection pulsing through the air. And standing beside Jack, I knew I wasn't just building a hotel; I was building a life, one I could finally call my own.

The evening unfolded like a carefully orchestrated symphony, the air alive with the laughter of townsfolk and the clinking of glasses filled with wine. Candlelight flickered against the walls of the hotel, casting warm shadows that danced in time with the soft music drifting from the small sound system in the corner. I surveyed the scene, my heart swelling with a sense of pride that mingled with gratitude. This was not just an event; it was a rebirth—a celebration of new beginnings, and I was at the center of it all, along with Jack.

"Hey, do you think we should start a line for dessert?" I asked, nudging Jack playfully as we stood by the dessert table. The selection was enough to make anyone swoon: chocolate ganache tarts, lemon meringue pies, and an assortment of cookies that looked like they had been crafted by angels.

Jack grinned, leaning closer as if sharing a grand secret. "If we don't start a line, I might just have to dive face-first into the dessert table. And frankly, I don't think Mrs. Elkins would appreciate that kind of chaos."

"Point taken. But we should at least save a piece of that chocolate tart for ourselves," I replied, a conspiratorial glint in my eye. "The guests will have to understand. It's a matter of life or death for us culinary adventurers."

"Culinary adventurers? You're sounding awfully fancy tonight," he teased, his playful smirk tugging at my heartstrings.

"I learned from the best," I said, gesturing grandly to him. "A master of pastry heists."

Jack laughed, his laughter weaving through the crowd, drawing more attention. "Well, if we're culinary adventurers, we better make our next stop the drink station before we get overwhelmed by all this sugar. I need to keep my wits about me."

As we made our way through the throng of guests, I caught glimpses of familiar faces—Mrs. Elkins chatting animatedly with Mr. Thompson, who had brought his grandchildren, their eyes wide with delight at the candy table. The sense of community felt electric, and I couldn't help but think how lucky I was to be part of it.

As the evening progressed, we took turns chatting with guests, Jack's easy charm working its magic as he effortlessly made everyone feel like old friends. I watched him from the sidelines for a moment, his animated gestures and genuine interest captivating those around him. It was a sight I never wanted to forget—Jack as the life of the party, glowing with confidence.

"Are you ready for a little toast?" I asked, raising my glass as he returned to my side.

"Always," he replied, his eyes sparkling like the wine in our glasses.

"Tonight is about coming together, about building not just this hotel but a place where we can all feel at home," I said, feeling the warmth of the moment wash over me. "To new beginnings, to friendship, and to a future that sparkles as bright as the stars outside!"

"To sparkling futures!" Jack echoed, and we clinked our glasses, the sound ringing with promise.

As the night wore on, the atmosphere remained buoyant, filled with the kind of laughter that only comes from a shared experience. I felt a pang of joy and melancholy as I glanced around the room, realizing how far I had come. I had planted roots here, and for the first time in my life, I felt truly grounded.

Just then, the front door swung open with a creak that sliced through the laughter like a knife. The room fell silent as a stranger stepped inside, dripping wet from the rain outside. He wore a dark coat that seemed to cling to him, his hair tousled and unkempt, a stark contrast to the cozy elegance of the hotel. My heart raced with apprehension; something about him felt ominous.

"Excuse me," he called, his voice cutting through the quiet. "I'm looking for someone."

Jack and I exchanged a quick glance, the atmosphere thickening with tension. "Who are you looking for?" Jack asked, his demeanor shifting to one of protectiveness.

The stranger stepped forward, scanning the crowd as if searching for a ghost. "I need to find Sarah. She's in danger." His words struck the air like a thunderclap, sending ripples of unease throughout the room.

"Sarah?" I repeated, my heart pounding. "Do you mean me?"

"Yes!" he said, his eyes locking onto mine, a desperate intensity in his gaze. "You don't understand. You have to come with me. It's not safe here."

Confusion twisted inside me as the crowd erupted into a flurry of murmurs. I felt Jack shift protectively beside me, his body a solid wall against the encroaching uncertainty. "What do you mean it's not safe?" Jack demanded, his voice steady but laced with concern.

The stranger hesitated, looking at the gathering crowd, and then back at me. "There's no time to explain. Just trust me! If you stay here, you could be in serious trouble."

My mind raced, thoughts colliding like a storm. "What trouble? Who are you?" I pressed, my instincts battling against the urge to flee or fight.

"Look, I know this is hard to believe," he said, frustration creeping into his tone. "But you're being watched. You've been drawn into something bigger than you can imagine."

The room felt suffocating, the air thick with uncertainty. I glanced at Jack, searching his face for guidance. His jaw was set, eyes narrowed as he studied the stranger. "If she's in danger, you need to tell us everything. Now."

The stranger's expression flickered with a mix of irritation and desperation. "There isn't time for details. You'll have to trust me—"

"Trust you?" I interrupted, my voice rising as the weight of the night pressed down on me. "You show up out of nowhere and expect me to believe you? I don't even know you!"

Jack took a step forward, his presence radiating strength. "If she goes with you, I'm coming too. You don't get to whisk her away without an explanation."

A flicker of something unrecognizable crossed the stranger's face—a moment of hesitation. "I can't explain everything right now, but I assure you, it's for her own safety."

My heart raced, caught between the pull of curiosity and the threat of fear. I wanted to scream that everything felt wrong, that the night had been perfect until this moment, until this man crashed into my life like a wrecking ball. "What does that even mean?" I demanded, stepping closer to Jack as a protective instinct surged within me.

Before the stranger could respond, a loud crash echoed from the back of the hotel, sending a jolt through the crowd. The room erupted in chaos as people turned, eyes wide with fear. "What was that?" someone shouted, panic seeping into the atmosphere.

The stranger's expression hardened. "They've found you. We have to go. Now!"

And as the lights flickered overhead, casting the room into eerie shadows, I felt the ground shift beneath me, the world I had just begun to embrace teetering on the brink of upheaval. Jack's grip tightened around my arm, and for a heartbeat, I was torn between two worlds—one rooted in love and belonging, the other swirling with uncertainty and danger.

"Sarah!" Jack's voice was urgent, pulling me back to reality as the crowd surged around us, the distant sound of breaking glass echoing ominously. "We can't stay here!"

With the stranger's gaze fixed on me, I made my choice—my heart pounding, knowing the moment would change everything. I could either retreat into the safety of the life I had built or step into the unknown, where danger lurked but perhaps also answers. I took a deep breath, ready to decide my fate, as the darkness loomed closer, its grip tightening around us all.